THE THIRTEEN BLACK CATS OF EDITH PENN

Sean McDonough

The Thirteen Black Cats of Edith Penn is a work of fiction. Names, characters, places and incidents are either products of the author's imagination or are used fictitiously. Any resemblance to actual people living or dead are entirely coincidental.

ISBN: 9780578996363

Cover Art by Vector Artistry

For Gatsby, Dinah, Harley Cat (Mrow), Sassy, Princey, and all of the good cats out there.

Chapter 1

THE TWO MEN STEPPED out of the frigid New England night and into the cozy heat of The Badger's Den tavern. Warm air swept over them the moment they entered, but the rookie still didn't stop shivering. The rookie would have still been shivering on a beach in Mexico.

Mike dropped a heavy palm on the kid's shoulder and guided him towards the bar. "Come on. This way. I've got 60 cc of anesthesia with your name all over it."

It was a slow crowd, even for a Wednesday night. Joy saw Mike and the whey-faced kid coming long before they made it to the bar. The kid was hard to miss. Hearty, New England stock, but his size didn't amount to much when it was carting around on legs quivering like jello. Not bothering to wait for their order, Joy poured out two shots of Jim Beam and set the glasses before a pair of empty stools. Mike nodded gratefully as he sat down and drained his shot in a single swig.

The kid did not drink. He raised the shot glass but merely held it at eye level, staring blankly into the amber well.

"Go ahead," Mike prodded. "It's medicinal."

Still, he did not drink. The kid was operating with tangled lines. He could lift the glass, but to get it to his mouth was a call that simply wasn't going through.

Joy leaned forward on the bar. She was past sixty, and time had done its work on a face that wasn't anything spectacular to begin with, but her eyes were kind and her crooked smile was reassuring. She read the name tag on the queasy young man's midnight blue uniform.

"Let me tell you a story, Davis. I may have aged a little more kindly than Mike over here, but me and him actually started our careers right about the same time. Way back then, ol' Jimmy Rooney brought Mike to this very bar and bought him a shot just like the one in front of you. That was after they pulled the Williams' family station wagon out of the river. I remember he was just about as pale as you, and look at the old cuss now."

"Cheers, Joy," Mike said.

She squeezed the young man's hand. "Take the drink. It'll do you good."

Brian Davis looked up at her. His eyes were far away, miles away, but something within them crawled hesitantly towards the light. He sighed, and Joy smelled fresh vomit on his breath. She nodded encouragingly, and he raised the shot to his lips with jittery hands and slurped it down. Brian coughed against the harshness of the liquor, and she patted his arm sympathetically.

"Another round if you don't mind, Joy," Mike said. He pushed the empty shot glass back towards her. Brian followed his lead. The rookie's hands were still shaking enough that he nearly knocked the glass over.

Beginning to feel uneasy herself, Joy obliged them and poured a fresh round.

"I gather it was a bad one?" she asked.

Mike finished the whiskey before answering. He rubbed at the gray stubble under his chin. "It'll make a helluva story one day. I'll probably still be telling it twenty years from now."

Joy poured them two beers and added a third for herself. "That your way of saying it's not a story for tonight?" she asked.

Mike accepted the beer and favored her with a wry smile. Joy felt a pleasant squirm in her stomach, even though it had been many years since they'd gotten up to anything like that. "No, I'll tell you," he said. "But before I do, you should pour one of these beers out for the poor, departed Edith Penn."

Joy's eyes went wide. Her jaw dropped to the taps. *"Edith Penn is dead!?"* she asked in a stunned whisper.

"Dead as her wicked sister in the West. I haven't seen the paperwork, but a heart attack would be my guess."

Joy looked from the rookie, still seeking refuge in his beer, and then back to Mike. Behind the veteran paramedic's rakish grin, there was a quiver in his lip and a queer sheen in his eyes. His facade was holding, but Joy could sense the supports behind it straining to keep it up.

"I don't get it, Mike. You've seen heart attacks before."

Mike chuckled. The sound rattled behind his teeth like a fish flopping in the dirt. "Did Wicked Edith have any roommates, Joy?"

The bartender shook her head. "No, she lived all alone. Edith Penn and her..."

And then she understood. Joy's eyes swelled to bursting. Morbid pictures filled her head as she realized what atrocity Mike was implying- gruesome, grisly imagery that belonged in the horror section of an old Blockbuster.

"Noo," Joy groaned. "No, no, no." They couldn't mean what she thought they meant. It was the kind of sick story that never really happened. Just a twisted urban legend. The old lady who dies all alone and then her...

"Thirteen," Brian whispered. "We thought she was still breathing. I got down to do chest compressions.."

"One had crawled under her nightgown," Mike supplied. "Poor Brian pushed down and the damn thing came out hissing like a snake. Nearly pissed myself too, if we're being honest."

"One of the damn things," Joy reflected.

One of her cats.

One of Edith Penn's thirteen black cats.

"How long do you think she was..."

"Days," Mike said. "They'd eaten her down to the bone in some places. Her fingers... her lips... My brother is a homicide cop in Providence. He usually beats me when it comes time to swap stories, but I think I might have the prize winner this time."

His beer was empty. Joy dispensed with the pleasantries and poured a generous stream of straight whiskey into the pint glass. She cast an eye around the bar. There were two regulars milking the same pints of Sam Adams, and there was the Spencer girl with a tumbler of Makers that looked just about done. It was a ruinously cold night, and custom was few and far between.

"I'm gonna close up early," she said to Mike. "Do you wanna stay and help me button up shop?" She brushed his knuckles. "We can swap some old stories."

She saw less queer in his eyes and more sheen. Mike turned towards his first responsibility before answering, but the kid was already finishing his beer. "Don't worry about me," Brian said. "I'm okay."

"You'll find a ride home?"

"I'll walk," Brian said. "I'm not far from here." He slapped the older man on the shoulder. "Thanks, Cooper."

The older man waved him off with a flap of his weathered hand. "You're buying next time, assuming they don't find you frozen on the sidewalk tomorrow morning."

"Take care, hun," Joy called out.

Brian flushed, and it had nothing to do with the drink or the cold. "Nice meeting you," he mumbled.

He left the bar but didn't set out right away. He stood there in the icy night, leaning against the wall beneath the cheap light mounted next to the door. Brian sucked in cold air and breathed out hot vapor. More satisfying than any cigarette. It was the kind of air that crackled inside of you with every breath. Living air.

Brian's career as a paramedic had been short, but not uneventful. Just last week, he and Mike had responded to a man who'd tried to unclog his snowblower by hand and lost three fingers for the effort. He'd seen gore. He'd even seen a death. None of it was fun, but he could handle it.

Brian couldn't handle this. There was no part of it to grab hold of. Not the hissing shadow crawling out of the dead woman's nightgown. Not the blood-drenched cats crawling all over the house.

Not the body of Edith Penn with chunks taken out of it.

The cats hadn't scattered as emergency services entered the home. Why would they? The house was theirs. The old woman was theirs. And they'd taken her. They'd chewed her flesh. They'd tracked her blood over the cheap linoleum in the kitchen and over the upholstery in the living room. They'd grown fat and sleepy off the meat from her bones.

He was shaking again. *Just the cold,* he told himself. Right. Just the cold. So bad that it had him frozen to the spot. That was all.

"Oh, my God. Are you, like, a paramedic?"

All two hundred and ten pounds of Brian Davis jumped. He avoided screaming by the smallest of margins.

The girl at his side laughed. "I'm sorry. I wasn't trying to scare you."

Brian took a shaky breath. "Don't worry about it," he said.

He took a good look at her. He'd been so wrapped up in his own bullshit that he hadn't even noticed her coming out of the bar, and that was a sure sign that he was fucked up because holy shit was she hard to miss. She was short, but not small. Her body curved generously in all the right places beneath her jeans and an unzipped North Face jacket. Her eyes were dusky amber set amongst skin that glowed like warm, sun-dried clay, even in the garbage light outside the bar. She smiled, and Brian felt the bands around his chest loosen for the first time all night.

"So... are you?" she asked.

"No, I'm fine. I was just thinking about something."

She fingered the stitching of his name tag and giggled. "I mean are you a paramedic?"

"Shit. Right. Yeah, I am. Station 19 out by the freeway."

"Do you like it?"

"Yeah, I do." And saying it out loud hit him with a tremendous sense of relief. Whatever he'd seen tonight, there was no question of whether or not he'd be at work tomorrow. "It matters. There aren't a lot of jobs where you can say that."

She clasped her hands together, inadvertently squeezing her generous breasts together and pushing them towards him. "I wish my job was interesting like that. You must have so many cool stories," she gushed.

"I mean, a couple. Like this summer, we-"

"What about tonight?" she asked.

Brian shrugged and turned his face away, suddenly interested in the bleak, snow-covered parking lot. "Tonight was regular. Nothing crazy."

Her beautiful, dark eyes narrowed and her lips turned in a knowing smirk. "It seemed like you were telling Joy a story."

"What, were you watching me?"

She curled a strand of hair around her finger. "A little. I'm just curious how you got iron-fist Joy Fenton to open up for free drinks like that." She leaned in close. "Come on. I can keep a secret."

Brian leaned away from her. Something Mike had warned him about early on the job suddenly rang through his head.

"Girls like the uniform. And they like stories about saving babies. But trust me, kid. Nobody looking to get laid will ask you about some girl who OD'ed in a bathtub."

"Tell me again what you do for work?" he asked her. But a sinking feeling told him he already knew the answer.

"Just be smart is what I'm saying. You don't want to get a reputation for talking to the wrong kinds of people. Even if those people have spectacular tits."

A different light suddenly glowed in the woman's eyes-amusement at being called out, but colder than the wind blowing between them.

"I can keep your name out of it," she promised. "I just feel like there's a story you want to tell... and I'm kind of a professional listener."

Brian recoiled. He knew it. A fucking reporter.

She saw his reaction. "Slow down, okay? Let's just talk. Off the record. Promise."

Brian stepped out on the asphalt. His first step away from her. "No comment. Understand? How's that for talk?"

She pulled a card from her jacket. "Rebecca Spencer. Look, take my card. That can't hurt, right?"

Brian didn't slow down. "Get fucked," he told her. He didn't even bother turning around to say it, he just kept his back to her and marched into the shadows beyond the small parking lot.

Rebecca waited, even after he faded out of sight, hopeful that he might change his mind. Minutes passed, and she finally gave up after the last few patrons filtered out of the bar and the door clicked shut behind them. The windows went dark as Joy turned off the lights.

Rebecca sighed and pulled up the zipper on her jacket. It was for the best, she supposed. She already had her hands full with the Hyde story... but the way those paramedics looked coming into the bar. And Joy Fenton offering up free drinks. There *was* a story there, and it killed her to miss out on it.

That's what she told herself. But as Rebecca cruised towards her apartment at the far edge of town, her eyes kept creeping along to the sidewalks to see if maybe her mystery paramedic was still out walking the streets.

Alas, it was not to be.

***

Back in the bar, long after she'd turned out the lights, Joy was scrounging behind the counter for her bra when the question occurred to her. "So what's going to happen to all of Edith's cats?" she asked.

Buckling his pants, Mike favored her with another dry grin. "Stop by Hunan Cottage tomorrow and see for yourself. They should be ready just in time for the lunch special."

Joy blanched. "Oh, Mike. Are they really going to kill them?"

He shrugged. "It's procedure. Once an animal gets a taste for filet of grandma, you can't just put them up for adoption. Those kitties are marked for the big sleep."

Chapter 2

TYLER ERIKSON NAVIGATED THE wheezy county van through the night-silenced streets of New Birmingham. Even with the heater rattling as best it could, his breath still fogged before his face as he drove. His fingers were numb, and the small of his back throbbed more painfully with every passing mile. It was hard to imagine this shift getting any worse.

On cue, his acid reflux flared suddenly, making Tyler wince and clutch at his chest. Vindictively, he took another deep swig from the mug of lukewarm chili in his cup holder.

Just another half hour, he consoled himself. *Maybe less if you're lucky.*

From the rear of the van, one of his inmates let loose with a pitiful *yowl*. The sound echoed in the metal interior like a prison inmate's mournful harmonica. Tyler didn't turn around, but he grabbed an empty coke can off the dashboard and flung it backwards. "Shut the fuck up back there!" he bellowed.

They drove another two blocks in silence except for Donovan playing on WBOS. Tyler noticed a few cars still parked in front of the bowling alley as he cruised by. A couple lucky souls taking advantage of two-for-one pitchers and grousing over the strikes they didn't make. Not for the first time, he cursed that bitch Glapin for scheduling him on the night shift again.

And then the sound came once more. That desolate, keening cry from the cages. It was incessant.

Jesus motherfucking Christ am I being tested, he thought. Tyler considered pulling over and making an example out of one of the little fuckers, but he fought down the urge. The County Wildlife Control building loomed up ahead. He'd be done with them soon enough.

He pulled into the parking lot. Miracle of miracles, the old minivan with the "Feel the Bern" bumper sticker was already there waiting for him.

Tyler brought his vehicle up alongside it and shifted his van into park. The girl was quick. Courtney was already out and halfway around to the back of the van before Tyler hauled his bulk out of the driver's seat.

"Courtney!" he greeted with leering sweetness. "How are you on this brisk evening?"

The girl only glowered at him from within her rat's nest of unruly brown hair. Tyler could feel her impatience, but he took his time ambling around to the back of the van. All of a sudden, it seemed that he had all the time in the world.

Finally at the back doors, Tyler put his hand on the latch. He knew what she wanted, but he took her no further. His grin just grew wider, exposing more of his teeth to the red glow of the tail lights.

He's so fucking ugly, Courtney thought. She felt like she was facing down a troll every time she dealt with him. But she kept her disgust to herself and took out the roll of twenties that he was waiting for. "Here," she said, offering up the money for him to claim.

Tyler reached out and grabbed her wrist instead of the cash. He turned her hand over, inspecting the deep scratches across the back of her knuckles.

"Which grateful little furball gave you those?" he jeered.

Courtney yanked her hand free and punched the mass of bills into his doughy chest. "Just open the van," she spat.

Tyler bowed in mock servitude and flung open the rear of the county van. The overhead light was broken, and the interior of the van was a yawning, black vortex of darkness... except for the array of glowing yellow eyes floating in the shadows.

Eye shine, Courtney told herself. *Totally natural.*

But even for someone familiar with nocturnal animals, the wall of glowing eyes was jarring. It triggered a primal urge to flee in Courtney's legs. There were just so many of them. Pair after pair of glowing, yellow swamp gas orbs with nothing anchoring them to a body.

Tyler saw her discomfort and grinned. "No returns, you understand."

Courtney gritted her teeth. She hated him. She hated him so much, but she kept her mouth shut. He was her only contact at animal control. It wasn't worth provoking him. Courtney climbed into the van. Up close, she could see the shelves and the cages. There was no more ethereal realm of eyes here. It was just the wildlife control van. Just a row of shoddy metal shelving lined with plastic carrying cages. Something moved inside the nearest cage, like a shimmer in black water.

Courtney shuffled right up to the cage, and the animal inside turned towards her. The angle was better here. No eye shine now- just a sleek, agile body and wise, regal features.

There was no yellow-eyed spirit here. Just a cat looking for a new home.

"Hey, baby," Courtney crooned. She stuck two fingers through the wire grating of the cage and stroked the animal's dusky fur. "You want to get out of here?"

Her fingers came away sticky, like she'd just touched a melting chocolate bar. She hadn't noticed it at first, but she peered more carefully through the gloom and saw that the cat's fur was covered in something stiff and tacky.

"I wouldn't do that," Tyler warned as Courtney brought her fingers up towards her face.

Too late. She caught the heady scent of pennies left too long in a hot car.

Blood. Courtney surveyed the other cages, and realized the cats were all like that. Blood-drenched, every one of them.

"Didn't have time to give out baths," Tyler said. "Hope you don't mind."

Didn't have time to give yourself one either, Courtney seethed.

The occupants meowed quietly, but stayed relatively peaceful.

"Charming as can be, aren't they?" Tyler opined. "You wouldn't even know they're feral."

"They're not feral," Courtney hissed, snapping just like she promised she wouldn't.

Tyler only chuckled. "Sure, not now they're not," he said. "Just wait until they get hungry again."

Courtney pushed her misgivings aside. She grabbed a crate in each hand, carried them into her old minivan, and went back for two more.

Tyler watched her without offering to help. He tucked the money into his pocket. “I’ve got some records to falsify. Close the van when you’re done.” He retreated to the comfortable warmth of the county building, leaving Courtney out in the cold.

Alone with Edith Penn’s black cats.

The same as you’ve been alone with animals in this parking lot a thousand times, she reminded herself, firmly refusing to indulge in any old stories from her childhood.

Courtney checked to make sure the animals were stacked securely and then closed the back of the minivan. The nerves she’d felt before were gone. Even in the dim light of the parking lot, even with the cats themselves dark as blackberry juice, Courtney could see the animals clearly now. She saw beyond the blood still caked around their muzzles and paws. She saw the souls underneath.

Someone else would too.

Driving back to her house, Courtney was already mentally reviewing her list of foster contacts. There was no way to keep them all together unfortunately. They would have to go to different homes.

Well, at least they’ll have tonight together.

She pulled up in front of her rental house. It was after midnight, and the homes up and down the street were all dark and silent, but she braced herself for a fight nonetheless. The snooping hag next door had called the police on her before, and doubtlessly would again.

If you wanna waste your tax dollars, bitch, be my guest. Courtney knew the local animal ordinances front and back.

As it turned out, the only fight was with her weary body to bring all the cat carriers into the house. After getting the last one inside, Courtney sighed heavily and dropped onto the couch. She rubbed her eyes and looked out over the jumble of cages cluttering her small living room. She had pulled a double shift at the shelter today. When Tyler had called her with word of the thirteen cats, she had already been in bed and poised to drift off into sleep.

Speak now or speak over the incinerator, he’d oozed. *These are real felons here, honey. I won’t be able to hold them long.*

The anger burned away her exhaustion. Thirteen cats, euthanized over some old BS claim that animals exposed to human flesh couldn’t be rehabilitated.

So she’d rallied. She’d made it out in the cold. She’d gotten the cats home, safe and sound. But she’d been awake for over 18 hours now, and she felt every minute of it in the soupy haze pumping through her brain. At that moment, the lumpy thrift store couch felt as decadent as a palace bed.

Courtney looked into the nearest carrier. A gorgeous Maine Coon stared back at her, but the poor thing's coat was still matted and sticky with the old woman's blood. Nobody had done anything for these poor animals.

That stops now, she promised.

Courtney heaved herself off the couch and knelt down to open the cage. The big black cat padded cautiously out. She looked up at Courtney with gorgeous golden eyes, unsullied by the matted gore all around them.

"Come on, baby." Courtney picked up the cat, unmindful of the sticky blood clotting on her arms. "You're not going to love this part, but I'll do my best."

She did the same with all of them. One by one, Courtney cradled the felines into the bathroom and into the bathtub. She didn't put them under the water, absolutely never, but she dabbed gently at each cat with a damp rag, blotting the sticky blood from their fur without causing any distress. She held their inky forms against her chest and patted each one dry. She set each cat down and did it again with the next one. She repeated the process again and again, until her white tank top was stained mottled pink.

As she finished, Courtney didn't bother to return them to their carriers. By the time she'd cleaned the last feline, the rest of the felines were sprawled throughout her living room and kitchen. Four black cats shared the couch. A fifth peered at her from on top of the fridge. Still more wound sinuously across the floor.

Courtney surveyed the animals, basking in their dark, glossy fur and their pristine innocence. A few hours ago, these same animals were feasting on a dead body. That might have made some people uneasy, but Courtney looked at them now and felt only vindication. One of the cats came and rubbed herself against Courtney's shin. The animal purred deeply, signaling its comfort.

Totally docile, every one of them. Perfect companions for a family or a lonely old woman looking for some company.

Courtney felt better now that she'd washed the animals, but she knew she wouldn't be able to sleep right until she had their pictures posted online. With luck, she would wake up to find a few forever homes already lined up for these kitties.

Stifling a yawn, she went to the kitchen first for a pick me up.

Hopefully, she reminded herself. It had been a long week, and tomorrow was supposed to be her shopping day.

Courtney pulled open the fridge and breathed a sigh of relief. There was still one more Mayocoba Bean energy drink in the fridge. The can was mercifully right up towards the front of the shelf, just waiting for her grateful hand. She closed her fingers around the cool aluminum and took the can out of the fridge.

The cat leapt at her before she could open the drink. Courtney shrieked as the bristling, black form struck her chest. The can dropped from her hand to the floor, and the black cat landed shortly after. She dropped with easy, stealthy grace, and sat before Courtney with the perfect poise of a sphinx statue.

Courtney let out a shaky laugh, even while her heart hammered in her chest. "You stinker," she chided.

There was a simple rope collar tied around the animal's neck. A worn, dented oval of tin dangled from it. There was no address and no phone number printed there. Just a single word, etched in crude capital letters:

Tituba.

Tituba is a playful character with lots of personality, Courtney composed. *Great for a family with kids who can give her lots of attention.*

The scare had certainly woken her up, but Courtney went to retrieve the drink anyway. The can had rolled over against the kitchen counter. She bent down to pick it up.

That was when the two cats lying in wait behind the microwave made their move.

Courtney's microwave weighed forty pounds. Edith Penn's cats were larger than the norm, most of them close to thirteen pounds each, but a single feline couldn't have done it alone. The two cats had to move in perfect tandem, bracing their back legs against the wall and uncoiling their muscular bodies as one, to shove the microwave oven off the counter and onto Courtney's head.

The appliance struck her in the back of the skull and smashed her head face-first into the tile floor. Courtney's nose broke. Her front teeth shattered.

She wasn't dead. She groped for the counter, struggled to her feet, and immediately reeled across the floor. Blood drenched her shirt in an ongoing torrent. The back of her head was dented inwards like an old car door. She'd gone blind in one eye. Her mouth fumbled open and closed, silently groping for words her brain couldn't find.

The cats paid her no mind. The felines gathered in the kitchen, gracefully avoiding the blood and Courtney's shambling steps with equal ease. They made no sound except for the occasional tinkle of their name tags: Danvers,

Oyer, Glover, Osborne, Hobbs, Wildes, Eastey, Deliverance, Dorcas, Morey, Sears, Bethiah, and Tituba.

They came in all breeds. Oyer was a Persian with a full, luxurious coat. Hobbs was a bristling, imperial British Shorthair.

Most impressive of all was Tituba. The massive Maine Coon was a black storm cloud of lustrous fur. She was the one the others gathered around, her golden eyes wordlessly noting each one as the felines drew together in a rough circle.

There was no noise, except for the clamor of Courtney banging into chairs and rattling the refrigerator in her cotton-headed stupor. Hobbs' pawed impatiently behind one ear. Deliverance yawned silently, baring a mouthful of teeth like nails. Tituba held still as a statue until dawdling Osborne finally fell into place.

Then, as one, the glaring of felines broke the circle and skulked forward together.

Tituba prowled in front. She led her sisters to the basement door, already partially ajar, and pushed it further open with her sleek, muscular body. Tituba padded down the unfinished steps with her tail held high, and the other twelve flowed behind her in a long, sinuous river of black fur.

They descended into the basement and kept moving with the same unerring purpose that had driven them this far. The cats spread to the four corners of the dingy room, weaving around piles of laundry and skipping gracefully over discarded boxes. They climbed over clutter and prodded cobwebbed corners, methodically surveying every inch of the unfinished basement's concrete perimeter.

Above them, there was a dull thud as Courtney finally collapsed to the kitchen floor and did not rise again.

The cats, focused on their search, didn't so much as flinch.

It was Eastey who discovered the window with the broken latch. The rusty hinge folded open with a squeal like a dying mouse as the cat butted her head against the glass.

The other cats followed Eastey out onto the sparse, frosted grass of the backyard. They lingered together for a last moment... and then they spread in every direction like spilled oil.

Wildes prowled behind the Green Valley diner. Osborne took advantage of a broken window in a nearby garage. Oyer huddled in the shrubs at the elementary school. Deliverance found shelter in the garbage cans behind The

Badger's Den. The others spread further still, deep into the heart of the town and all the way out to its farthest edges.

They were not stopped. They were not noticed. The late hour and the cold season had wiped human eyes from the streets. The people of New Birmingham slept with blankets up to their chins, completely unaware as the thirteen black cats of Edith Penn made their way through the night.

Chapter 3

MARTHA BREATHED A SIGH of relief when she heard her husband rumbling down the stairs.

At least, she wished that she could have breathed a sigh of relief. Her breathing actually hadn't varied at all. It marched on in the same unerring pace of inhales and exhales. The same as when she was screaming.

"Back!" Tom called out cheerfully. He was almost always cheerful. His broad, slightly chubby features seemed ill at ease with any other expression- so unlike Martha and her narrow, hawkish face. Like everything else, they complimented each other almost perfectly.

"Sorry, hun. You know Ed. A four-minute update turns into an hour-long conference about third quarter 2023." He sat down on the couch across from her. "He's thriving, though. Handling the business like-" He cut himself off and sprang back up as he realized his voice was the only sound in the room. He ran to the tablet by the speaker and hastily punched away at the touchscreen.

"It is a truth universally acknowledged..." Scarlett Johansson began, narrating the opening lines of *Pride and Prejudice* before Tom's blabbering drowned her out.

"Oh shit, I guess it doesn't matter now." Tom paused the audio book and went back to her side. "I'm sorry, Marty. I swear I'm going to figure out a way to set it so the next book starts automatically. I promise." He squeezed the limp dough of her hand. "I hope you weren't stuck for too long."

"I had two pages of Jane Eyre left when you got up, Tom. I've been staring at that wall in total silence. I've memorized the order of the books on that shelf. I counted the petals on every flower in that vase.

I screamed. I screamed and I don't even know how long I was screaming for, you idiot fuck!"

Martha Lindquist told her husband none of this. Her mouth couldn't convey her fury. Her eyes slouched in their sockets with the same glazed indifference. Tom did not recoil from her anger. He simply leaned over and dabbed away the drool from the corner of her mouth. While he was there, he lifted her dress to make sure she didn't need a diaper change.

From beyond the den that encompassed Martha's moon and stars, she heard the front door open and slam shut.

"Don't slam the door!" Martha screamed reflexively in the prison of her skull.

"Dad!" a voice cried, ringing through the house with gleeful exuberance. Sneakers squeaked against the wood floor in the living room. "Dad, where are you!?"

"Down in the den, Ginny!" he called.

The cacophony grew closer. It sounded to Martha like the way her daughter used to move. Thunder and lightning with a ponytail. Never slowing down. Never silent. Her mother's stroke had tamed the lighting, dimmed the thunder, but something had reignited it.

Virginia came bounding into the den. The girl hadn't even bothered to take off her backpack. She rumbled towards her father with eager eyes and with something dark and fuzzy clutched tight to her chest. At first, Martha thought it was a handbag, the kind of hideously designed monstrosity that Ginny inexplicably adored, but then the bag blinked and Martha saw the thing for what it was.

A black cat.

"Dad! I got off the bus and she was waiting under the bushes!" Ginny cried. She cradled the cat against her chest as if she'd loved it since birth. "Can we keep her? Pleeassseee?"

Always so direct. Martha felt a surge of pride.

Tom's face twisted indecisively. "It's got a collar, Ginny. It belongs to somebody."

Virginia was prepared. "I'll put up signs so her owner can call us. But we can't just leave her on the street, Dad! But, I mean, if nobody claims her...."

Ginny held up the cat, truly a sleek, lovely specimen, and bribed her father with a smile that was shameless in its intent, but still no less lovely.

"Virginia. We've got enough going on in this family right now. We don't need another thing to deal with.

"Let her have this, Tom," Martha willed. *"She is a ten-year-old girl with a cardboard cutout for a mother. Let her have something to tell her friends about that isn't more misery."*

"It's a cat, Dad!" Ginny implored. "We won't have to walk her or anything. She just needs food and a litter box, and I can do that. Pretty please, Dad? I promise to take care of her."

Tom heaved a heavy sigh, but Martha could tell he didn't really mean it. In her heart, she cursed him for that. That he had the luxury to waste facial expressions on things that he didn't even truly feel.

"We'll try it for one night and see what happens. I'm not promising anything."

Except he was promising plenty. Ginny knew it and Martha knew it. And Tom sealed the deal by picking the cat up and carrying it over to Martha in her recliner for inspection.

He held the feline too close to her. The same way he held everything too close. Martha's early, glowing evaluation of the cat dimmed with every inch it drew closer. The sickly yellow lanterns of the cat's gaze hovered mere inches from Martha's face now. There were flecks of leaves in its fur, and god knew what kind of parasites were lurking underneath. The collar around its neck was a frayed braid of rope. *Hobbs*, read the name inscribed on a cheap, tin pendant.

"What do you think, beautiful?" Tom asked her. "Any interest in a new face around the house?"

"I think its breath smells like an old lady's asshole," Martha thought and was then immediately struck by a bizarre, but irrefutable certainty.

This cat knew exactly what she was thinking.

Martha pushed the wild thought aside, but not without some dread for even having it. It had been a little more than a month since she had the stroke. Ever since then, Martha's greatest fear had been going insane while trapped in the lifeless mannequin of her body.

But that wasn't what mattered now. Now, she dwelled on the surge of warmth in her chest as she watched Virginia take the cat from her father and cradle it to her chest. The cat reciprocated by craning its neck and nuzzling up against her daughter's chin.

She was a beautiful child with a large mane of golden hair and a lean, coltish frame that would spring into a beautiful woman in the fullness of time. And all of those advantages were just window dressings around the spirit of a wonderful, precocious, intelligent child.

Martha didn't expect to live much longer. But this child, this miracle, made that okay. Martha had already achieved the greatest wonder of her life. She took comfort from that.

And then she felt a different warmth between her legs as her bladder let go.

Chapter 4

THE NEXT MORNING, REBECCA finally got the story she'd missed out on at the bar the night before.

It was relayed to her in the slack channel she shared with the other two Gazette reporters young enough to know what a slack channel was. Tom Senzer had gotten the assignment, and he was all too happy to furnish the gory details.

TommonSense: Eaten by her cats. It's only front page news because budget cuts killed the Food and Recipes section.

Jill Baldwin replied with a vomit emoji while Rebecca typed out her response.

ReblogSpencer: OMG. I could have gotten you an eyewitness statement. I was at The Badger last night with these two totally freaked out paramedics. I bet they were there.

TommonSense: Thanks, but I got everything I needed from the cops and the neighbors. There's no shortage of people happy to spill on Evil Edith Penn.

ReblogSpencer: ???

TommonSense: Oh, yeah. I forgot you're "From Away."

JillNye: Edith Penn is the lost Sanderson Sister. She's the town witch. Everybody here grew up scared to walk past her house after dark.

TommonSense: My dad used to tell me that if I didn't do my homework, Edith Penn would creep into my room one night and take my insides for her soup.
ReblogSpencer: So what was she really? Just some non-christian, closeted lesbian?
JillNye: LOL. Probably.
TommonSense: WAIT.
TommonSense: Our parents scared us with some weird old cat lady...
TommonSense: And now we'll get to scare our kids with the GHOST of some weird old lady who was EATEN. BY HER CATS. How's THAT for an upgrade?!
JillNye: LMAO!

He was just warming up, Rebecca knew how Tom was once he got on a roll, but she didn't get a chance to see what he typed next. It was at that moment that she glanced up in the rearview mirror and saw her target coming out of his office. She hastily swung out of her car and sprinted to catch up with him as he crossed the parking lot.

"Senator Hyde!" she called, jogging up on him from behind.

Senator William Hyde spun towards her with the genial smile already locked across his ski-tanned cheeks. For a moment, it was easy to see how his charm outpaced his homeliness. Hyde's hair had receded in a drastic widow's peak and his shrunken, beady eyes were overwhelmed by livery lips and a massive, rounded nose, but there was a jovial charm that washed all of that aside. There was just an aura of charitable warmth around him. It invited you to go easy on his shortcomings.

That warmth wavered for a moment as Senator Hyde recognized exactly who was chasing after him. The smile stayed, but the manner of his bared teeth shifted. The glint in his eyes might have been an errant reflection of the sun, or it might have been a hint of his feelings toward a reporter who refused to just drop the fucking bone.

In that moment, it was very easy to think of him as ugly.

"Miss Spencer," he boomed. "I believe my secretary already emailed a statement to you. There was no need to come down and collect it in person."

Rebecca grinned right back. "Well, Senator, I came down because there must have been some confusion. You see, the statement I received didn't address any of the questions I posed to your office."

Senator Hyde shouted a response over his shoulder without breaking his stride. "I have to say, I didn't think that a young woman of your ancestry would object to the full legalization of marijuana in the fine state of Rhode Island."

Rebecca kept pace right beside him. "Senator, your Cannabis Authorization Act sets licensing requirements for a dispensary that are wholly impossible for small entrepreneurs to comply with. Meanwhile, the most likely applicants are all investment firms that you have an ownership stake in. Wouldn't it be preferable if the bill afforded fair opportunities to people of my age and... ancestry?"

William opened the door of his Cadillac, but deigned to favor her with actual eye contact. "You're not going to make that into some kind of 'thing' are you? I gave you my statement, Miss Spencer. Beyond that, I have no further comment."

Hyde got into the car and slammed the door behind him. It was a damn tragedy what the Gazette had become, he thought to himself. Somebody ought to look into that.

He shifted into reverse, but his foot held on the brake. Hyde looked at the backup camera with an expression torn between cynical humor and pure, unbridled fury.

"Unbelievable," he murmured. "Un-fucking-believable."

The snooping bitch was standing behind his car. Trying to block him from pulling out of his spot. The grainy feed from the backup camera was clear enough to show the defiant jut of her lip, as if she were the one who got to decide when they were finished talking.

State Senator William Hyde didn't dither. He put his foot on the gas and the big Caddy surged backwards with a ferocious snarl of combusting gasoline.

The girl got the message. Hyde saw it in her wide eyes just before she leapt to the side. William looked up in the rearview mirror so he could see her properly. The low-res camera just didn't do justice to the scene of that mouthy bitch down on her tits in a snow drift.

"Teach you not to bluff with an empty hand," he muttered before shifting into drive and making the rubber scream like a teething infant as he roared away from his office.

Cruising onto Route 27 and suddenly overcome with good cheer, he tapped up Spotify on the infotainment system and brought up his "Grillin' and Chillin'" playlist, never mind the snow mounds on the lawns outside his window. Dire Straits had just begun the Walk of LIfe when the music abruptly cut off and the blaring ring of an incoming call echoed through the sedan. Hyde normally would have let it go to voicemail, but the memory of the reporter swan-diving into a snowbank was such that he actually smiled as he answered.

"Hello, dear." he said.

"Willlll," his wife moaned. "Lexie found a cat hiding under the porch."

Hyde's smile withered like a rose sprayed with weed killer. It was his own fault for assuming his wife would call for any reason other than to bitch about something.

"So get my .22 and shoot the fucking thing," he instructed. "Leave it where it lies and Hector will collect it tomorrow. You don't have to do anything except move your finger a couple inches."

"No, Will. She's already brought it inside. You have to tell her no."

"Jesus, Torrie. What the fuck do I care? Let her keep it if she's already got it." In truth, his first instinct would have been to kick the damn fleabag out into the cold, but if Torrie thought she could make it into his problem then she had another fucking thing coming. Clearly, she needed a reminder of how things were done in this house.

Hyde's other phone chirped from the passenger seat. The one he didn't sync up with the car. He glanced at it and saw a different kitty trying to get his attention. A pretty little Siamese with fake tits up by her chin.

"Listen," he said to his wife. "You can let her keep the cat, you can drown it in the backyard, you can do whatever you want to do... but *you* do it, Torrie. I don't care enough to get into it and have the kid hate me for two months. And I've got a committee meeting tonight, so don't bother setting me a place for dinner."

He hung up the phone and brought up Google Maps. The Proctor Hotel was already there waiting for him in his recent destinations list.

He'd put the reporter in his place. He'd put his wife in her place. Pretty soon, he would put "Lovergirl92" into a very different kind of place. All of that, and his financial and political futures would both be secured once the legal weed bill passed. He looked out over the sunny sky and reflected it was a very good day to be an American.

"What's new, pussy cat, whoa-uh-ohhh," he crooned to himself as he pulled onto the freeway.

Chapter 5

FOR THE THOUSANDTH TIME, Brian tucked his chin down and tried to smell his own chest.

He'd taken a shower after work. And he'd stopped at CVS on the way home and bought some no-brand cologne just so he'd have *something* to layer over the stench, but vomit carried a phantom smell that no amount of showering or aftershave could totally hide.

A waiter appeared beside the table, pen and pad at the ready. "Would the gentleman like to start with an appetizer?" he inquired.

Brian sat up, trying to look the part in the sport coat that he'd never gotten around to taking to the dry cleaner. "Uh, not yet. But could I get a bottle of red for the table? Whatever you think is good."

"Very good, sir." The waiter departed as smoothly as he'd arrived, leaving Brian to drum restlessly at the table. He sat back and checked his phone. 7:38. His "date" was technically late, but only by a few minutes. He sipped at his water glass and tried to relax. If this girl didn't show up, then so what? He could tell his mother that he'd done his part and that was the thing that actually mattered. In the meantime, he pulled up his fantasy league to see who was available for trade.

"Uh-oh," a feminine voice suddenly murmured from across the table. Brian's head was still down, but the raspy timbre of that voice was enough to send gooseflesh up his neck. The girl sounded uneasy, but still unable to suppress a smoky amusement.

Brian looked up from his phone with a charming, self-deprecating smile. *"Hoping I wouldn't show?"* is what he'd been planning to say, but then he laid eyes upon his blind date and lost the ability to speak.

He was dumbstruck. First, by a figure that could have stopped a train in its tracks. Then, by her inescapably deep, incredibly beautiful eyes. And then, finally, by the hammer-blow realization that he had seen her before. Brian finally found his voice, but all that came out was a blunt, unintentionally harsh declaration:

"You."

Her.

The reporter from the bar.

"I don't suppose you'd believe that I've got a twin sister?" she winced.

She tried to smile, but Brian was no longer there. He wasn't at the only decent Italian restaurant in town, smiling at a stunningly attractive woman in a tastefully low-cut dress. He was back outside the bar in the freezing cold. Trying to shake off the worst call he'd ever received and wondering if he should stop somewhere for a twelve pack because the sight of the old woman and her bloody cats still wouldn't shake itself out his head.

And then, out of nowhere, this vulture cawing in his ear. Trying to pry the morbid details out, asking him to relive it when he still wasn't over living through the situation the first time.

Brian said none of this out loud, but Rebecca was a student of people. She heard enough of what Brian wasn't saying to jerk a thumb towards the door.

"Okay, so I'm gonna bounce," she said. "Don't worry about my mom. I'll say I had to work late. She's heard that before."

At that moment, the waiter appeared with a bottle of Cabernet. He smiled as he saw Rebecca standing by the table. "Ah, excellent. I'll give you two a moment to look at the menu." He set down the bottle, added two glasses, and was gone as quickly as he appeared.

The two place settings yawed wide between them. At last, Brian waved her towards the empty chair. "You're here," he said. "Might as well have a drink."

With only the slightest hesitation, Rebecaa settled into her chair as Brian filled both their glasses.

"So. You're Rebecca," he said.

"And you're Brian," she supplied.

"Your mom knits?"

"About as much as yours, sounds like."

That was how they got to be here. Their mothers lived five hundred miles apart, but they were friendly in a sewing group together on Facebook. Chatting in Messenger, they realized that they both had children living in the same Rhode Island town and OH! Wouldn't it be just darling if the two of them hit it off?

Brian had been browbeat into it. *"Six months since that bartender broke up with you, Brian. You're going."* Rebecca had accepted the offer with a casual shrug. There was a retro charm to the idea of a genuine blind date. It beat getting another dick pic on Tinder, and there was the possibility of an article in it. She could always use another freelance check from the HuffPost or Refinery29.

"I guess your mom didn't show you a picture of me beforehand?" Rebecca asked.

"She told me that I was being shallow for asking and that you were a lovely girl."

Rebecca swigged half of her glass of wine in a single gulp. "Man, they *really* brought you here under false pretenses, didn't they?"

Brian laughed. "What did your mom say about me?"

Rebecca put on a heavy Carribean accent. "Rebecca, he's sooo good to his mother! And *handsome,* my lord. And Rebecca.... He cooks!"

Brian waved it off. "I make a good pressure cooker chili. Ribs if I'm feeling ambitious. Nine days out of ten it's just a sandwich in an ambulance." He sipped at his own wine. "My mom said you moved here from Miami. What the hell made you want to do that?"

Rebecca finished off her glass, and Brian poured her another. She tipped the glass at him and took a sip before answering.

"Just work. The Gazette was hiring when most other papers were just offering internships. I'm not going to lie and say that I don't miss wearing shorts year round, but at least here I'm getting real bylines. And there are some good stories around if you're willing to talk to people."

Brian couldn't help but snort. "I'm sure you're doing just fine," he said, and was then surprised by how immediately he worried that she'd think he was rude.

Her companionable chuckle put him at ease. "Don't worry. Edith Penn is already in print, so I've got no reason to pump you for any more information. And I'm not 'sorry' for the routine I pulled on you, but I do understand why you might have found me... less than forthcoming."

"Oh," he chortled. "Is that what we're calling it?"

"Perks of being a writer," she said. "I have a voluminous assortment of efficacious and antipathetic synonyms for most idioms. Not that 'get fucked' doesn't have a certain blunt charm to it."

He blushed, but Rebecca took mercy on him and changed the subject. "My mom said you guys were an Army family. You lived all over too, so how'd you wind up in Rhode Island?"

Brian shrugged. "I finished high school here. In-state credits made it the easiest place to get my paramedic certification. And then it was just like you said, New Birmingham was hiring."

"You didn't want to enlist?" she asked.

"I thought about it," Brian said. "Y'know. Legacy. But I was fourteen and we moved to some bullshit army town. My dad was only there for training, so I just wanted to keep my head down and get out.... But this kid in my homeroom just decided that I rubbed him the wrong way." Brian folded his arms on the table. His biceps strained against the sleeves of his sports jacket. "I was already a big kid, and army brat schools are always aggro. He probably just wanted to make a name for himself. Anyway, it escalated into some shitty little shoving match after school..."

"And what happened?" Rebecca pressed.

Brian didn't answer, suddenly lost in the memory. Joey Collins. Not a small kid, just smaller than the guy he chose to pick on. Brian had nailed him with an uppercut and left him spread-eagle on his back. Joey had gone limp with his open, unblinking eyes staring blankly up at the sky.

To Brian's mind, Joey was looking past the sky. Joey was communing with God himself while he waited for his body to yank his spirit back into it. Meanwhile, Brian stared at his own fist, overwhelmed by what a single punch had done, but mostly just wishing that Joey would do something. Cough. Roll over.

Just give me something so I know I didn't kill you. Come on, Joey. It was one fucking punch. Come on. Please.

Brian jerked back to the present. A restaurant, ten years later. Brian had graduated without consequences. And Joey Collins had turned out fine after his broken jaw healed and people stopped calling him "One Punch" in the hallways. Brian shook his head and finished his own glass of wine.

"It turned out I wasn't a fighter," he settled for. "Being a paramedic felt like a better way for me to serve."

"Nobody was disappointed?" Rebecca asked.

That's what Brian had feared too. He remembered being piss-scared as his 18th birthday rushed forward and he wasn't asking for a lift to the recruitment center.

"Honestly, I think my dad was relieved," Brian said. He refilled his own glass of wine. "I'm sorry. This is probably a little too heavy of a story for a first date."

Rebecca smiled back. It was a small one, just a gentle lift at the corners of her mouth, but it made Brian realize that she was so sexy it was easy to miss how beautiful, how truly and incredibly beautiful, she really was.

"It was probably a heavy question for a first date," she said. "Sometimes I just can't help myself. We can talk about anything you want. Stupid stuff. You wanna know my favorite TV show? Childhood best friend? Hey, do you wanna hear about my new cat!?"

Brian tilted his head skeptically.

"You want to talk to me about... a cat?" he asked.

Rebecca's eyes bulged. "Oh! Oh shit!"

Brian laughed. On impulse, he reached out and touched her hand. It was entirely unplanned, but it felt perfectly natural. His skin settled against hers in total compatibility.

"We don't have to talk about it," he said.

***

They didn't talk about it until two weeks later, lying together in Rebecca's lumpy, full-sized bed with the sweat of passion cooling against their skin.

"...I really should have given you that interview," Brian panted.

Laughing, Rebecca grazed her nails over his exposed hip. "I think it worked out for the best. If you were a source, then we wouldn't be able to do *this*." She leaned forward and planted a trail of kisses down his chest. "That would be very. Very. Unprofessional."

He pulled Rebecca up to claim her mouth. His broad, powerful hands slid under the sheets and squeezed her backside. "The story was a real mood killer anyway."

She let her head fall against his chest. It was not sex now, but a deeper comfort. His body beneath hers felt as solid as the earth.

"You must have a lot of stories like that," she said quietly.

"A couple, but this is a quiet town. Car crashes, sometimes a farm accident, but what happened to Edith Penn..."

Pressed to his chest, she felt his heart hammering. His skin had turned cold with a suddenness that gave Rebecca her own case of goosebumps.

"You don't have to talk about it," she told him.

"I think I want to," he said. "The thing is, I keep waiting for it to feel fake. That's how it is for me with the bad ones. It's real when I'm in the thick of it, trying to help, but give me some distance and whatever happened starts to feel like a story. Just something I'm telling instead of something that happened to me. But Edith Penn..."

The memories slammed into him again. The images didn't feel like a story. They felt vivid and suffused with a living, nuclear heat; stamped into his brain like a tattoo he'd carry around for the rest of his life.

She's on the kitchen floor. Dried up oatmeal and a spilled bowl next to her head. Some of it is in her hair. So is the blood.

"This town talks about her like she's some child-stealing freak, but she looked like she weighed about twelve pounds. She wasn't a witch. She was just some old lady who lived out on the edge of town with her cats. And then she died. Heart attack. Embolism. Whatever. And those cats chewed her to pieces."

Rebecca took her ear away from his heart. She wanted to see his face.

The bites are everywhere. The soft places are the worst. Her lips are gone and her teeth gleam out at them in a permanent smile. Her ears are mashed up orange rinds, gnawed until all the juice was gone. But her arms and legs are fair game too. All the blood's turned her white cotton nightgown into red satin.

"You know who called 911?" he asked. "The mother of some kid who went by every few weeks to do chores for pocket money. There were no pictures in the house. No friends. No family. If some kid didn't need twenty bucks, she'd be a skeleton before anyone called."

And the cats look happy as can be. Well-fed. Sleek. They parade around the house- bloody prints on the couch and the counter top. They look at Brian and the others as the interlopers. And why shouldn't they? Edith Penn owned them in life, now they own her in death.

He felt Rebecca's lip press gently against his. Her tongue gently opened his mouth and caressed his, wiping away the furious, raging voice at the back of his thoughts.

All too quickly, she pulled back. Her hands went to the back of his neck.

"You do what you do because you don't like seeing people get hurt," she said. "It sounds like Edith was hurt a lot in her life. Not just at the end."

She straddled him again and sat up in his lap. She worked her hips back and forth against his until he began to stir beneath her. "I've got bad stories too," Rebecca said. "I'll listen to yours if you listen to mine." She saw Brian grin in the dark.

"Really? Still in the mood after that?" he asked.

"It didn't seem to bother your partner or Joy."

It was hard to think with the steady, liquid-lightning pendulum of her hips short-circuiting his brain. Harder still because Mike was old and....

He got it.

"Noooo," Brian groaned. "No! Come on!"

"You should have seen them looking at each other as she pushed everybody out the door," Rebecca teased.

"Nope. I definitely don't need to see anything like that," he stressed.

"What?" she teased. "You're not still going to want it when you're sixty?"

He squirmed beneath her, the angle was close... God, so close. "It would be nice if I wasn't still going to bars looking for it," he said.

Rebecca shifted with him. Brian slid up and in, exactly where they both needed him to be.

"Really?" she breathed. "That's good to know."

Afterwards, Rebecca fell asleep quickly. Brian stayed awake, resting his hand against the curve of her ass and savoring her warmth nestled against him. The room still smelled faintly of sex and the sandalwood candle she'd lit.

He liked it. He liked the feel of her satin pillowcase. He liked hearing from her during the day. He liked the way he felt right now, like he was floating in a warm bath.

He really liked Rebecca.

He didn't like the rancid yellow eyes that suddenly opened in the shadows over Rebecca's dresser. The sight splashed over him like ice water and nearly made him jump out of the bed.

He stopped at the last moment and tried to quell his thumping heart. He warily watched the cat stretch on top of the dresser and then curl up into a ball. The glowing eyes disappeared as it settled into sleep. *Get it together,* he chided himself. *You can't almost shit yourself every time you see a cat for the rest of your life.*

Maybe, but he couldn't deny the coiling tension in his back and shoulders every time he saw Rebecca's cat lurking in the kitchen or behind the sofa.

There was nothing he could do about it. All he could do was try to ignore the cat. Ignore his jitters. Ignore the way he felt like those sullen yellow eyes knew exactly how much he disliked it.

Ignore the nagging certainty that Rebecca had put the cat out into the hallway before closing the door.

Chapter 6

1965

THEY ALWAYS CAME IN the middle of the day.

There was logic to it, Edith supposed. They couldn't come before nine AM, not with kids to get to school and husbands to wave off to work. Then there was always some hesitation to contend with- an hour or two's delay while they reasoned that they were just being silly. And then yes, a little more time just to be afraid. But if they waited too long, then it was already two o'clock. The kids would be home soon, and there was still housekeeping to finish and dinner to get in the oven. Put it all together and twelve o'clock seemed to be the, ha ha, magic hour.

Edith understood it, but that didn't mean she had to like it.

Regardless, the furtive knock came at her back door, and Edith Penn obliged. She set aside her chicken salad, turned down the volume on *Jeopardy*, and put her day on pause so she could see who had turned up on her doorstep with a problem.

This time, it was Janine Walton. She stood there on the back steps, trying to make herself look as small as possible. No small feat given the blonde woman's hefty stature.

"Good afternoon, Edith," Janine said formally. As if the two of them hadn't grown up scurrying for aluminum cans in the same ditches during the war.

"Janine," Edith greeted in a calm, neutral tone. She stepped aside, allowing the other woman to come inside. If she wanted to.

Janine did, stepping tentatively over the threshold as if the tiles below her feet might be hot with hellfire.

She really had gotten fat, Edith thought. Too many years of prosperous living. Edith had been all elbows and knees as a child, and not much had changed. She was a tall, sunken-chested woman with the proportions, long beak, and large eyes of some kind of water bird.

"Oh," Janine said in soft surprise as Tituba bounded up onto the counter. She was a small Maine Coon, which still made her bigger than most house cats, and her thick mane and broad snout lent her a wildness that most people found off-putting. A few of Edith's other cats also crept out of their hidey-holes to get a look at the new visitor. Yellow eyes regarded Janine with unabashed curiosity. Noses twitched as they took in the newcomer's scent.

"Don't mind them," Edith said. "Would you like some tea?"

"*No.* I mean, no thank you." She sat down at the kitchen table and folded her hands in her lap. Edith set a pot to boil anyway and then joined the other woman at the table. Janine nervously fluffed at her freshly-dyed hair. She'd clearly been to the salon recently. Edith's own hair was clean, but the same river-water brown it had always been.

They sat in silence, except for the hiss of the gas stove behind them. It was not Edith's way to begin the conversation. These women could ask for themselves.

It took a try or two, but Janine found her voice. "My... my son is a senior in high school," she said.

"A football player, I understand."

"A *quarterback!*" Janine seethed with sudden vehemence. "He's taking Quill High to the state championship, and they're going to *win.* I see the college scouts already. They're always in the back, trying to blend in, but I *see* them seeing my boy."

"He sounds very fortunate," Edith said. The teapot on the stove was starting to bubble.

"And he says he wants his father to get him a job at the mill!" Janine erupted. Edith was strictly incidental at this point. A random bypasser in front of Janine Walton's street pulpit. "He could be a doctor! Or a lawyer! And with a scholarship, it won't cost him a *cent*! But no, he just wants to chase some cheerleader's skirt. I've begged him. His father's threatened him. We've tried everything to make him understand that his *future is at stake*, and all he wants to do is spend the rest of his life breaking his back while that leech in a skirt drains the life out of him!"

"But there's still one thing you haven't tried," Edith said quietly. "Isn't there?"

The tea came to a boil. It screeched in the silence between them while Edith waited for Janine to make a decision.

Not trusting herself to speak, Janine reached into her purse and threw an envelope onto the table.

Edith didn't bother to count the money. It was always enough. She went to the stove and silenced the howling tea kettle. From the cabinet, Edith produced a steel thermos. From the same cabinet, she laid out an array of glass jars with cork-stopped tops. Some of the containers held colored powders. Others contained murky fluids. A few, disturbingly, held things more easily identifiable.

Edith unscrewed the thermos lid and put the ingredients in first. Some powdered black widow leg. A splash of Falcon's Eye. A trio of dead flies. Edith felt Janine's heavy gaze at her back as she worked, but the other woman asked no questions.

The hot water came next. The stench, barely noticeable at first, grew stronger as the thermos filled and the brew steeped. Edith checked that the color was satisfactory before screwing the cap back on. She brought the thermos to Janine, who took it gingerly. As if the contents could explode at any time.

"Bury this in your yard until the next full moon," Edith told her. "Then dig it up. You'll have two days to persuade your boy to drink it. I suggest trying to hide it in a clam chowder. Do *NOT* give it to anyone after the second day. Is that clear?"

Janine had gone white as a daisy. Her doughy hands were clamped tight around the thermos.

"He's going to be sick," Edith warned. "Fever. Vomiting. He might bleed from his eyes. If you want to take him to a hospital, that's your business, but it won't make a lick of difference. He'll recover in a week. And he will never, ever mention the name of his beloved again."

Janine clutched the thermos to her swollen bosom. She looked equal parts ecstatic and repulsed. She'd entered the lair of the witch and discovered that it was all true. The good and the bad. Her cheeks quivered and she pushed the chair away from the table. She retreated from the table in hasty, stumbling steps and fled through the back door. Another unspoken ritual, they always came and left through the back way. And their only parting words were always the bang of the door.

Edith returned to the chair in time for Final Jeopardy. Her lunch was where she'd left it.

Osborne jumped into her lap. Tituba joined her on the armrest. Others leapt onto the headrest or coiled at her feet. Greedy little Sears mewed and nosed at her lunch bowl. Edith let her take a taste.

"Another satisfied customer," Edith remarked to the cats.

On the TV, Art Fleming posed the Final Jeopardy question.

Chapter 7

THE DONKEY SOUNDS BEGAN the moment Maura walked into school.

"Hee-aw!"

"Hee-aw!"

She kept her head down. After so many years, the taunts were like walking around with broken glass in your shoes. It never stopped hurting, but you eventually realized that you just had to make your peace with it and keep walking.

She was spinning her combination lock when the fingers nipped at the back of her neck. Sharp nails made Maura wince. Briana Warren flicked a stray piece of straw into her face. "Forget to shower when you rolled out of the barn this morning?" she asked.

Lily Greenhall stuck her nose in Maura's face and sniffed twice. "Smells like it to me. Hee-aw!" They departed, cackling. Maura heard them casually change the conversation to a planned shopping trip before they faded out of earshot.

The abuse roared in and swept out like the tides. Morning classes were low tide as her classmates feigned attention to lectures. High tide came again at lunch. Today, someone thought it would be cute to steal her sandwich. Maura came back from the bathroom and there was a fist-sized mound of dirt waiting on her plate instead. A lone worm wriggled up, tasting the air.

The other outcasts at her table, not friends, simply looked down in shamefaced silence.

The bell rang for afternoon classes. Another low tide.

Then the bus. High tide again. Her stop was the last on the route, giving everybody one last lick at her before retreating to the comfort of their own homes. The driver didn't even favor her with a nod as Maura stepped down.

Maura squelched her way from the corner to her house. In the spring and summer, the small farmhouse had a quaint charm to it as the sun beamed brightly and the earth bloomed lush and proud. But against the grey February sky, the paint alway seemed more faded. The muddy pens surrounding the property seemed to creep larger and the animals living there always seemed filthier, no matter how many times they were washed.

She finally reached the door. Her father was running the petting zoo at an elementary school carnival. Her mother was teaching ice skating down at the lake. The house was empty.

Maura went for the oreos. They did her thighs no favors, but it was part of the after school ritual that iced her scorched nerves. Half a sleeve of oreos up in her bedroom while she worked with one of her candle-making kits.

She set out the candle wicks, hot wax, and the melting plate, and popped another cookie into her mouth while she waited for the hot plate to warm. Her phone buzzed just as Maura swallowed another oreo. The sound soured the taste, making it so that the sugary sweet cookie landed in her stomach like a ball of porcupine quills.

They'd found her again. It didn't matter what name she changed her online profiles to or what website she jumped to. They always found her. 1..3... 7... the notifications piled up in her phone like pigshit piled in the pens outside.

Maura didn't need to look. She knew what they said.

"Hee-aw!"

"Donkey!"

More taunts. There would be pictures of her head photoshopped onto 2 donkeys having sex. There would be links to websites where she could buy bleach to kill herself.

She knew it. She didn't need to read it.

She reached compulsively for the phone anyway.

A blur of black fur beat Maura to the punch. The cat hopped on the desk and playfully swatted her paw at the rush of notifications. The stray tilted her head to the side, clear confusion in the animal's green eyes as she batted ineffectually against the glass screen.

Maura laughed through her pre-emptive tears. She picked up the black cat, leaving the phone to buzz into the void, and hugged the feline tight under her chin. The cat's fur somehow always smelled like autumn leaves.

"Oh, how rude!" she crooned to the cat in baby talk. "All this food for me and none for you. Are you hungry, Eastey?" she said, addressing the cat by the name she'd read off its collar when she found it. "Come on, I'll take you downstairs."

And that's exactly what she did. The phone and the oreos sat, forgotten, on her desk.

Chapter 8

SENATOR HYDE MADE IT a point to conduct as much business as possible in public.

Part of it was optics. Business carried out in the town square was surely business carried out for the town's good.

The other part was simple love for the town of New Birmingham. His father had been Mayor here, and while William Hyde's own ambitions were set a trifle higher, old Papa Hyde had instilled in him a love of this town that ran deep and true.

He began his day at the drugstore, conscientiously wiping snow off his boots on the mat by the door before venturing inside.

"William!" Joseph Savall greeted as soon as the tarnished bell chimed to announce his arrival.

"Morning, Joe," Hyde replied, seeming to fill the narrow aisle as he approached the counter. He shook hands with the proprietor, careful to exert enough of a grip to show respect, but mindful of the fragility of the seventy-year-old man's bones. It was a careful balance honed by years of practice.

"Good to see ya, Senator." Joseph tried to pull his hand back but Hyde held it firm. He had his phone out in his other hand.

"Don't mind, do ya, Joe?"

Joseph rolled his eyes. "I suppose not, Will." But his free hand clasped the Senator's shoulder, and his smile for the selfie was genuine.

"Okay if I get your prescription now? Or do you need me to knock on some doors first?"

"By all means," Hyde said as he posted the photo to Instagram. *#shoplocal #lovemydistrict.* He perused the shelves while he waited. A lot of business had moved to the CVS on Montauk Way, but Joe Savall had been filling Hyde's prescriptions since he was a kid. And he wasn't shy about slipping in a few trial packs of Valium or Viagra in with your Lipitor.

The crinkling of paper alerted William that his order was ready. Hyde paid cash for his prescriptions along with the pack of condoms he'd grabbed while he waited. Joe rang him up for both and tipped him a wink to let him know there were a few double Vs along for the ride in his bag.

"Best RX in town, Joe," Hyde said on his way out the door.

He left his Cadillac where it was, deciding to take a walk even though his final destination was at the far end of Milwaukee Road. William Hyde's breath fogged before him. The bitter cold tried to seep through his bomber jacket, but it couldn't touch the warmth in his chest as he nodded and waved to the shopkeepers shoveling and salting their storefronts as he passed.

"Call me next time before you get out here, Joy!" he called as he passed the Badger's Den. "I'll come shovel you out."

"Why don't you just do your own job!?" the bartender shouted cheerfully back.

He stopped at Sherman and Son's to inquire about some cross country skis. Sarah Clarke pushed open the door to her bakery as he passed and complained about changes to the health code. Hyde promised to work on it. "But it won't be done by November, so make sure you get to the polls!"

Senator Hyde finally reached the diner a few more handshakes and back pats later. He hung his coat on a peg by the door and saw that Duncan was already waiting for him in their usual booth. He was not surprised to see that his special assistant hadn't waited to order. Nor was he surprised that Duncan did not look up from his heaping serving of pancakes as the Senator sat opposite him. He'd poured so much syrup on them, the hotcakes were little more than soggy islands floating in a sea of molasses.

"Good morning, Mr. Carter," Hyde greeted.

"Senator Hyde," Duncan muttered before stuffing another chunk of flapjack into his gullet.

Hyde waited... and waited.

"Do you have any updates about the new swimming pool?" he finally prompted.

Duncan cleared his throat with a hefty slurp of his milkshake before responding. His voice was surprisingly high and strangled for a man with such hefty jowls and wide neck.

"I have an update, but I can't say that it's a good one. We seem to have discovered an old septic tank on the property."

The Senator's smile didn't fade. It locked into place, a gate to hold back whatever else he might be feeling.

The waitress came up to the table. Hyde's smile broadened at her approach, even as he tightened his grip on his spoon until the cheap metal sank into his palm. "Sam, I know it's early but I think I'm gonna do a burger. Tell Pedro not to skimp on the tomatoes. Thanks."

She left with his order and Senator Hyde turned his attention back to his special assistant. "Do we know what we're going to do about this development? I promised my daughter she could spend every day in the pool this summer. I'd hate to disappoint her."

There was a smear of syrup at the corner of his mouth. Duncan dabbed at it with a movement that was absurdly prim for a man with balloon fingers and a wrist as thick as a coke can. "I have some ideas," he said. "There might be a delay on our timetable, but I think we can sort it out in time to be open for Memorial Day."

There was no visible change in his demeanor, but Hyde loosened his grip so the spoon handle embedded in his hand could slip free. The blood pounding behind his eyes returned to a normal level.

"While you're waiting for me to sort this out, you might want to start looking at flowers," Duncan suggested. "Landscaping brings the whole thing together, you know."

"If you say so, Duncan. Goodness knows I wouldn't mind an excuse to stop and smell the flowers."

Samantha came back with his order and Hyde offered up a genuine smile of thanks. Sam was waitressing to get by while she was working on her teaching degree. Her mother was a receptionist at the firm where Hyde practiced law before being elected to the Senate. The possibility that he might actually be Sam's biological father had occurred to William Hyde more than once.

He touched on a few other important matters with Duncan while they finished eating. Endorsements. A scheduled tour of his office with some grade school class. Pete Benson, a longtime donor, had choked to death eating breakfast of all things. Hyde directed a deli platter be sent to his family.

"It all sounds good, Duncan," Hyde said. He signaled to Sam for the check. "Let's plan on meeting Monday for a status update on the pool."

As was his custom, he left a stack of bills on the table before the check even arrived- enough to cover his tab and a generous tip for the server. Sam arrived quickly to retrieve the tab and clear the plates, but only once she was sure that Duncan was in his car and Hyde was halfway down the block did she bring the dirty plates back behind the counter.

She took the dishes past the wash station and all the way to the far end of the counter, where a young woman sat with her full head of curly, dark hair pushed underneath a baseball cap. Sam set the plate down and the woman reached out and stuffed some stray fries into her mouth.

"That's gross," Sam said.

"Reporter's salary," Rebecca mumbled through a mouthful of starch. "What have you got for me?"

Samantha responded by dutifully ripping the top page off her order book and handing it over. She waited while her friend carefully read the notes scribbled on the back. Samantha had kept a careful log of the two men's conversation. Not just what she'd overheard while taking Senator Hyde's order, but also what she'd picked up as she unobtrusively filled the water glasses at the table behind them. And when she brought a takeout order up to the check-out table. It hadn't been that hard. Senator Hyde made little effort to keep his voice down.

Rebecca finished reading. "This is everything?" she asked.

"As far as I can tell," Samantha said.

"Thanks, Sam."

"Just make sure you're available Friday night. I need you to help me make a fake Tinder profile. I think my boyfriend's cheating on me."

"I know the guys you date," Rebecca said. "Let me save us both the trouble, he's cheating on you."

Samantha stuck her lip out. "Yeah, you're probably right."

Rebecca folded up the paper note and stuck it into her front pocket.

"Did I find anything good?" Sam asked.

"He's hiding something," Rebecca said.

"How do you know?"

"Because he talked about everything *except* the dispensary bill. The CAA is the biggest move of his entire career. The vote's in three weeks and he wants to talk about some field trip? Bullshit."

"So what are you going to do?"

Rebecca shrugged. "Boring stuff. Chase paperwork. Send emails. And I want to dig into that aide."

Samantha shuddered. "That guy creeps me out."

"Me too," Rebecca admitted.

Her friend gently touched her wrist. "Beck, you're being smart, right? Promise me you're not going to get hurt."

Rebecca rolled her eyes. "The guy's just a petty thug in a suit."

"That doesn't make me feel better."

"You don't have to worry about me, Sam. I'm fine."

Rebecca's phone buzzed. She glanced at it before starting to type. Samantha loomed over her like a ravenous wolf.

"Is that your boyfriend? Have you called him your boyfriend yet?"

Rebecca's answer was a slow, sly grin. Samantha squealed. "Rebecca! When can I meet him?"

"When you're not asking me to help you spy on your loser booty call, Sam!"

"Well, don't lead with that. Duh. You haven't told him that, have you? He's not going to set me up with his friends if he thinks I'm a hot mess."

Rebecca stood up and slung her messenger bag over her shoulder. "What are you doing tonight after class? If I go out with Brian, can you stop by my place and feed my cat? I'll give you the key."

Samantha sighed. "At least I'll get to meet *somebody* new in your life."

Rebecca laughed. "If Tituba likes you, we can talk about Brian."

***

Senator Hyde got back to his car and found there was a voicemail waiting for him from the septic tank himself.

"Bill! Ryan here. Give me a call when you can. Let's talk about this weed business and see if we can work something out. You've got my number"

He jabbed his middle finger at the voice playing through the car speakers, wishing that he had the genuine article in front of him. *I've got your number all right, you slimy son of a bitch.* Duncan had already given Hyde the heads up. State

Senator Ryan Cooper planned to kill his marijuana legalization bill in committee unless Hyde agreed to whatever bullshit qualifiers Cooper had in mind. The kind of backroom dealing that might fly if you were a career benchwarmer looking to rename a town park, but it wasn't the sort of bullshit you tolerated when you were dealing with a legacy-making legislation. It certainly wasn't the level of ass-kissing you sank to if you wanted to be President-elect in 2032.

I know what you want to do, Cooper. And I know what I'm going to do too.

Flowers. Duncan had told William that he ought to consider some landscaping options while his aide took care of his situation with the septic tank. Hyde understood exactly what that meant.

As a colleague in good standing, Senator William Hyde would be expected to send his condolences.

The next voicemail was from his wife. William barely recognized her voice. Torrie's normal, hectored shrieking came out muffled, as if there were a pillow stuffed over her face.

"Willum! You haff to geth rihd uf thith *CAT!* I can't breef!"

William shook his head. *Give her this much,* he thought. *She knows how to cheer me up.*

Chapter 9

MARTHA WATCHED HER PRETEEN daughter clamor up onto the counter and open the spice cabinet. Blood throbbed in the abandoned highways of her brain as she seethed in her wheelchair, insignificant as the bag of Nestle chocolate chips that Ginny pushed aside.

Get down from there before you fall! She yelled in the hollow behind her slack features. Oh, how she wished she could rise up from this wheelchair and grab the girl herself. *You come down right this instant, Ginny!*

Virgina, obviously, did no such thing. She dug through the cabinet in a clatter of rattling plastic and glass. Her vantage point on top of the counter gave the young blonde easy access to the farthest reaches of the cabinet. Ginny read labels, sniffed at contents, put some jars back and placed others down on the counter. When the girl had what she wanted, she gathered the ingredients up in a disorganized clutch and carried them over to where she'd set a large sauce pot on the counter.

Hobbs followed behind her. The cat was never more than a few inches behind Ginny's heels.

This is torture, Martha thought. Not for the first time since the stroke had ripped her life away from her. *I'm being tortured.* She thought back on her life. The test she cheated on in sophomore Spanish. The one time she'd tossed an idle rock at a seagull and broken the bird's wing. She repented of every wrong she'd ever done in her life, and it didn't make a whiff of difference. She was still in the chair.

Ginny set the jars and vials in skewed lines like drunken soldiers. Martha had loved to cook, and her collection of spices had been accumulated over years of travel and hours spent chasing down authentic suppliers and rare ingredients.

Stop it, Ginny! Please, baby. Please stop.

In her head, Martha wept.

Ginny heard nothing. She actually sang snatches of pop songs as she haphazardly threw flurries of spices into the mixing bowl. Ancho chile, whole Anise seeds, Baharat. Oh God, nearly half a can of White Sage.

I've had that Cardamom since before you were born!

The cat was up on the counter now, peering inquisitively into the bowl. Her whiskers rose as she took a sniff.

"Get back, Hobbs," Virginia murmured, distracted. For a moment, the child looked adrift. Her unfocused gaze swept across the kitchen before something seemed to click behind her eyes. She skipped to the fridge and came back with lemon juice, chicken stock, and three eggs. Virginia emptied both bottles of liquid into the pot before cracking the eggs and throwing them in as well, shells and all.

She mixed the concoction vigorously, heedless of the spatters of murky brown swill spattering onto the floor. Like most things the child did, there was no obvious pattern to it. Ginny stirred the pot clockwise several times, then abruptly stirred in the opposite direction three times before moving on to jerky, half rotations from twelve o'clock to six o'clock and back again.

At last, to her satisfaction and to her mother's horror, she put the pot on the stove and set it to boil.

"Hey, Google, set timer for 19 minutes."

While the flame hissed, Ginny came over to her mother's wheelchair. The blanket over her knees had come loose and Virgina reverently tucked it back under her thighs.

Don't touch me! Martha raged. *Just leave me alone, you thoughtless little bitch!*

Ginny dallied at her side. "Tracee Trance is gonna be at the DnD Center next month. Dad said he'd take me, but he never knows the words to any of the songs. Do you want to come with us, mom? We could get you a ticket."

...I would love that, Ginny. I would love that very much.

Ginny patted her mother's slack hand, and Martha's anger collapsed into a chasm of sorrow. It was tears her glorified corpse of a body held back now, not anger. She would have traded the rest of her life for just five minutes of singing along to some god awful pop song with her daughter.

Virginia prattled on, unruffled by her mother's inability to respond. It was a queer reversal of when the girl was a baby. Ginny had been a quiet infant. Quiet, but alert. She would sit silently for hours while Martha narrated what she was doing.

"We're cutting the carrots now, Ginny. Yummy, yum, yum!"

"This is tumeric, honey. Your Uncle Mason is dating a woman from India, and she was nice enough to tell me about a shop in Providence that sells it authentically."

Martha lost track of time. She drifted off, willingly floating along to the steady stream of her daughter's voice."So Madison says we're going to play spin the bottle at her birthday party, and Bee's flipping out because-"

Ginny broke off from her story as the melodic chiming from the timer echoed through the kitchen.

"Oh, it's ready!" she cried.

As if the volume were suddenly turned up, Martha could again hear Ginny's monstrous concoction boiling away on the stove. But her anger had not returned with her sense hearing. It was a small cost for the minutes she'd spent feeling normal with her daughter again.

And at least I won't have to clean it up, she laughed in her head.

Ginny ladeled her concoction out into a measuring cup. It spilled forth in a color like rotting leaves. Martha smelled the stench of it from all the way across the room. It made her eyes water. For the first time, she wondered what Virgina planned to do with that cup of slop.

...And then, Ginny took a funnel from the cabinet.

She skipped back towards her mother, carrying the funnel and not spilling a drop from the noxious brew in the measuring cup.

No, Martha realized.*Jesus no.*

Martha willed her body to move. To crawl from the chair. To fly. She struggled more desperately than she had since those first hellish days after the stroke. She tried to call out to her husband reading in the den. She wanted to grab her daughter and make her throw away that brimming cup of rancid dreck.

The only thing that moved was her neck. Ginny pushed gently under Martha's chin, tilting her head back in the chair without resistance. Martha's eyes rolled backwards, leaving her staring up at the ceiling. The harsh glare from the lights narrowed her pupils to stinging pinpricks... until the light was eclipsed by Ginny looming over her.

She stuck the funnel into her mother's mouth. The dry plastic neck depressed her tongue, leaving Martha's throat wide open for whatever might come.

NO! Martha begged. *Ginny Stop! Don't Dont No No!*

Virgina slowly tipped the measuring cup down into her mother's mouth, pouring slowly to ensure that the funnel didn't overflow. The mixture oozed down Martha's throat with excruciating slowness. The chili burned. The salt scraped her throat lining raw. The taste overwhelmed her. She wanted to retch, but her gag reflex was as living dead as the rest of her motor functions. Martha was screaming into a dead phone. She could no more throw up than cry. Or push the funnel from her throat.

Or scream out loud.

Ahhhh!

AHHHH!

OH GODDDD!

Deprived of the ability to retch or spasm in disgust, Martha clawed at the walls of her skull. She went temporarily insane with revulsion.

Ginny fastidious shook every last drop of the concoction. When the measuring cup was totally empty, Ginny plucked the funnel from her mother's throat. She took the funnel and the cup to the sink and carefully rinsed both, exactly as her mother always told her to do, before returning the items to their respective cabinets. She put the spices back too, working carefully to make sure everything was exactly back where she'd found it. By the time Ginny had finished cleaning up, Martha was still mentally wheezing but had at least managed to regain some semblance of coherence.

What... What...

Virginia bounded back to her mother's wheelchair. She kissed Martha on the cheek before spinning the wheelchair around.

"You want to watch Queer Eye, mom? Come on."

Ginny pushed her mother out of the kitchen. Hobbs followed behind them, the cat's tail held high in the air.

In the living room, Virginia sat on the couch beside her mother and brought up Netflix. If asked, the young girl would have had only the haziest memories of what had happened in the kitchen. She knew she was with her mother. She knew she'd put something together on the stove. Other than that...

But she'd done well, that much she was sure of.

Hobbs bounded up into her lap. The cat purred happily as Ginny rubbed her back.

Chapter 10

1984

EDITH WOUND THE LONG strand of blond hair around the bullfrog's leg bone. Once the yellowed bone was completely wrapped in golden hair, Edith held it out over the black candle, muttering a few choice phrases in Early Mandarin as the follicles crackled and the stench of burning hair filled her nostrils.

After the fire did its work, Edith was left with a charred stick the length of a stubby pencil. She set the candle aside and unfurled a roll of parchment paper on her kitchen table. Edith put the burnt piece of bone to paper and held it loosely between her fingers. She breathed calmly in and out, emptying herself of consciousness and being. Her lidded eyes were half open, but she no longer saw. Edith Penn had gone out for coffee. Her body was left behind with the door open just a crack.

After a few moments, her hand began to move across the parchment, scrawling out words in the ash left by the burning hair. Edith herself had no idea what was being written. She had only posed the question. She was not answering, she was merely taking down notes.

It hurt after a while. Her knuckles burned. Icy cold set into her wrist.

Edith wrote on.

She knew when she was done. The burnt piece of bone fell from her hand of its own volition. The force that had pulsed through her departed as quickly as it came. Edith slumped back in the chair. Her heart hammered in her ears.

Her joints ached like an invalid. Something gurgled and revolted in the pit of her stomach, and her bowels trembled fitfully.

"Well?" Tanya Mathers pressed. If she was aware of Edith's struggles, the other woman didn't care enough to allow her a moment to recover. "What does it say?"

Edith managed to shake off the lingering effects from the minor possession. She pushed her chair forward and bent over the parchment. Flickering candles crowded together on every available surface, and Edith had no trouble reading the ash markings in the golden light filling the kitchen.

She looked up at her client, aware of how she must look in the glow of the candles. The bony town witch, hunched over yellow parchment with doom in her eyes. Tanya saw it plainly too. Her hands were fused and rigid under her chin like a knot in an oak tree. Her eyes were bulging owl eyes hidden behind the curtain of her blonde hair.

Such pretty hair, Edith mused. And then she shook her head.

"It's terminal," Edith said. "Eight months. Maybe."

There was little shock. Edith wasn't surprised. Tanya had likely heard the same from her doctors already. It was her true motivation for coming that made the brawny gym teacher lunge across the table. Her chair fell behind her with a heavy clang. She grabbed Edith's arms. Nails dug into thin flesh. Her powerful grip squeezing bone until it creaked.

"How much will it cost!?" She yelled. "You heal me! *You stop this!"*

Edith shook her head. "There's nothing I can do for this."

"I told you I'll pay!" Tanya screamed. She released Edith and feverishly pulled at her own wedding ring. "Anything you want is yours!"

Edith gently cradled the younger woman's hands before she could remove the diamond and platinum band. "It's not about price," Edith said.

It's about cost. What this poor, doomed woman was asking for could technically be done, but Edith knew from painful experience that it wasn't worth doing. It was better to just close that door.

"Some things are beyond me," Edith lied. "I'm sorry."

The punch was unexpected. Edith was prepared for the possibility that Tanya might try to slap her, but the mother of four hit her with a clenched fist that knocked Edith from her chair and squirted blood from her nose like a smashed ketchup packet.

"Bullshit!" Tanya screamed. She stalked around the table. She pulled back one sensible Reebok sneaker and drove it into Edith's ribs. The witch groaned.

Tanya kicked her again. "You're lying," she raged, blood flushing her tan cheeks an ugly shade of mud."You and your magic tricks, and your potions, you're going to *fix me*! I'm not-"

She screamed as Oyers battened onto her back. Claws dug into her sweatsuit and the cat lunged forward to take a chunk out of her ear lobe. Tanya screeched. She stumbled around the kitchen, leaving a spattering blood trail behind every step. Oyers hissed and raked a set of claws down the side of the young mother's face. Her cheek opened in four matching, gushing gashes.

Tanya stretched back, groping for the cat, but Oyers dropped nimbly to the ground first. The feline sprinted across the floor and took her place alongside her sisters, forming a line between the woman and their fallen mistress.

Tanya stumbled back. Fear of the cancer, anger at Edith, everything was eclipsed by the immediacy of what was facing her.

Thirteen black cats held the ground before her. Thirteen sets of teeth bared, a chorus of thirteen hissing cries clawing at her ears. Thirteen baleful, furious cats with their hair standing on end. They fixated on Tanya with sheer hatred in their gemstone eyes.

Tituba advanced first. Her sisters prowled close behind.

The warm blood running down Tanya's back was overwhelmed by the chill running down her spine. She searched fitfully for something to defend herself with, but she could never take her eyes away from the prowling cats long enough to focus.

Most fearsome of all was Tituba. The big Maine Coon's eyes held Tanya in their sway. The cat's snake slit pupils yawed deep as twin gorges. They seemed to swell, growling larger with every thud of Tanya's pounding heart.

In her terror, it took her too long to realize it was no trick. The cat's pupils were widening. Her eyes had turned completely black. And not just Tituba. All thirteen cats stalked closer with eyes of pure, inky blackness.

No. Nonono. NO.

But it was happening. Black smoke poured from the cats' eyes. They began to hiss again, the sound rising with the thick smoke.

"Enough!" Edith yelled.

Her cats immediately ceased their advance. The smoke disappeared as quickly as it had appeared, without so much as a lingering stench. It was thirteen normal felines that scattered at the old woman's cry.

Edith wiped blood from her face and hastily forced her aching bones up. She leveled a crooked finger towards Tanya.

"Just get out!" she screamed. "Get out and never come back!"

Tanya wheeled towards the back door. She lost her balance and stumbled against the counter. Her elbow glanced against a dirty drinking glass and knocked it to the floor in a haze of broken glass. The dying woman swung back towards Edith, eyes wide with fear.

"I said leave!" Edith shrieked. The cats echoed her displeasure in a cacophony of shrieks.

Tanya found the door. She fumbled over the knob, but eventually flung it open and slammed it shut as soon as she skittered out of the house.

In the silence that followed, Edith slowly and painfully made her way to the bathroom. She opened the vanity. There were no prescription bottles or Advil inside, but there were knotted pouches and glass bottles with cork stoppers.

Edith stuffed some Wormsworth up her nose to quell the bleeding. She swallowed a handful of Moonbeam petals for the pain and retired to the couch with a tall glass of lemonade.

Her cats lurked in the corners of the living room and the kitchen. Edith felt them watching her reproachfully.

"It's okay," she told them.

Absolved, her cats came forward. Some wound around her ankles. Others leapt into her lap or up on the couch by head. Tituba clung to her chest, but never painfully, and was rewarded with some gentle strokes along her elongated back.

"You wanted to protect me," she said. "I understand. That woman... she got some bad news. And she lashed out. We know how that happens."

Tituba yowled, as if to show what she thought of *that* line of thinking. Edith chuckled. She picked up the TV remote, a convenience that she still marveled at, and turned on *Cheers*.

More cats creeped closer still as they sensed their mistress relax. Danvers nestled against her thigh and Edith scratched behind her ear.

"She was rude, though, wasn't she?" Edith brooded. Her nose throbbed with thirty years of resentment, dirty looks at the grocery store, and Halloween vandalism. "This whole town. They treat me like a vending machine. And what do you do when a vending machine gets stuck and won't give you what you want? Give it a few whacks, of course."

Perhaps picking up on the undercurrent of Edith's thoughts, Bethia gently took one of Edith's fingertips into her mouth. Pointed teeth pressed on her finger pad

Edith quickly but kindly took her finger from out between the cat's teeth.

"No, no," she chided. "Oyers protected me, and that's okay. But that's all. Let's just enjoy the rest of our evening."

Perhaps. But for the rest of the night, Edith's cats sulked with a bitterness that could not be ignored.

Chapter 11

AS WAS HER CUSTOM, Rebecca knocked as a passing courtesy, but did not wait to be invited in. She strolled into Jerry's office and dropped into the threadbare vistor's chair before his mahogany desk.

"I need to take Kyle on Saturday," she announced. Her editor had called the meeting, but it was also Rebecca's custom to begin a meeting with what she needed to say before allowing her boss to get a word in. "I've got a tip about the Hyde story in Boston."

Jerry didn't look up from the article he was proofreading. Rebecca saw the block of text reflected in the square-rimmed frames of his glasses. He took a sip of his coffee and made no secret of the dollop of whiskey he poured into it while his employee watched.

He continued with his work as if he hadn't heard her. The only sound was the dull chatter squawking from the police scanner he kept behind his desk.

Rebecca evaluated her editor's massive, mahogany desk while she waited. It probably would have gone for six hundred dollars in an antique store by the coast. Jerry had grabbed it for forty dollars at a church rummage sale thirty years ago, and he'd been working to equalize that price difference ever since, one cigarette burn and one whiskey glass ring at a time. The desktop was almost totally impersonal. The only humanizing detail amongst the sweeping rat's nest of draft articles and lawyer's statements was a playing card-sized photo in a cheap CVS frame. That was Jerry's daughter Mary, a freshman at Dartmouth. *"Smart enough for a full ride, and yet still damn fool enough to be a journalism major,"* he always said with a mournful shake of his head.

"Kyle's got to shoot the town fair Saturday," Jerry finally replied. He closed the article and opened up another, never interrupting the flow of his routine.

"Crap," Rebecca groused. But it wasn't the end of the world. She'd taken her own photos before. She could manage it again.

"You're going with him," Jerry added, almost as an afterthought.

Rebecca slammed her hands down on his desk. Papers flew everywhere.

"I'll liveblog your colonoscopy before I cover the goddamn town fair!" she shouted.

The old editor swiveled away from his computer. He was not a large man, nor an angry man, but his displeasure was clear as he stared at her from over the rim of his glasses. Rebcecca scowled, but grudgingly bent down and retrieved the papers she'd scattered.

When she finished, Jerry was leaning back in his chair with his hands folded over his ample stomach. "Jill is covering the Salve Regina Game, and Tommy has an interview with Senator Hyde's campaign manager."

Rebeccca opened her mouth, but Jerry was quicker. "-A request we're obligated to agree to as a legitimate news operation," he said, derailing Rebecca's colorful objection. "And Angelo is on vacation, so I find myself lacking for coverage. Whatever Lois Lane scheme-"

"Iris West," Rebecca said.

Jerry raised an eyebrow at her.

"Iris West is black," Rebecca clarified.

Jerry sighed before continuing with his point. "Senator Hyde. Do you have any reason to believe you're going to catch him in Boston with another woman?"

Rebecca scowled. "No."

"Another man?"

"No."

"Murder?" Jerry pressed. "Extortion? Do you have any reason to believe anything newsworthy will happen? Or are you just shaking trees?"

"...I'm shaking trees." Rebecca admitted.

"Admirable," Jerry said. "That instinct is going to serve you well when you shake my rinky dink paper off your heels and settle in at the LA Times or the Washington Post. But for now, please cover the town fair so I can make the advertisers happy and keep the lights on for another six months. Thank you, Rebecca."

***

She was still grumbling about the assignment later that night.

"I thought you liked your boss," Brian said. He was cutting onions, but he kept an eye on her as he did it. She was sitting up on his counter in a skirt, legs crossed in a way that made her very easy to keep an eye on.

"I do," she said. "Jerry's been running this paper for thirty years. He holds us to major newspaper standards, even if we're not one. I've learned more from him than I would have learned anyplace else. But this gig is a waste of my time!"

Brian put the onions into the pressure cooker and gave the sizzling pan of ground beef another shake. "Because you want to follow this Douglas guy who's working for Hyde?"

"Duncan," Rebecca corrected. She hopped off the counter and grabbed two beers from the fridge. "Officially he's just a personal aide, but I did some digging and he's not local. All of Hyde's staff comes from inside our zip code. Part of his 'Our Town' bullshit. Except this guy. If there's anybody who picks up the dirty laundry, he's the one."

"You really think Hyde's into anything that nasty? I'll take your word that he's an asshole, but you're pushing this pretty hard. What do you think you're going to find?"

Rebecca shrugged. "I'm investigating. This marijuana legalization bill is completely rigged for a couple rich old guys to reap all the profits. That's crap, but it's, you know, normal crap. That story is what got me involved, but the more I look into Senator Hyde- he won't answer softball questions. He bristles when you try to corner him... There's more to whatever he's doing. Or maybe there's just more to how he's getting it done. But something's up. I feel it."

"So what's this other guy doing Saturday?"

"Picking up some package for the Senator over in Boston."

Brian took the ground beef off of the flame and added it to the cooker. "How do you know that?"

Rebecca offered him an open beer before taking a deep draught from her own. "Like I said, his staff's local. Nobody's too good to trade fifty bucks for the occasional inside line. I just want to see what he's getting and who he's getting it from."

Brian cut two jalapenos, carefully removing a third of the seeds before dropping them in amongst the meat and the other ingredients.

"So why don't I go?" he asked. "I'm off that day."

"What do you mean?"

"I mean give me the address. I'll take a drive to Boston and sit in the car with a thermos of coffee and your tiny camera."

"You don't drink coffee on a stakeout. It makes you pee and there's nowhere to go."

"I have... more options when it comes to that problem," he said.

She cocked an eyebrow. "Privilege, you mean."

Brian laughed and put his arms around her. They rocked gently back and forth in the kitchen, but her resistance to his offer was mirrored in the tension in her body. "Let me do this," he said.

"You could be there all day. I don't want you to do that."

He shrugged. "I do."

She finally relaxed against him. He really was the perfect height. She had to arch up just enough to kiss his mouth.

"You're hired," she said.

He grabbed her under the thighs and set her back on the counter. Rebecca luxurated back on her elbows, curly hair in a glorious halo around her head. She bit her lower lip and favored him with a look that glowed with dusky heat.

Brian turned on the pressure cooker before sliding his hands under her skirt to toy with the waistband of her underwear. He met her look with a hungry smirk. "When do I start?" he asked.

Rebecca pulled him into a heated kiss.

"Anytime you want," she said.

Chapter 12

VIRGINIA DID NOT KNOW she was dreaming.

That was the way of it, ever since Hobbs had come into her life. Her dreams ran through her mind like an underground river; unseen but immensely powerful and unrelenting. The young girl slept deeply and darkly, unaware of the things filling her mind as she slumbered.

She was equally unaware as her bedroom door swung open. Hobbs lifted her head as a narrow crack of light fell across her inky pelt, but the cat didn't retreat from her perch at the head of the bed.

The midnight visitor came to the foot of the bed. Bare feet soundlessly crossed the carpeted floor, and a long shadow fell over the sleeping child.

Ginny had shifted in her sleep. The covers dangled half off of the bed, exposing the girl's legs to the early March chill.

Careful not to wake her, the visitor's hands pulled the blanket back up so the down comforter rested snugly just below the girl's chin.

Hobbs was left where she was, curled up on top of Virginia's head. The slumbering child's eyes, nose, and mouth were completely enveloped by the feline's coiled body.

The cat earned a scratch behind the ears before the departing visitor closed the door

***

Tom was very much aware that he was dreaming.

It was a very familiar type of dream by now. He had them often since Marty's stroke. Dreams of tongues and sweat and silk negligees. No wet dreams, thank God, but all too often he woke up with a hard-on straining to split the skin. Masturbating didn't seem to make a difference, and Tom knew why.

It was Martha he needed. His wife. Not the gaunt mannequin confined to a chair, but the Martha he was dreaming about now. Twenty-five years old. Lean, trim, and still full of high-test fuel from her four years of college volleyball. Their daughter wasn't even a whisper then. It was just the two of them, hard-scrabbling it out together in a small, basement apartment. Not a lot of money for outside entertainment, so they made do as often and as frantically as they could.

He was half-awake. He sensed that he could pull out of the dream if he wanted to, but the dream was much better. Martha pressed hard against him, her body baking hot and brimming with living, vibrant need. He cupped her breasts and she purred with delight in his ear. Every inch of her was active. Her lips were on his neck now... and then his chest... past his paunch... Tingling lower... Lower...

He screamed in guttural agony and sat up. For the first time since he was twelve, Tom woke up to the sensation of hot glue filling his boxers. Panting, he fell back in bed with a hand thrown over his eyes, heart still racing with shame and exhilaration.

I can't go on like this, he thought. He didn't know what that meant. A prostitute. Or maybe, God help him, sending her away. But something had to be done.

...That was the moment the blanket rose up. A shadowy head and long, spidery limbs crawled up his body. Hands held down his shoulders.

Tom screamed. Lank hair fell over his face. On cue, the clouds parted and moonlight poured in through his bedroom window.

"Darling," his wife said.

Chapter 13

REBECCA ALLOWED HERSELF TO get a funnel cake. She deserved it for slogging through this crap assignment.

Not that she was slacking off. Hell no. Rebecca interviewed farmers about their prize hogs, and she quizzed bakers about why *their* apple pie was the best in all of Rhode Island. She spoke with the carnival game operators to get their impressions on how the fair had changed over the years and she listened to a first grader with very strong opinions about whether candy apples tasted better than caramel apples.

In the parlance of Lisa Simpson, an early idol, Rebecca had enough sap to keep the readers blowing their noses with pancakes for a month. She'd earned her damned funnel cake.

"The Main Street School Dancers are performing at the bandshell," Kyle said. "You want to get some pictures?"

Rebecca glared at him from the corner of her eye.

"*You* can," she said.

All right. Maybe she was slacking. A little. Kyle went off to take his pictures while Rebecca enjoyed her carbs and sugar.

Her phone buzzed. Rebecca took it out and was greeted by a text from Brian:

Agent 9, reporting in. No sign of the target.

She typed back, unaware of how broadly she smiled as she did so.

HOW ARE YOU HOLDING UP?

Fine. There's a nifty alley right here in case I need to pee.

She sent a laughing emoji. COME STRAIGHT TO MY PLACE WHEN YOU GET BACK. I WANT A FULL REPORT.

He responded with a GIF of a soldier saluting. Rebecca put her phone away, still amazed at how just plain *good* it felt every time she heard from him. She polished off the last of her snack and then got up to find Kyle. As she walked, she found herself thinking about her planned June trip home to Florida. *If* she wanted to ask him to come, he would probably need to book a ticket soon.

Her attention snapped back to work as she passed the petting zoo. There was a young woman, fifteen or so, taking tickets beside the gateway to the pitiful ring of goats, donkeys, and pigs. At first, it was her glum expression that caught Rebecca's eye. This gloomy teen at least offered some contrast to the merry fair-goers crowding the promenade. There could be something here. Worker's rights, maybe. Class dichotomy. Hell, even some simple teen angst would spice things up.

Then the cat curled up in the girl's lap raised its head to be scratched, and suddenly Rebecca couldn't see anything else.

The cat, black as shadows, with blazing yellow eyes, purred contentedly as the girl's fingers curled behind its ear.. A collar of grey rope dangled at its neck, and the battered, metal name tag glinted like fish scales in the afternoon sun.

Just like Tituba, she thought. Tituba's tag. Tituba's coloring.

The cat had lived with Rebecca for a month now.

And you never thought to put up signs. Never wondered where she came from or who put a collar around her neck.

...Could that really be possible? It didn't seem compatible with how Rebecca thought of herself, but it was true. She'd woken up one morning to find Tituba on the balcony, scratching at her sliding door, and she just... kept her. She certainly never stopped to think that the cat might have had an owner that was looking for her.

The black cat nestled in the girl's lap was a different breed than Tituba, but the similarity between them ran deeper than that. Rebecca saw it in the animal's reclined poise and watchful gaze. There was a spiritual kinship between the two cats that flashed out at Rebecca like a neon sign.

Tituba had a life before she was in mine.

The girl paid Rebecca no mind. She was lost in her own world, absentmindedly scratching the cat behind the ears. She was probably supposed to be paying a little more attention to the petting zoo, but it was a handful of scrawny goats, idle pigs, and one docile donkey. There wasn't much to mind.

Rebecca wasn't so far removed from high school that she couldn't recognize this kid. A little fat, a little unattractive. Working at the petting zoo probably didn't do her any favors. Her cat probably meant a lot to her.

Cats. Not cat. Cats.

Rebecca took a step closer, but no further. The thought of even possibly giving up Tituba suddenly loomed large in Rebecca's mind, and she was unprepared for the fierce resistance to the idea that suddenly surged in her chest. Rebecca liked having Tituba waiting for her at home. She liked having the cat jump into her lap while she was working. If the cat had lived somewhere else before, so what? Rebecca was her home now, and nobody would-.

Jesus Christ, she chided herself. *It is a cat. And you are talking about a fucking child.*

Right. Rebecca pushed her weird, unwanted maternal feelings deep down, a task that she was perfectly capable of thanks to years of practice. At a minimum, she could at least try to suss out if the damn kid was even missing a cat before she had to prepare for any tearful goodbyes.

Rebecca walked up to the petting zoo. "Excuse me," she said.

The teenager looked up from her pet. *"Maura,"* read the name on her name tag. "5 tickets," she said to Rebecca with utter disinterest.

"That's okay. I'm with the Gazette and I just wanted to know if I could ask you a few questions?"

Rebecca never got an answer. Something sickly green and brown splattered against the back of the teen's head first. It hit hard enough to drive the kid out of her chair and down to her knees. The cat scampered away with an indignant shriek. Rebecca jumped back as a spatter of something like mud dappled her shirt.

Something that looked like mud... but didn't smell like it.

The girl stayed down on all fours. The poor kid's head was caked with the murky slop. The black cat had a dusting of it across her back.

Meanwhile, the fuckface teen with donkey shit on his hands laughed and laughed from inside the petting zoo pen. His chucklefuck pals crowded outside the fence and laughed right along. Some of them had their cameras out to capture the moment.

"Hee-aw!" the boy in the pen brayed. "Hee-aw!"

Rebecca saw red. She stomped through the mud towards the railing. "Hey! Shithead!" she yelled.

The teen swung towards her in a cocky gunslinger's stance. He met Rebecca's furious scowl with a look of smug dismissal. A big, handsome kid with an unblemished face and an expensive ski jacket. On the far side of the pen, his pals lined up like hungry jackals, excited for the next act of the show.

She was slipping into a role. The indignant "adult" whose outrage just made the cruel antics that much funnier. Rebecca knew it, but she was too livid to care. She slammed the top of the metal enclosure like a pro wrestler waiting to be tagged in. "You belong in that fucking pen," she yelled. "Take the Lexus your daddy bought you for your birthday and shove it up your ass."

The kid just folded his arms. "I got a Corvette for my birthday," he gloated.

What little restraint Rebecca had left snapped. She got one foot up on the bottom rail.

"Feroces Bestia!"

The guttural bellow stopped Rebecca in her tracks. The ugly smirk disappeared from the punk's face at the same moment.

It was the girl. She rose up with shit dripping from her hair. The black cat perched, hissing, on her shoulder. The animal's back was raised. Her fur stood on end.

"Feroces Bestia Ultionem Meam Facti Sunt!" Maura roared. The cat screeched behind her words. Conjoined fury blazed between their two pairs of eyes. Brown and yellow, bonded in hatred.

What happened next happened fast. A person less confident in their senses might not even believe they saw it.

Rebecca saw it.

The donkey loitered in the background of this tawdry after school special, seemingly unconcerned with the drama unfolding before it. But at the girl's cry, the donkey's placid brown eyes flooded with a murky yellow like spilled urine. Its pupils narrowed into black knife slashes.

It kicked.

The donkey's rear hooves slammed hard into the boy's back, wrenching his body backwards and turning his spine into a horseshoe.

The kid was lifted off his feet. The entire cheap, aluminum pen rattled as his body smashed into it.

"Craig!" one of the girls outside the pen screamed.

The boy dropped into the mud and stayed there, settling into the muck like something waiting to be fossilized. Onlookers jumped into the pen. Some of them came to scoop up their wailing children, others turned over the unconscious teenager. They wiped mud from his closed eyes and cleared more from his nostrils. Somebody called for a paramedic.

Some people screamed.

Others cried.

The girl with the cat only watched.

- -

Brian was grateful when he saw the bridge looming ahead of him in the fading light of dusk. More than the estimated arrival time on the GPS, the rusting span across Booth river was the surest sign that he was almost back to Rebecca's apartment.

The day had been exhausting. It wasn't just the discomfort of sitting in a car for nine hours, it was the added tension from being *watchful* at all times. He could never settle into a show or take a bite to eat without constantly looking at the entrance to the shipping company, fearful that this Duncan guy had somehow slipped in and out while Brian was putting mayo on his sandwich.

When Duncan finally did show up, Brian had to laugh. The guy was about as easy to miss as an ocean liner plowing through the wharf.

He didn't laugh long. Two months ago, Brian couldn't even have told you who his state senator was. He hadn't volunteered for this assignment out of civic duty, he was just trying to impress his girlfriend, but the distaste that twinged in his gut at the sight of this guy was real and immediate. There was something about the way Duncan Carter oozed from step to step with the smooth, flowing motion of an octopus; something in how his grimy eyes stayed fixed dead ahead at all times. It made Brian's molars ache just looking at him. The fat around him felt necessary. Like it was insulation separating the world from some noxious, decaying substance.

Surreptitiously holding the small camera Rebecca gave him, Brian took four photos. Two of Duncan entering the shipping company, and two of him leaving with a small box tucked under his arm. The package was roughly the size of a cracker box. Brian figured that Rebecca would probably be interested in that. Why would the guy drive three hours to pick up something you could ship overnight for ten bucks?

He climbed the stairs to her apartment with the spare key she'd given him the night before. He'd offer to give it back, but if she told him to keep it.... Well, there was an extra key to his place that she was welcome to have.

"Rebecca?" he called as he entered. "Beck, you home?"

The living room was empty, but he heard a keyboard chattering from her bedroom.

"Back here," she answered.

Brian heard the distracted, monotone timbre of Rebecca's voice. It was a vocal tic he was already familiar with. She was working on a story.

He found her sitting on the bed, cross-legged with her laptop in front of her. She'd taken a shower, and her still-wet hair was pulled back in a messy bun.

He admired the view for a moment before speaking. "How was the fair?"

Rebecca's focus didn't sway from the screen. "Interesting," she said.

"Really? And here you thought it was going to suck."

She shrugged. "I've occasionally been known to be wrong."

He cocked an eyebrow. "Really? Good to know. You wanna hear what Hyde's guy was doing?"

Rebecca came back to earth. She looked up from the computer and truly saw him for the first time. She sat up. Her face broke into an eager smile that hooked him through the gut. "Yes. Please tell me it was something I can use to take this story to the next level."

He came towards the bed with the camera in hand. "Well, that's for you to tell me. I will say that it's weird to drive all that way for something that fits into a shopping bag. And I'll tell you one other thing. You're right- that guy that works for him is creepy." He sat on the rumpled comforter and put a hand around her waist.

He jumped up just as quickly. The comforter *hissed* at him. Brian screamed.

"Don't hurt her!" Rebecca yelled. She reached under the covers and pulled out Tituba. The massive cat curled up in her arms as if she were no larger than a loaf of bread. She didn't hiss again, but the animal glowered at Brian with sullen eyes.

Rebecca checked Tituba over- fine, thank God, and then turned reproachfully towards Brian. He looked about ready to climb up a wall. What the hell was he scared for? He wasn't the one who just-

CPR, Rebecca remembered. *Edith Penn.*

Rebecca's resentment evaporated. She gently set Tituba on the covers and knee-walked to the edge of the bed so she could put her arms around his sturdy middle. Jesus, he was shaking. She squeezed tighter until his arms came around and encircled her back.

"The plot thickens," she said. "Tell me about it over takeout?"

He grinned. It was shaky around the edges, but genuine. "You're buying. Boss." He followed her out into the living room, trying to ignore the genuine relief he felt when Rebecca closed the bedroom door, separating himself from Tituba's bitter glower.

Chapter 14

THE POUNDING BEATS OF Tracee Trance echoed through the house, loud enough to make the dishes rattle in the cabinets. Martha and Ginny had been at it for hours-holding hands and laughing, dancing together to album after album.

Tom did his best to keep up with them. He, who had barely danced at his own wedding, plunged in eagerly. How could he not? It was Martha, shaking her slim hips with graceful ease as if she weren't growing bed sores a mere two days ago. She pulled him close and kissed him. She lifted Ginny up and swirled her in matching twirls of golden blonde hair.

Tom danced with them as long as he could. Not as graceful, but he lifted his legs and waved his arms with all the exuberance the moment deserved.

It wasn't the pulsing beat of Tracee Trance's "I Bug You Because I Love You" that Tom danced to. In the chambers of his mind, it was the new hit single, "I Can't Explain It," by Dr. Ellen Lopez, that drove Tom into a flurry of movement that bordered on cardiac arrest.

"I can't explain it," Dr. Lopez said. "There's no longer any sign of tissue damage. Her motor functions are perfect. The MRI is clear. It's like the stroke never even happened."

A Christmas miracle two months late. He felt like more people deserved to know. The church, or the news, or *somebody*.

But not tonight. Tonight belonged to the three of them.

Tom finally collapsed back on the couch. His heart hammered in his chest. Sweat shimmered on the bald dome of his head.

Ginny and Martha danced on without him.

How long? How many songs? Tom didn't know and he didn't care.

"I'm hungry!" Martha bellowed. "Who wants cheeseburgers!?"

"Me!" Ginny cheered. She raced for the coat closet.

They'd already eaten dinner, but the thought of refusing them never even crossed his mind. "Get my coat too, Ginny," he called.

They were stopped at the door by a distressed *"mrow."* Hobbs pouted disconsolingly at them from the stairs.

"Sorry, Hobbs," Tom said. "We'll bring you back a tuna sandwich."

Ginny stuck out her bottom lip. "Aww," she moaned.

Before Tom could speak, Martha tipped her daughter a wink. She spun towards the cat and opened her voluminous handbag.

Hobbs needed no further invitation. The cat was a black blur, slipping between the railing and up into Martha's bag before the clock could tick twice. Tom glimpsed yellow eyes in the bag's shadowy confines before Martha clipped it shut and raced Ginny out to the car.

At the diner, Tom ordered a cheeseburger. Ginny got a tuna sandwich and surreptitiously slid pieces into the handbag.

Martha ordered a shepherd's pie. And a french dip with a side of onion rings. Also a plate of chicken tenders. For dessert, she wanted two oreo milkshakes and a slice of cherry pie.

There were no leftovers.

Ginny never actually agreed to go to bed. It was past midnight when she finally slumped over, passed out on the Monopoly board. Tom got up to carry her to bed, but Martha gently pressed him back into her seat.

"Let me," she said, and Tom had never been happier to oblige a request. He watched Martha hoist their daughter up, as effortlessly as if the preteen were still a toddler. Her arms flexed as she cradled the child close. In sleep, Ginny instinctively burrowed into her mother's shoulder. An arm came up and wrapped around Martha's neck.

It's back, he marveled privately. *Your family was a vase broken into a thousand pieces, and it's somehow good as new again.*

While Martha put Ginny to bed, Tom weighed what to do next. It was almost one o'clock, Martha had to be exhausted. He even felt his own eyelids dragging beyond the surge of joy-driven adrenaline that had kept him going for the last twenty-fours hours. They both ought to get some rest.

Fuck it, he opened a bottle of wine.

Tom heard Martha coming back down the stairs. He turned towards her with a glass of cabernet in each hand, and literally stopped in his tracks.

The sight of her hit him like a freight train. *This is a miracle*, he realized. He had known that intellectually for hours, but this was the first time he had a quiet moment for the totality of that notion to strike him square in the soul. His wife was there. His beautiful wife, leaning against the door frame with a playful smirk on her lips.

Whole.

Back to him again.

"I would have stayed," he told her. "Even if... even if this had never happened, I never would have left you alone. I love you, Marty. Always."

She was suddenly right in front of him. Incredibly quick. Martha grabbed his face, nails hooking him in place, and devoured his mouth. Her tongue forced its way between his lips and poured into his soul like a stream of lit gasoline. He yearned to touch her, but the wine glasses were still in his hands. Powerless to stop her kiss, he reached blindly for where he thought the counter was. Twin explosions of broken glass told him he'd guessed wrong.

"Oh, shit," he laughed, muffled by her lips.

Martha didn't laugh. She bit his neck, sudden hot pain in his throat, and pushed him back towards the counter. He stepped in broken glass, a red pool expanding instantly against his white sock.

"Ah!" he cried. "Stop, Marty. Hold on."

Martha didn't hold on. She tried to jump up into his arms, forcing Tom to stagger to the side and driving another shard of glass into his foot. "Jesus, Martha! I said stop!"

His wife hissed. She gripped his collar and whipped him the opposite way. Tom reeled. He slipped in blood and wine and his feet flew out from under him. His head hit the stone floor hard enough that he went blind for a moment.

His vision returned in time to see Martha's face looming over his own. She was straddling him with a look of hunger in her eyes that would not be denied. He reached for her hips and felt only bare skin. She'd already taken off her pants. He felt damp heat searing against his waist.

Tom's head was barely there, but his body was. His hands squeezed flesh. Her hands undid his belt and pulled his jeans down just low enough.

Tom tried to remember how badly he'd wanted this.

Chapter 15

SENATOR RYAN COOPER STOOD up in the bleachers and pounded his hands together until the stinging pain raced all the way up to his shoulders. He shouted loud to be heard above the roar of the crowd. “That’s it, Matty!” he yelled. “Keep it up!”

His son didn’t look up, too busy hustling back down the court, but Ryan knew that the boy had heard him. He saw it in the extra burst of speed to get ahead of his opponent as the Hornets switched to defense. Ryan sat back down, where his wife excitedly squeezed his arm. “He’s doing so good,” she gushed.

Damn straight he was. Twenty points, five rebounds, and the first half wasn’t even over. Ryan could see the scouts across the court, hastily jotting down notes as Matt Cooper stole the ball off a pass and drove it down the court for an easy layup.

Not that it was really easy, but that was how his son made it look. The adrenaline surged through Ryan. He felt it as powerfully as if he were twenty-five years younger and down on the court himself. He clapped savagely.

Duncan clapped along with the rest of the hometown crowd. Basketball wasn’t really his game, but appearances were important. He was more interested in the timeclock. The seconds were slipping away towards the end of the half. 8... 7...

Matt Cooper grabbed a rebound and surged down the court again. He was truly a handsome kid. Wavy blonde hair and a lithe sinewy body that moved like he had liquid mercury pumping in his veins.

5... 4...

Matt pulled up just short of the three-point line and threw the ball up in a neat arc. The kid made it look like anyone could do it. The ball flew through the air, accompanied by the howl of the buzzer, and slipped through the hoop without so much as brushing the rim.

The home crowd erupted. Not just for the three points, but for the artistry that delivered it. They shouted and roared because they recognized they were in the presence of a special talent. Matt Cooper had the spark that was going to kindle into an inferno. In a way, they were cheering for themselves. Ten years from now they would have the privilege of saying that they saw superstar Matt Cooper play in high school, and they roared in celebration of that knowledge.

And while they cheered, Duncan leaned forward from his front row seat and replaced Matt Cooper's red water bottle with an identical copy.

Nobody batted an eye. Duncan moved with a fluid, guileless calm that cloaked him from even a shred of suspicion. He stood up with the same even, placid ease and was halfway towards the exit before the team even made it back to the bench.

Halftime passed like an eternity for Matt Cooper. He measured the seconds like he was measuring the growth of a Bonsai tree.

He wanted to get back out there.

He needed to get back out there.

His coach droned on. Matt barely heard him. He barely heard anything until the buzzer sounded, signaling the next half. Matt took another deep draught from the water bottle that wasn't his and stepped back onto the court.

The crowd roared with approval. Heroin in his ears.

The two teams lined up. The ref blew the whistle and tossed the ball up into the air. The players surged forward, but none with the born speed of Matt Cooper. He palmed the ball off the tip off and drove down the court.

He heard sneakers slapping the wood slats behind him, but it didn't matter. He had open court in front of him and nobody had a prayer of catching him. His path to the basket was clear. A scout loomed in his peripheral vision on the right.

Matt turned on the jets. He was cleared for take off. He was going to *nail* this dunk. He could feel it.

He stumbled. The ball slipped from his hands as Matt skidded across the gym floor on his hands and knees. Friction burns seared his skin, but that didn't hurt nearly as much as watching some dickhead from Saint Timothy's scoop up the ball and wheel it back the other way.

Shit! Matt slammed the ground and sprang back up. He saw the scout jot something down in her notebook.

Forget it. Yeah, brush it off. Lot of game still to play. Christ, he needed to calm down. His heart was beating out of control. He should have been already running back down the court, but he took a couple breaths first to steady himself.

But Matt's heart only kicked up another notch. The reckless pounding shook the boy to his foundations. His legs quivered.

Ryan Cooper groaned with the rest of the home crowd as his son sprawled across the court, but he recovered faster than most. "It's okay!" he clapped. "Shake it off!"

Don't get hung up, he urged silently. If his boy's game had one real weakness, it was a bad habit of getting flustered by small mistakes. Ryan saw it coming already, and it made his stomach clench. Instead of hustling back to get on defense, Matt lingered on the far side of the court, huffing and walking in small circles. His son's face was tomato red with frustration.

No, Ryan moaned. *No, no. Come on, Matt.*

And then Matt collapsed flat on his back. He dropped completely in one utterly fluid motion, as gracefully as anything else he'd ever done on the basketball court. He did not get back up.

"*Matt!*" Ryan screamed. The Senator ran, dimly aware that his shrieking wife was right behind him as he vaulted down the bleachers, maniacally shoving people out of the way. All around him, the cheers were turning into screams and horrified gasps. The sounds followed him like a swarm.

The coach and Matt's teammates had gotten there first. They stood around him in a circle, Ryan shoved teenagers aside, and there was his son. He was no longer red, but bleached an awful shade of white. His entire face matched the white of his bulging, unfocused eyes. The boy's hand (*A boy. Please God, he's just a boy)* had clutched his jersey into a tight knot over his heart. Matt clawed for air with shallow, sucking breaths.

Ryan dropped to his knees and gathered up his son to his chest. Matt trembled in his arms and the sensation of it nearly undid the older man. "Took a spill, eh?" his words cracked like thin ice on the lake. "It's no big deal. We'll get it straightened out. Just relax, ok? In and out. That's all you've got to do, Matty. Just breathe."

He sought out the coach's eyes. "Where's the ambulance?!" he screamed.

The initial pandemonium from the stands had decayed into deathly silence. Ryan Cooper's desperate, whispered pleas could be heard all the way in the furthest corners of the gymnasium.

"Hang on, Matt... Hang in there for your dad... please, Matt..."

His screams could be heard all the way in the parking lot.

***

The knock at his door came at about the time William Hyde expected. He answered the door and stepped back to allow Duncan entry into the foyer. His special assistant came with a large Baja Burger cup in his hands. Hyde didn't need to ask about the content. It was a vanilla milkshake. Duncan always ordered one after completing one of the Senator's.... special assignments.

"Evening, Duncan," Hyde said. "Can I fix you a drink?"

Duncan responded by inserting the straw between his swollen lips and making a sound that resembled a sump pump working overtime.

"I've already had a refreshment, actually," he said. "I was over in Hutchinson Port when I heard the saddest story at the bar. It seems your colleague Senator Cooper suffered a personal tragedy tonight."

"Oh, dear. Is that so?" Senator Hyde questioned. His voice carried just the right note of surprised concern.

"Mhm. His son dropped dead in the middle of a basketball game. Some sort of undetected heart defect is what they're thinking. A million-to-one, freakshow kind of thing."

Hyde shook his head mournfully. "What an awful thing to hear. I guess Ryan won't be at the Capitol on Monday."

"No, I don't suppose he will," Duncan agreed.

"A shame. There were some adjustments he wanted to see added to the Cannabis Authorization Act. I'm sure his proposals would have been to our state's benefit, but I suppose now the bill will have to proceed as is."

Duncan's only reply was the mournful gurgle of air bubbling in his straw as the milkshake ran dry. He set the empty Baja Burger cup on Senator Hyde's oak credenza.

Hyde fought the urge to ask him to move it before the cup left a ring on the table.

"I should be getting home, Senator. I just thought it best to tell you in person. It didn't seem like the kind of news to deliver over the phone."

"I agree. Much less painful this way. Thank you, Duncan."

They didn't shake hands. Duncan preferred not to be touched. That suited William Hyde just fine. Once Duncan had left, Hyde fought back the urge to run to the window and make sure his special assistant was really gone. You could summon a demon to do your dirty work, but it seemed unwise to then look and see how the demon returned to its lair. Much better just to have another drink.

"Daddy?"

Hyde jerked up from his stupor as light flared up from the staircase. Lexie stood at the top of the stairs in her footie pajamas. *Probably the last year for those,* he thought, and quickly forced the thought back down. The thought of his four-year-old daughter being too old for ice cream cone footie pajamas was too much to consider. Better to think of her as she was now, even with that ugly cat hugged tight to her chest. The living room was dark, and the hallway light set behind her threw her features into deep shadows. It looked like the child didn't even have a face. Hyde walked closer until the disturbing effect receded. It was just Lexie. Round cheeks. Bright eyes. Her brow set in a stern line as it typically was. The child seemed born perpetually dissatisfied. He loved that about her.

"What is it, baby?" he asked.

"Oyer keeps waking me up," she complained.

Oyer. The feline in question stared at him unremorsefully from her daughter's arms. It was a weird name for a cat. He'd explained that the kid could rename the cat however she wanted, but Lexie insisted on sticking with the name on that shitty twine collar.

"Really? What's she doing?" he asked. "Chasing mice around your bed? Eating stinky tuna?"

Lexie did not laugh. "She keeps talking to me."

"Yeah?" he grinned. He turned his attention to the black cat and her squat, ugly face. "You meowing at the moon? You figure my daughter is too pretty to need her beauty sleep?" He reached out to scratch the cat's head and recoiled just as quickly. The fleabag hissed and showed him her tiny fangs.

You're lucky my wife hates you, he thought.

"She's not *meowing*, daddy," Lexie explained patiently. "She's talking to me. It's keeping me up."

He smiled indulgently. "Really? What's she got to say? Anything interesting?"

The little girl crinkled her brow. She tried, genuinely tried hard, to remember.

"I don't know," she said finally. "It's fuzzy in my brain. But it was *loud*."

William gently spun her around, back towards her room. "I think that means you were dreaming, kiddo."

"I wasn't dreaming!" Lexie protested. But she undercut her own argument with a tremendous yawn.

Hyde walked her towards her pink-painted door with the unicorn door hanger. "I'll tell you what," he said. "Lay back down. If Oyer talks to you again, you tell me all about it in the morning."

"Okay, Daddy," she agreed.

"You want me to tuck you in?"

She rolled her eyes. "That's for babies, Daddy."

Hyde suppressed a laugh. "All right, kiddo. You go ahead. I'll see you in the morning."

He lingered to take one more look at her before closing the door, leaving it open just a crack. She was so small and yet he marveled at how large she'd become.

Such a precious thing, being a father.

Chapter 16

IT BEGAN WITH TY Hodgins.

Ty got on the bus right after Maura. For the ten minutes that it was just the two of them, Ty was usually content to leave Maura alone until there was more of an audience.

On Monday, the first day of school after the incident at the fair, Ty boarded the bus and poured a thermos full of milk over Maura's head. No pretense, no theatrically pretending to trip. She stopped just long enough to dump the liter of milk into Maura's hair, seemingly deaf to Maura's sputtering shock, and then casually took her seat at the back of the bus.

It continued at school. Maura went straight to the bathroom, hoping to rinse out the worst of the milk before it curdled in her hair. She dunked her head under the sink, and that was when Lily Greenhall hip checked her. The soccer play threw all of her muscle behind it. The impact ran all the way through Maura's ass up her spine and was joined by a twin flare of pain as her thigh bone struck the porcelain edge of the sink.

Like Ty, Lily didn't stick around to hear Maura's pained gasp. She left the bathroom without so much as a glance in the mirror.

First period. Craig Johnson's usual seat in the back of class was conspicuously empty. Supposedly, it was too early to know if he'd ever walk again.

Maura kept her head down and shuffled to her own desk. She expected for the seat to be pulled out just before she sat down. It was clearly that kind of day.

What happened instead was Maura actually settled into her desk, and then Billy Pullman lashed out hard with one foot and toppled the desk with Maura still in it. She fell to the floor, landing painfully on her elbow.

Mr. Edwards at least spun away from the board, but he turned back with weary acceptance when he saw the source of the commotion.

At lunch, her table was empty. Rules be damned, the word was out. Sitting too close to Maura was like sitting at ground zero of an incoming air raid.

That was what was coming next. Maura sensed it as she sat there and methodically plowed through her leftover casserole while her bones still throbbed and the stench of sour milk filled her nostrils.

Her weary eyes swept the cafeteria. Milo Teller was palming a pear as if it were a hand grenade. Jenny Havermeyer had a slice of pizza stealthily cradled against her chest, waiting for the right moment to let it fly. Maura felt the tension thick in the whispered murmuring all around her. They were all waiting for the right moment to bury her in a barrage of flying food.

The thing was, Maura sensed no joy in their anticipation. There were no smothered grins or stray chuckles masked behind fake coughs. This wasn't sport for them anymore. They weren't torturing her for the same fun they usually did. There was a predatory urgency driving her classmates forward.

Because they're afraid now, she realized. She looked around the cafeteria at the pale cheeks and bulging eyes of her classmates and understood that they feared her. They feared Maura the donkey fucker now. They knew what had happened to Craig. Maybe not consciously, but they knew the truth in their bones, and their only choice now was to strike first. Strike hard. Hope that they could break Maura before she came for them again.

But I didn't do anything! I didn't kick him. I just...

Just what? Just nothing. She'd done nothing except get hit with an earful of donkey shit!

She threw her fork down. It clattered off of the tray and skittered to the floor. Glumly, Maura bent down under the table to retrieve it. She reached out her hand, groping for the feel of cheap metal.

Instead, she felt warm, bristling fur beneath her fingers.

Maura looked down. Eastey was there. The cat pushed herself more firmly against Maura's palm. The steady vibration of the cat's purr raced up her arm.

Maura felt her breathing steady. She let her fingers run up and down the cat's spine. Back and forth, back and forth.

There was new tension in the air around her. Maura felt it coming. This was their moment. She was going to pop her head back up from under the table, and then the onslaught would begin.

That was okay. Maura had some things to say.

Chapter 17

1944

EDIE WAS ALREADY AWAKE when her mother came for her at midnight. The girl was sitting up in bed, looking at a book that she wasn't actually reading. Waiting was what she was actually doing, and her eager gaze sprang up the moment Genevieve cracked the door open.

Her mother was not surprised, but the child's eagerness pleased her nonetheless. Work ethic and talent counted for a lot with spellcraft, but it was desire that truly fulfilled potential. Nobody learned the craft unless they felt the need deep in their bones... and Edie most definitely had the need.

"Is it time, Momma?"

"Get your makings," her mother said. "And let's get on." She did not need to tell Edith to get dressed. The child was already wearing jeans and a plain blouse.

They stepped out the backdoor and into the moist summer night. Genevieve Penn tasted the air and found it good.

"You feel it too?" she asked.

The answer came from the damp earth under the backsteps. A single, cheerful croak from the darkness before the shoebox-sized frog hopped out into the dim light. Movna did indeed feel it too. A storm was coming. The air was heavy with the power hurtling towards them.

Another good sign, Genevieve thought. She guided her daughter towards the narrow country road. Movna the

Bullfrog followed along, nipping at their heels with every leap of her powerful back legs.

Edith walked beside her mother, diligently upholding the woven bag so that the contents didn't scrape along the road. The girl worked to convey solemn dignity, but trying to keep her mouth in a straight line was like trying to keep an earthworm still. The corners of her mouth kept twisting into a smile.

"It's all right to be excited," her mother said. "I know I was when old Nana took me out to get Movna." The frog croaked heartily, confirming her Mistress' account.

"I just want to *know*," Edie squealed. "I hope I get a frog, like Movna. I wanna do everything just like you, Momma."

Genevieve pulled her close into a one-armed hug. "That's sweet, but I hope there's more ahead for you than brewing Lilac potions for girls who want a baby and black moss draughts for the ones who don't. You've got real ability, Edie. If you stay focused, you've got the potential to go much further than I ever did."

"You mean like a shop downtown?" Edie asked. "With an awning and a glass front and all kinds of ingredients on the shelves!?"

Her mother chuckled. They walked in silence through the warm night before Edith's anticipation got the better of her.

"But do you think I'll get a frog?" she asked.

"There's no telling," Genevieve said. "And there's no complaining either. Whatever you get, it's exactly right."

They came to the edge of the woods and stopped. The bullfrog hopped in line alongside mother and daughter. Genevieve knelt beside Edie and pointed towards the thick wall of trees.

"You see that?" she asked. "Do you see how dark it is?"

Edith saw immediately. There was a full moon overhead, and the new streetlights blazed at the edge of the road, but the woods beyond the street were cloaked in a thicket of pure shadow. There was no perceiving anything beyond the first line of tall pine trees.

"The woods know you're coming," her mother said.

Genevieve cupped her daughter's face. Edith savored the sensation of her mother's rough hands. They always smelled of her work. Tonight, it was Motherwort and Nettle wafting off her fingers.

"Repeat it to me," her mother said.

"I spark no light," Edith said dutifully. "I walk. I don't look. If something makes a sound, I do not hear it."

"Until?" Genevieve pressed.

"Until something takes the bag."

"And then?"

And then I can see."

"That's right," Genevieve said. She was being silly, but she opened Edie's sack one final time to review the contents.

The corpses were all there, exactly as they were the last five times Genevieve had compulsively checked. The still, dead forms stared back at her from their burlap tomb. A frog, a newborn kitten, and a raven hatchling. All of the dead things were there in perfect, unblemished form. Just as they were supposed to be.

Satisfied, Genevieve kissed her daughter on the forehead and smoothed her hair one final time.

"I'll be waiting for you here," she said.

As was expected of her, Edie didn't reply. She hitched the sack higher on her shoulder, and Edith Penn took her first steps into the deep, dark woods.

It felt like a curtain was drawn the moment the girl stepped into the forest, cutting her off from everything that was familiar only footsteps ago. The moon overhead disappeared as the ground beneath her feet shifted from grass to fallen leaves and underbrush. The streetlights should have been visible behind her, they had been only a couple steps earlier, but the lights had blinked out as easily as spent match heads. It was just Edie now. Edie and the darkness.

Somewhere, distant, her heart pounded in her chest. Cold sweat ran down her back. Edie knew not to acknowledge these sensations. She marched deeper into the suffocating black, trusting that no root would trip her. No gopher hole would snare her ankle

I am expected.

I am welcome.

She had walked through these woods for as long as she'd been able to walk. She knew them intimately. The smell of Baneberry patches, the babble of the stream that cut through the trees, those touchstones were as familiar to her as her own bedroom.

She did not sense them now, and that was more disorienting than the darkness. This blackness, wherever it was, was not her woods.

I am expected, Edie repeated. *I am welcome.*

I am expected.

I am welcome.

Something screamed in the darkness. It was the earth itself crying out- soil rupturing in a tortured bellow of ground torn asunder and then branches shattering in a dozen tiny deaths as a massive tree slammed into the ground.

Edie flinched. She breathed in a scream, but smothered the sound before it could escape her lips.

I do not hear. I do not hear. Idonothear. Idonothear.

Something else shook the ground beyond her blindness. Something too measured and deliberate to be another falling tree. Something living. Edith smelled it on the breeze blowing in her face. It smelled like some of her mother's ingredients. Racoon guts and salamander skins. Components long past their shelf life.

It was coming closer.

Edith stood her ground.

I do not look. I do not look.

The thing was before her now. Edith sensed it though she could not see it. It wasn't the smell, it was the *force* of it. The thing baked with heat like the woodstove in the deep of winter.

The sack was still in her hand, the burlap soaked with sweat and greasy in her grasp.

I do not hear. I do not look. I do not hear. I do not look.

The rough material rubbed against her leg.The sides of the sack twitched and writhed as the dead things inside fought to get out.

Edie did not look. She did not hear the undead hisses, croaks, and squawks coming from the bag. She did not hear the hefty *whuff* as the thing radiating its terrible heat pressed closer to her face.

I do not hear.

I do not look.

I do not hear.

Oh, please, I do not hear. I do not look. I do not hear. I do not look.

The bag was torn from her hand, so forcefully that the burlap ripped a scorched strip of skin from her palm.

But the pain was also a release.

Edie looked.

She heard.

***

Genevieve Penn sweated under the moonlight and tried to quell her pounding heart. She'd gathered Movna up in her arms and clutched the frog like an overgrown stuffed animal.

She'd heard the thunder as the tree fell. Nothing with that kind of power should have been stalking the forest, not for a ten-year-old girl seeking her first Familiar. Edie was going to be strong, Genevieve knew that, but the power she sensed stalking her daughter was obscene. It was too much. Surely too much. Genevieve could feel it easily, even here by the road.

Edie's been taught, she consoled herself. *No power can hurt her so long as she remembers her lessons.*

And so long as Genevieve remembered her own lessons as well. She herself could not enter the forest. No matter what. This was Edie's trial. If Genevieve tried to interfere, then both of them were forfeit.

The wind howled. It began in the woods and exploded outward like a spilled bucket of whirlwind. It blew Genevieve's hair back and molded her dress tight against her slim body. Flying dirt battered her face. Genevieve shielded her eyes and gritted her teeth... and then gasped as her upturned hand turned red.

The rest of the world followed suit. The grass, the tree line, everything around her was suddenly cast in a shade of rusty, autumn red.

Geneveive looked up, knowing what she'd see but refusing to believe she actually would.

And yet, there it was. The full moon had become a blotted strawberry, hanging high overhead, ripe for the picking.

"This can't be," Genevieve uttered as she gaped at the blood red moon in the sky.

The animals started next. The crickets. The owls. The raccoons. Even Movna squirmed and squealed in her grasp. The laconic music of a summer night fractured into a frenzied squall of panic. The natural world was spasming in terror of what walked among them.

And my daughter is what it wants. Oh mercy, what have I done?

The silence came without warning. The moon peeled away its bloody film. The noise from the forest ceased. The croaking from Movna in her arms changed, becoming steady and soothing even as the frog's heart hammered beneath her touch.

"Edith!" Genevieve screamed. She ran and stopped just short of the treeline, still afraid to enter the woods. "Edith, follow my voice, baby!"

Genevieve waited.

Nothing answered her call. No answering voice, no footsteps dragging through brush. Genevieve plunged into the brush, the rules be damned.

"Edith!"

And then her daughter was there, seemingly materializing all at once. Untouched, unhurt.

Alive. That was Genevieve's first thought. Alive. She didn't even pause to wonder if the offering had been accepted... until the night behind her daughter lit up in a marching line of glowing eyes at ankle height

Edie had gone into the woods in search of a Familiar. The Trial had been called so she could prove herself worthy of a companion that would help the girl strengthen her natural abilities. Just as Movna had done for Genevieve ever since she was a little girl. If a witch was found worthy, a Familiar would present itself to serve as her companion.

Thirteen had found Edith worthy.

They'd come as cats. Each one of them inky black. Kittens on the verge of adolescence, large enough that they could walk on their own, not so old that they should have stood behind her daughter with the eerie obedience they showed.

"Look, Mom," Edie grinned. "They already told me their names."

Genevive saw. More than the Familiars, Genevieve saw that she had been right.

Edith Penn had power that would take her far beyond the walls of New Birmingham.

Chapter 18

BRIAN DROPPED ONTO THE bench and exhaled three lifetimes' worth of exhaustion.

He knew what came next. Undress. Put his uniform in a biohazard bag. Shower. Get the hell out. But he was too damned drained to do it. His elbows propped on his thighs were the only things keeping him from melting into a puddle right there in the locker room.

The onslaught had begun right after Brian clocked-in and hadn't stopped until only a few moments before the end of shift. Brian looked around the locker room and saw that he wasn't the only one splattered in blood and vomit and staring into space. Nobody seemed to have the energy, and why the hell should they? Their bodies were beat to hell after an eight-hour relay race of hauling victims, and their brains were still shuddering under the mental load of watching kids, so many fucking kids, puking until blood ran out of their eyes. What kind of maniac had the energy to move after that?

The door swung open and struck the tile wall with a rattling bang. Mike rolled into the locker room, bouncing on the balls of his feet, supremely unconcerned with the beige bloom of vomit on his chest and the bloody slime clinging to his sleeves.

"Did I make a wrong turn and end up in the morgue!?" Brian's partner bellowed. He clapped his hands, as solid and unshakeable as he'd been the night they found Edith

Penn. "Clean up and clear out or I'm gonna start slapping toe tags on the lot of you."

Chastened, Brian's fellow paramedics jerked from their malaise and slowly began the process of wrapping out. Still, there was no chatter, no friendly back and forth of gossip. They were just burnt out automatons going through the motions. Brian rose up to join them before Mike came to his side and slapped his shoulder.

"I'm all right, Mike," he said.

"Never said you weren't."

"This is the job, right?" Brian asked. "I had my first rough one..."

"And now you've had your second."

"Yeah," Brian said. "But I'm handling it. I'm good."

Mike let it drop. "I'll take your word. A little burg like this only gets so many ugly days in a year. Hopefully this was our allotment and the next six months will be kids falling off of slides and middle-aged ladies giving each other stitches over the last open pew at church." Mike hesitated, but plowed ahead anyway. "But I'll tell you, this one really was fucking weird."

Brian laughed harder than he had to. He needed to. It was desperately needed after the spine-clenching tension he'd battled through all day. "Yes," he agreed. "It was definitely a fucking weird day."

"You want to get a beer after we clean up? Joy's bartending at the Den."

"Thanks, but I've got plans."

Mike winked. "Say no more. Word of advice, take some extra time in the shower. You're never actually clean the first time you think you're clean. And let me get out of the shower before you get in. The last thing my self-image needs is you shirtless next to my flabby gut."

***

Brian finally made it back to his apartment and found Rebecca had already let herself in with the key he'd given her.

He meant to ask if she'd heard news, and he got his answer as she immediately crossed the living room and pulled him into a tight embrace. Brian went with it, willingly sinking his heavy frame against her. He let his head drop into the generous tangle of her curls, the stench of blood and vomit swept away by the scent of coconuts.

"You were there," she said. Not a question.

"I was actually kinda surprised you weren't. A whole cafeteria full of sick kids? Seems like front page news."

"Jerry had me covering the unveiling of some solar panel farm. I didn't even know what was going on until I checked the Slack. Was it really that bad?"

He could have answered her very clearly if he wanted to. The memory of it was still perfectly preserved in his mind. The sounds of retching and splattering, the kids who were able to talk begging for help. He remembered that first, frozen moment where he tried to determine who to treat first. There were so many of them. So much pain.

He went to the kitchen for a beer and found a whiskey neat waiting for him on the counter. He picked it up gratefully.

"It was a lot," he decided on telling her. "A lot of kids."

"Was it food poisoning? That's what we're hearing."

"We won't know for sure until the tox screens come back. It's always a risk with buffet-style food. One tray left out of the fridge too long is all it takes"

"But all those kids ate cafeteria food?" Rebecca pressed. "Nobody had a bag lunch from home?"

Brian threw his hands up. "I don't know, Bec. Nobody could stop puking long enough to tell us what they ate. And if you want to be honest, 'why' is a doctor's game. Paramedics just try to keep people alive long enough for them to figure it out."

And we had a lot of kids to keep alive. The cafeteria was a fucking war zone. There wasn't a section of the floor that wasn't covered in vomit or some kid spasming. Usually both. Promethazine didn't stop it. Neither did Prochlorperazine. And then a lot of them started throwing up blood and it didn't matter anymore. All we could do was lift them up and relay race them to the hospital. One after another. For hours.

He was brooding. Brian snapped out of it, not wanting Rebecca to worry, but she stood there looking just as distracted as he felt. Her brow was twisted in dark clouds.

"Bec, you okay?"

Rebecca took out her phone. "When you were at the school, did you see this student?"

Brian took the phone from her and looked at the open photograph.

His first instinct was to say, "No." The picture wasn't that clear, and the faces he'd seen today had all blurred together as he ran from one hurling teenager to the next.

...But he looked at the photograph for another minute. There was something familiar there. The girl looked to be about 16, but that could just be her size. She wasn't fat, but she was *solid.* Broad shoulders, big hips, a square jaw framed by a severe, blonde bob. She had a cat clutched to her chest, but Brian discarded that. And he told himself to ignore the denim overalls. For her sake, he hoped she didn't go to school like that.

It was the girl's expression that he lingered on. It wasn't an animated face; there was no snarl or burning stare there. But there was a bitter, ugly satisfaction lurking behind her stolid features. It was the look of someone who hadn't stuck a foot out, but was happy to watch somebody else trip over a stone and drop face first into the mud. He'd seen that expression-

"Yes!" he blurted. "She was on the sidelines with the handful of kids that didn't get sick."

They were all watching, but she was the only one who didn't seem revolted. She watched her classmates throwing up blood and she looked... satisfied.

"She was there," he confirmed. "And she wasn't sick. Who is she?"

Rebecca took the phone back. "I don't know. I saw her at the fair and something weird happened. And now again at the school. You said she was fine?"

Brian considered. "Not fine," he concluded. "She wasn't upset by what was happening. And she stayed for the whole eight hours. By the time we loaded up the last kid, she was the only one still watching."

Rebecca made a note in her phone. "Something's weird. I don't know, I'll look into it."

"Oh, good," Brian said. "You weren't busy enough trying to take down a State Senator. It's good to know you've got a few more irons in the fire."

She rolled her eyes. "You left out all the random backpage stories Jerry has me chasing. It's a miracle I can get anything done." She held up her phone. "But this... it's funky. Oh, and good news. Tomorrow I'm getting some customs records. Maybe I can figure out what Hyde had shipped to Boston."

Brian smirked. "Sounds like you've got a busy day planned. Does that mean you need to go home early?"

She laughed and pressed her forehead to his chest. "I never sleep better than when I sleep next to you."

...She said it before she realized what she was saying. He heard it before really realizing what he'd heard.

Both of them came to the same conclusion at the same time, and the silence that followed was anything but quiet. They communicated in the warmth of her arms around his waist and the strength he used to pull her body against his.

When they kissed, it went off like a match dropped into gasoline. Their lips hungrily slid together, meeting again and again in different configurations, each more perfect than the last. Rebecca's tongue met his and massaged it with incredible finesse. He breathed into her with the sweetest air Rebecca had ever tasted.

Brian picked her up and slammed Rebecca into the wall. Her legs went up around his waist. Primal moans of urgency passed back and forth on their tongues. Rebecca's kisses migrated across the side of his face, savoring the taste of his skin until her lips brushed his ear.

"The bed," she said. "Take me to the bed."

She didn't need to ask again.

***

The sex was exquisite. The relaxation, the sheer contentment that came after, was even better.

For Brian, most of that had to do with Rebecca's fleece-soft skin molded against his. Still, there was a small but very real part of his perfect contentment that came from the knowledge that they were in his apartment and not Rebecca's. Even more thoroughly satisfied than he'd ever felt in his life, Brian would not have slept quite so soundly if he knew that Tituba was out prowling the corridor.

Just us, he relished. It was his final coherent thought. Rebecca was already asleep; her gentle, steady breath keeping pace against his neck. He kissed her temple and willingly followed her into blissful darkness.

Brian did not wake once that night. Not even when his bedroom door opened slightly like a malignant, half-awake eye and Tituba came creeping into the room. The cat approached the bed, inexorable as midnight dreary, and leapt up onto the comforter to take her rightful place atop her mistress.

Spread out across the New Birmingham night, the rest of Edith Penn's thirteen black cats slept in much the same way. Oyer had a $200 cat bed in the Hyde's family den. Maura believed that Eastey slept on a pool of blankets under her desk. Joy, the bartender at the Badger's Den, let Deliverance sleep in an open drawer stuffed with clean terry cloth bar rags.

The other nine cats each had their own supposed sleeping arrangements, but all of them slept in the exact same place.

Each cat slept curled up over her mistresses' face, burying their features beneath a mass of warm black fur. As it was every night, the women and girls never stirred. Their own chests rose and fell, easily taking air beneath their black face covers.

In medieval times, it was believed that cats slept this way to steal a person's soul as they slumbered.

...The truth in New Birmingham was not quite the same.

Chapter 19

"I DON'T UNDERSTAND," REBECCA said. She used her shoulder to keep the phone pressed against her ear. Having her hands free to play with a pen or fiddle with paperclips helped keep Rebecca calm. Specifically, it kept her from driving down to Boston to grab this woman by the ears and smash the placid tapioca brains right out of her head.

"I was told the records would be available today for review. The last person I spoke to was very clear about this. I made sure of it," she said.

"I understand that, ma'am," the artificially pleasant voice said from the other end of the phone line. "You submitted the C-2 petition. That was cleared today. But you also need the B-19 form-"

"I submitted the B-19 form," Rebecca said through gritted teeth. She doodled as she spoke. Doodling was soothing. Doodling kept her from getting her car keys and looking up the traffic conditions to Boston.

"-And the B-19 form takes another week for review."

I don't have a week. Hyde's dispensary bill goes up for a vote in three days, you apathetic cunt.

Rebecca put down the pen and picked up a staple remover. She methodically pinched the sharp-mouthed tool between her thumb and middle finger, focusing on the soothing sensation of mechanical fangs snapping open and closed in her hand.

Open.

Closed.

Open.

Closed.

"Ma'am," Rebecca continued. "There are first amendment and freedom of information concerns here. Perhaps there's an expedited request form I can fill out? Some kind of emergency appeal?"

"There is not," the customs agent said.

Rebecca saw red. She snapped the staple remover shut. It wasn't until the pain raced up her arm that Rebecca realized she'd left the pad of one finger between the tool's snapping jaws. Blood flowed immediately as the metal points sunk into the tip of her finger.

Fuck! Rebecca screamed inside her head, keeping the curse away from her lips by only supreme force of will. She scrounged around on her desk for something to staunch the blood flow. With no other options, she ripped the top page off her notepad, jammed the piece of paper over the wound, and turned her attention back to the voice still rambling on over the phone.

"I'm sorry," Rebecca asked with remarkable poise as the paper pressed to her finger turned red. "You broke up for a minute there. Could you repeat that."

"I said that there's nothing to be done on your end, but there might be some procedural motions I could use to speed things along."

"Oh, my God," Rebecca thrilled. "That would be amazing!"

"I'll follow up with you once I have an update," the customs agent said. "Would this be the best number to reach you at?"

"...I might be away from my desk." Rebecca pressed her luck. "Could I give you my cell phone number?"

"That would be fine," the agent replied.

Dazed, Rebecca recited her phone number and then hung up. It was very likely she'd just been fed a line of bullshit, but it still felt like a more positive outcome than anything she could have hoped for. She checked her cut finger and saw that the bleeding had slowed to an oozy crawl. Good enough. She threw the bloody piece of paper into the trash, pushed away from her desk, and strolled into Jerry's office with her usual bombast.

"Jerry!" Rebecca boomed. "Two things."

Her editor, who had been about to cap his bottle of rye, sighed and poured an extra two inches instead. "By all means, Rebecca. Let me set aside the five things I need to do so that I can give your two things my undivided attention. Please..." His sheened eyes focused on her hand. "Are you bleeding?"

She waved it off. "Stationary accident. Forget it. Do you remember that stupid-ass carnival last weekend?"

"Do I remember making you do your job? Yes, I seem to recall."

"Funny you phrase it that way. I actually *was* making sure that my real job got done. Even while I was getting Melvin Porter's statement about which bakery makes the best cinnamon raisin bread in the state. I had somebody go down to Boston and stake out that package Senator Hyde was waiting for."

Jerry's face turned red to match his bloodshot eyes. "You did what? Spencer, If you hired some Philip Marlow wannabe to sit in a car all day and think you can expense it-"

"Relax, I called in a favor. I just wanted you to know that I put in a FoIA request for Hyde's customs manifest, and I'm hoping to hear something back soon. That's the first thing. The second thing is I need a little time this afternoon to chase a story."

"What story would that be?"

"Well, I'm not sure yet. It could be nothing. But I've got a hunch."

She watched Jerry turn the idea over in his head and hoped that he wouldn't ask her for any details yet, because the details were fucking insane. She didn't think that he would. Once you had his confidence, Jerry was usually willing to see what you could come back with.

Usually.

"All right," he finally relented. "Take an afternoon, but don't expect your leash to run forever. I need headlines, not hunches."

"Thanks, Jerry."

"Don't leave yet," he said. "We still have to talk about your first thing. Senator Hyde. You're dead set on pushing this expose out before this vote on the grass bill."

Rebecca rolled her eyes. "Nobody calls it grass anymore, Jerry. Be current."

"*-IF* you tie him to something more nefarious than, 'Politician wants to make money,' just be ready to stay on the train. The big breaking story isn't the ending. It's just the beginning. There could be a resignation, a trial... if you break open this pinata, make sure you're ready to grab every lollipop that comes out of it."

She smiled. "I'll make sure to save one for you."

He waved her off. "If you're in a grateful mood, all I ask is that you let my daughter shadow you when she comes home from the summer. I want Mary to learn from the best. Now go. Shake trees. Don't listen to what I tell you to do."

"Never do, boss."

Rebecca practically floated out of her editor's office. She maintained her careful, aloof veneer, but she cradled every glowing word deep in the center of her heart.

It wasn't until later, while she was in her car and driving out to the farm country outside of town, that the nervous breakdown hit.

Shit, shit, shit. The thought raced circles in her head as she tried to quell the anxiety suddenly broiling her insides. For the first time, it occurred to Rebecca that all the strings she'd pulled together on Senator Hyde actually didn't look like much at all. The sturdy rope of facts and evidence she thought that she'd been braiding suddenly looked like about six inches of fishing line. What the hell was she going to do if she went through all of this only to come up empty?

You won't get to find out, because that's not going to happen, she chastised herself. *You've pulled plenty of pieces together and you're still waiting on another one. Once you've got the full puzzle, you're going to nail his ass to the wall and you're going to write your own ticket.*

She shut off the spout of negative thoughts as the GPS announced that her destination was coming up on the right. Rebecca turned and shifted into park at the end of the long gravel driveway leading up to Manor Farm & Petting Zoo. There'd been an early March warm snap, and her boots squelched through melting snow and grass as she got out of the car and trudged towards the farmhouse.

The home was modest, but respectably kept. The same could be said for the pens and the small barn surrounding the property. A solitary, mottled grey horse regarded the new arrival and then trotted up to the fence to be pet. Rebecca indulged the old mare with a couple pats on the nose and then decided to check around the fields before knocking on the front door of the house.

Her instincts paid off. She found the teenager out in the pig pen, shoveling slop into a wheelbarrow. Rebecca didn't need to take out her phone to check the photograph. It was the same girl, right down to the overalls and the perpetually gloomy frown set into her pale features.

And, of course, the same black cat napping on one of the fence posts.

Despite her suspicions, Rebecca's heart went out to the girl all the same. She was just an overweight, pimply kid shoveling literal pig shit after school. Even the handful of pigs milling around in the muck didn't give her the time of day.

"Excuse me? Hello?" Rebecca called out with a wave and her most charming smile. She made an exaggerated show of lifting her feet as she trekked through the mud to the wooden fence, making herself look as awkward and out of her element as possible.

The teenager looked up from her chores. "Help you?" she asked.

"I hope so," Rebecca said. She rested an arm on the gate. When the young woman didn't object, Rebecca pushed it open and stepped into the pen. She cast a cautious eye at the animals, but the four hogs only took a casual glance at her before going back to their late lunch of corn cobs and apple cores.

Rebecca took another step closer, the slop oozing up to her ankles. She winced internally and tried not to remember that these boots were a Christmas present to herself. She held up her press pass for the teen's inspection. "Do you work here?" she asked.

The kid shrugged and spoke in a dull monotone. "Work here. Live here. I'm Maura."

"Rebecca. I'm with the Gazette. I'm working on a story, kind of a thing with older industries and the new economy. Are your parents around?"

"Sorry. We've got two shows this afternoon. They're both gone until dinner."

Rebecca shook her head ruefully. "Serves me right. Nobody picked up when I called, but I thought I'd take a chance and ride out just in case." She paused for a moment, just long enough to seem natural, and then brightened as if she'd suddenly gotten an idea. "Hey, you probably go to Roger Williams High, right?"

Clutching the shovel a little tighter, Maura jerked her head in what could charitably be called a nod and not the death spasm of a twitching animal. "Yeah, I'm a sophomore."

"That was insane what happened there yesterday. In the cafeteria I mean, with all those kids getting sick. How are you feeling?"

"I'm fine," Maura said. More forcefully than she had to. "I'm one of the ones that didn't get sick."

"Wow, that's really lucky," Rebecca said. "There must have been only like ten of you in the whole school from what I heard. Most of the kids are still in the hospital. I heard they're spread all over the county. Nobody had enough beds."

For somebody so fine, Maura had begun to look distinctly ill. Her already pale complexion was curdling. She scratched imaginary hives at the back of her neck. "I've got to get back to work," she mumbled. "I'll tell my parents you came by."

"Did any of your friends get sick?" Rebecca pressed.

Something in Maura's face twisted into an ugly knot. "I don't have any friends," she spat.

"Right, you've just got pricks like that douche who got donkey-kicked at the fair?"

"I never touched him!" Maura thundered. She threw the shovel against the wheelbarrow. A flock of black birds fled to the sky as the ugly clang echoed across the grey field. "What!? Am I supposed to feel bad for what happened to him? Because I don't!" she raged. "You don't know how they treat me. He deserved whatever he got!"

That's what she said, but Rebecca recognized the rising panic in the girl's haggard eyes. Maura stood before her, twitching and shivering. Desperately afraid.

Rebecca put her press pass away. "Maura, talk to me. Tell me what's happening to you."

Maura only shook her head. "I can't..." The girl dropped down like half-chewed refuse from a hog's mouth, sinking to her knees in the slop.

"I don't know what's happening to me," she moaned. "I hear words... I hear them in my head. And then I say them out loud and I can make things happen. Bad things."

"Is that what happened in the cafeteria? Is that why all of those kids got sick?" Rebecca asked.

Tearfully, Maura nodded. "I just wanted them to feel how they make me feel. And then, just like that, I knew words that could make them. But..." She trailed off as another sob wracked her body. Maura's back heaved up and down.

"Something's happening to me," she whispered.

Rebecca crouched down beside her. "What words, Maura? What did you do? Who's talking to you?"

The young girl only whimpered. She buried her face in her filthy hands.

"Maura. Tell me. What words?"

Maura lifted her head. Long, grey streaks of slop ran down her face from jaw to forehead. Rebecca saw her eyes, writhing in pain and confusion. The girl's lip trembled.

"Luto exaudi me!" Maura snarled.

The fury flared in her face, a viper lashing out from its hiding place. Rebecca tried to recoil away from it, tried to leap back, but something grabbed her by the ankle and rooted her in place. Rebecca overbalanced and flopped on her back in the mud as Maura rose up over her.

There was no distress now. No confusion. There was only righteous fury, The high school girl's hair hung in lank curtains around a face that had gone deathly white. Her arms were twisted, crooked crone's limbs at her sides. Her dark, sunken, angry eyes stabbed through Rebecca's soul.

But Rebecca saw none of that nuance. Her horrified, disbelieving gaze was fixated solely on the thing keeping her fleeing back to her car. The thing holding her captive was not subtle. It was not nuanced.

It was a thick, powerful hand risen up from the earth to snare her ankle. And it was not a human hand. The four-fingered limb was a damp, misshapen thing composed entirely from grey, pig-shit soaked mud.

"Teneat eam luto!" Maura howled. Her voice echoed in the frigid air and made it shudder like vibrating glass.

At the girl's command, half a dozen more limbs of grey slop rose up from the earth around them. Questing hands of muck grabbed Rebbecca's back. Her shoulders. Her thrashing legs. One gripped a fistful of hair and yanked her head into the filth until it oozed into her ears.

There was no time for denial. No time for Rebecca's professional skepticism to weigh in that this was impossible. The experience assaulting her was too much, too fast. The damp cold at her limbs, the stench in her nostrils. The *power* holding her in place while blood and adrenaline raced in her head and her own screams filled her ears.

And Rebecca was screaming. She couldn't stop the panicked, mewling plea, not even if she wanted to. Her desperate terror came from a depth of soul that she was powerless to control.

"Help!" Rebecca shrieked as the arms anchored their grips and shackled her that much more tightly. "Please God! Oh Jesus! Jesus fuck, *OVER HERE*! *HELP ME!"*

Nobody heard her except for the pigs. The animals had fled to the edges of the pen, their anxious squeals and their bulk thudding against wooden posts adding to the thick clatter of terror in the air.

While Rebecca struggled against the arms constraining her, Maura lurched to the wheelbarrow. Her steps were stilted, dragging things, pulling furrows through the mud. But she moved towards the shovel with relentless purpose.

Rebecca's eyes huddled deeper in their sockets, as if for protection, as Maura swiveled towards her. The scum-crusted shovel hung low by the girl's hips.

"Maura, listen," Rebecca begged. "Just listen to me, ok? People know that I came looking for you. They know where I am. You can't do this here."

But, yes, Maura could do this if she wanted to. The hands holding Rebecca down told her so. The almost casual calculations in the girl's eyes said that she could if she wanted to. She sauntered closer to the captive reporter, her dull gaze fixated on the ridge of bone between Rebecca's eyes as she trudged forward with the shovel.

Squelch.

Squelch.

"Nooo!" Rebbecca moaned. She fought to break free, but the arms of earth held her firmly in their grasp.

Maura came to a stop at the soles of the reporter's feet. Rebecca saw her coming and realized then that there was no reasoning with Maura. The girl, or what was left of her, raised the shovel over her head. Her face was as immovable as something carved from ice. Maura would not be dissuaded. She would not reconsider.

Rebecca gave up. She scrunched her eyes shut and waited for the pain, or the *cracking* sound as her skull shattered. Whichever came first.

Instead, she heard the wail of a cat. Rebecca chanced to look. The black tabby stood with legs spread and her ears pressed flat to her skull in the space between Maura and Rebecca. The cat looked up at her mistress and let out a warning hiss.

Just as inexplicably as they'd risen, the hands of mud holding Rebecca down collapsed back into the filth from whence they came. Rebecca scrambled away as soon as she could, watching Maura. And the shovel.

The girl's dazed expression never changed. The shovel fell from Maura's hands and she crouched down and picked up the cat in the same motion. She hugged the animal close to her chest, smearing the feline's muddy fur against her shirt.

"Leave," Maura said to Rebecca. "Just leave."

The girl retreated to her house with her cat. On trembling limbs, Rebecca picked herself up and ran back to her car. She threw herself inside, locked the doors, and stomped on the gas.

She forced herself to make it around two curves before pulling off onto the shoulder of the road. Rebecca barely flung the door open and made it out before her stomach revolted and she spewed a pulpy mess of half-digested pizza and garlic knots into the melting snow. She stayed there on her knees, shivering uncontrollably.

"What the fuck," Rebecca mumbled. She wiped her mouth. "What the fucking fuck?" She felt like she was on drugs. She wished she was. She wished she was insane and she could put herself in a rubber room. But there was no denying the truth of what had just happened to her. Even if she wanted to.

The muddy hand prints were still there. Stamped around her wrists like shackles chaining her to the reality of what she'd lived through.

Chapter 20

SHOWER. THAT WAS THE first thing on Rebecca's mind after she staggered back into her apartment. She stripped the dirty clothes quickly as she could and then lingered in that chamber of steam and scalding water until long after the last smudges of grey mud had been scrubbed off her body. She stayed until she felt like her mind had been scrubbed clean.

Rebecca emerged from the bathroom, steady if not stable. She still had no clue, *no clue*, what the hell had just happened, but she was at least removed from the situation enough to remind herself of the one thing that hadn't changed-

She could know. She could find out what had happened. That was the way she was built.

Close to home. That was the place to start. Rebecca retreated to the bed with her laptop and logged in remotely to the paper's server. She went to the Gazette's archives and opened up the editions from the last few weeks.

She skimmed the PDF files, not exactly sure what she was looking for. She was prospecting, sifting through sand in search of gold. She didn't bother with the front page, focusing instead on the back pages. She looked through the filler. The odd little stories that cluttered the back pages and back roads of every town in America.

She found the first piece of treasure in the February 16th edition:

LOCAL WOMAN ASTOUNDS IN MODERN MIRACLE

It was Thanksgiving when Martha Lindquist suffered a massive stroke.

"I thought she was dead," her husband Tom recalls. "She went into the kitchen to get the turkey and just didn't come back out. I went to check on her and found her sprawled out in a puddle of gravy. I mean it, I really thought that she was dead."

Martha had not died, but the news doctors confirmed was almost as dreadful- she had suffered a cataclysmic stroke that left her unable to move or speak. She would need to be fed through a tube. Her husband was told that there was no hope for rehabilitation.

Tom's voice cracks as he recalls what his family went through. "They told us that she was never going to get better. I'm a religious man. I prayed for weeks for her to be made whole, but eventually… I'd lost hope. I really had."

It's difficult to find a non-religious explanation for what occurred three months after that fateful Thanksgiving. Without warning, Martha regained complete and total control of her facilities.

"I just woke up to find her in bed with me," Tom recounts. "She was talking… moving. She was my Martha again."

Her doctors agree, though they are at a loss to explain Mrs. Lindquist's complete recovery from a stroke that should have left her an invalid for life.

"I haven't even seen anything like this in a medical journal," is what Doctor Herman Crane said when called for comment. "Her MRI results- there's nothing in her brain except healthy tissue. There were no experimental treatments, no incremental improvements. It's inexplicable."

There was a photo next to the article. A pleasant man with thinning hair and a slight paunch standing with his arm draped around a slender blond woman with incredibly bright eyes and a smile that showed a little too much teeth for Rebcca's liking. Their daughter stood between them. A gangly pre-teen radiating with sheer, unadulterated joy at her mother's miraculous recovery.

"Oh, shit," Rebecca breathed.

The young girl had a black cat clutched in her arms. A cat with a plain rope collar.

Rebecca dug back into the papers, a little more eagerly now, and found another story dated February 20th.

CHOKING VICTIM'S SORDID PAST REVEALED

At his funeral, Peter Benson was eulogized as a devoted father and husband.

In the week since his interment, his wife has come forward with a different story.

"He abused us," his widow Elaine revealed. "He hit me. He hit our daughter. I had to send Cassidy to school in a cast last year. I made her swear to me that she would tell everyone she broke her arm falling out of a tree."

Peter Benson was held in high regard throughout the area as a prominent local businessman and philanthropist, and his widow's accusations have generated significant tension in the community. Some have called her credibility into question.

"Let them," she says. "I'm not trying to convince anyone. I just don't want to have to lie for him anymore. Me and my daughter, we've got a new home and a new life. We've even got ourselves a little cat named Morey. Lying to protect him was the last piece of our old life, and I refuse to carry it around anymore."

A little thin by itself. There wasn't even a picture of the cat. But Rebecca backtracked a few editions and found the article on Peter Benson's death. He had choked to death, the coroner was able to confirm that much.

How a completely healthy adult man choked to death on a fistful of Fruit Loops was not elaborated on.

There were others. An Alzheimer's patient in the Calla Valley Senior Community seemed to have all of her memories back. Ecstatic family members attributed her improvement to pet therapy with her new cat, Sears.

Alice Lowry was chosen to be the new president of the New Birmingham bank, succeeding former President Marshall Evans after his sudden mental breakdown during a board meeting. The article didn't mention much more, but one quick search of Ms. Lowry's social media and what does she have in her profile picture?

A black cat.

Abruptly, the pattern ended in January. Rebecca scanned all the way into September and found no unusual stories or references to black cats. It all hinged on one story that acted like a border line. The rational on one side, the inexplicable on the other.

The death of Edith Penn.

"And her thirteen black cats," Rebecca murmured. Maura and the petting zoo. The stroke victim. The dead husband. The bank president and the Alzheimer's patient. That was five after just a short search. She could probably track down the other seven with just a few hours' work.

Only seven? You only have a lead on five cats so far. Who's the sixth one you know about?

Rebecca shook her head. She was getting ahead of herself. The first thing to do was try and confirm what had happened to Edith Penn's cats after she died. According to Brian, they all should have been put down that same night.

Easy enough to follow up on that, though, Rebecca mused. The roadmap was already forming in her mind as she jotted down some notes.

***

The icy shower was paradise. Martha lay beneath the frigid deluge and watched the water run in streams over her naked flesh. She was too numb to feel it, but the sight was enough. It was blissful oblivion watching the water. Easy to watch the neverending torrent and forget... everything. Martha would have happily stayed there for the rest of eternity. The peace... the soothing hiss of water...

The knock at the door came then, dragging her back to hateful reality.

"Mom?" Ginny called through the wood door. "Mom, are you ok? You've been in there awhile."

Martha didn't answer. She willed herself to be even more immobile. It was an impossibility; Martha was already as totally inert as an abandoned teddy bear lying on the side of the highway, but she forced herself to greater stillness all the same.

Ginny jiggled the doorknob fruitlessly, and Martha was thankful that she had locked the door before getting into the shower.

Not that she had actually been the one to turn the lock. Nothing Martha did anymore was truly her choice, but she was grateful to the whirlwind for locking the door and ensuring that she could have peace until whenever Tom came home to force the door open. And Tom was putting in a lot of hours these days. It was easier for him to work late than it was to share a house with the tornado pulsing through his wife's flesh.

"Resero," her daughter commanded. Martha heard the thumb lock spring open like a cracking bone.

Nooo, Martha moaned in her cocoon behind the shower curtain. She saw the silhouette of the door swing open. *Please, Ginny. Don't do it to me again.*

The shower curtain rattled back. Martha thought her body was numb after her hour in the icy torrent, but an electric bolt of terror rattled her bones as her daughter looked down on her. Hobbs was with her. The black cat was perched on the toilet, regarding Martha with her murky, yellow eyes. Martha saw contempt there, whether for the water or the woman, she did not know.

Virginia frowned. Her mother was slumped in the tub, slack and motionless. Like she was after the accident.

"Mommy, what's wrong?" Ginny asked. "Did your medicine stop working?" The girl thought about it for a moment, and then brightened considerably. "That's ok, I can get you more!" She raced out of the room with her familiar Ginny exuberance. Her feet pounded down the stairs and receded into the kitchen, leaving Martha alone to scream in the confines of her skull. Leaving her lips to turn blue in the frigid water.

Leaving her alone with the cat.

It had happened while Martha was taking a shower. The water had been scalding hot. It felt merely lukewarm to the thing Martha had become, but it was the best their water heater could manage. She was scrubbing herself with manic vigor, grinding the terrycloth into her skin like she was scouring a pan, pouring herself into the act with the same thrumming force she put into everything these days.

And then, easy as a tissue swept away by an errant breeze, the storm suddenly departed from her brain. Martha felt it lift like a physical thing. She was herself for a beautiful moment; aware that the terrible lighting driving through her had departed and her choices were her own again.

Even as her brain tissue withered and her limbs became vestigial once again, even as she collapsed into the tub, even as she first blistered, and then shivered, beneath the running shower, Martha wept internal tears of joy. She was free.

"I'm back, Mom!" Virginia called all too soon. She had the funnel in one hand and the steaming kettle hanging by her side.

Ginny, her mother willed. *Ginny, I'm begging you. Take that kettle and smash my fucking head in.*

Ginny lifted the iron pot, but she also lifted the funnel as well. She turned off the shower.

"Say, 'Ahh,' Mommy."

***

There were others in the night. In the Calla Valley Senior Complex, Melissa Addison sat in a rocking chair with Sears nestled in her lap. The old woman stared at the moon as memories grew anew in the suddenly fertile soil of her mind. Some of the remembered stories and histories were her own recollections, rediscovered once again.

Others were not.

Alice Lowry fumed behind her desk in her new corner office. She'd just spent an excruciating two hours trying to convince the board to throw their support behind her investment strategy. Some had eventually come around, but not a majority. Not yet.

They would. Alice had plans to make sure of it. A cutting of raspberry sapling, raven's liver boiled in a cup of lake water taken on the new moon.

How exactly that would persuade the board, Alice couldn't rightfully say, but she knew it as surely as she knew what would happen when she'd dunked former President Evans' picture in that brew of pomegranate pulp and Beechwood ash.

Maura slept peacefully in her bed as Eastey coiled over her face. She had only the dimmest of idea of what had happened in the pigpen with the reporter. That knowledge lay buried deep, hidden along with all the other things Eastey was nurturing inside of her.

While she slept, the goats, pigs, and the other animals waited in a patient line at the side of their pens closest to Maura's bedroom window. They stood with their heads turned uniformly upwards, their heated breath misted before their shadowy eyes beneath the cold moonlight.

They waited patiently for a signal that had not yet come and would not come. At least, not this night. The force growing in Maura's small bedroom had no use for them yet. It called them simply for the exercise of it.

In truth, that was what all of their activity throughout the town amounted to- Martha's return, the poisoning in the cafeteria... they were all just muscles limbering up in anticipation of what was to come.

Chapter 21

THE QUIET BETWEEN REBECCA and Brian was uncommon. They usually talked non stop in the car, bouncing back and forth between anecdotes and stray observations in a constant stream of effortless chatter.

Today was different. The only sound between them was the hum of tires over asphalt. Rebecca sat in the passenger seat with her knees up by her chin and her forehead pressed against the glass. She kept the hood of her coat up, even though the heater was on full blast.

"I'm not secretly taking you to the psych ward, you know," Brian finally said.

Rebecca swung towards him. She smiled, but it didn't quite reach her eyes. "I wouldn't blame you if you did," she said.

The whole thing was weird. Brian couldn't pretend otherwise. Rebecca had called him over last night and told him what had happened to her at the farm. She started all the way at the beginning, at the petting zoo, and reconstructed the entire chain of events for him. She relayed everything in a straightforward, coherent manner, and at no point did she make any excuses for how batshit crazy she sounded.

And when she had told him what she wanted to do, braced for him to absolutely refuse, he had agreed with the same even-tempered calm.

Now he reached out and squeezed her thigh. "I was at Edith Penn's house on the night she died, remember? You don't have to push me hard to believe that something weird could be happening there. That's part of it."

He waited. She just waited right back. But Brian could see the corners of her mouth struggling to stay down.

"You're supposed to ask me what the other part is," Brian prompted.

"I refuse to give you the satisfaction," she said primly.

He said it anyway. "The other part is you, Rebecca. You're not crazy."

"I don't think so either," she sighed. Their destination was coming up on the left, growing bigger as they came closer. "But we'll find out soon enough."

They pulled into the lot. Brian put the car into park and nodded through the windshield. "That's his van," he said. He pointed to the white county van parked closest to the entrance.

Not that he needed to. Rebecca could easily read the words printed on the side of the van in the grey light of the dreary day.

Wildlife Control.

Rebecca took a deep breath. "All right, let's go talk to him."

They approached the squat, unassuming building that housed the local shelter and the county's Nuisance Wildlife Department. They went through the front entrance, and the interior was just as faceless. White floor tiles, beige walls, and dingy ceiling tiles in need of replacement. The plump woman behind the reception desk saw them coming and set down her macrame.

"Yes, how may I help you?" she asked.

"Hi, we're looking for Tyler," Brian said. "Is he around?"

They didn't offer any more information. Brian wore his paramedic uniform and they hoped that, and small-town consideration, would be enough.

It was. The woman pointed a manicured finger down the hall to the right. "Down that way, he's taking inventory in the supply room."

"Thanks."

Rebecca waited until they were out of earshot to murmur, "You're holding up your end already."

"Off to a good start," he muttered back.

But the real challenge lay ahead. Brian remembered that Tyler Morrison had claimed the cats from the scene, and he knew the animal control technician from various calls for dog bites and other incidents. The guy was an asshole juggling about a dozen petty side hustles at any given time. He ran numbers, he dealt a little ketamine when he could get his hands on it. The idea that he had some racket selling off animals marked for destruction was far from impossible. The hope was that he might be a little more forthcoming with somebody he recognized instead of some random reporter.

They found him inside the supply room, marking down numbers on a clipboard. To Rebecca, he looked exactly like the kind of person Brian described- doughy and unshaven with a fresh jelly stain on the collar of his coveralls.

"Hey, Tyler!" Brian called out. "You remember me? Brian Davis?"

Brian spoke, but it was Rebecca that Tyler noticed first. His gaze stripped her of her jacket and clothes, and his smirk said he didn't mind what he saw. Only after he'd gotten his fill did Tyler's focus swivel towards Brian. It took a second, but Tyler lit up in a broad display of yellow teeth. "Sure, Mike's protege! What's goin' on, kid?" His smile broadened, but it hung with his canines bared. For all his bonhomie, it was the bared teeth of a wary animal.

"This is Rebecca," Brian said. "She wanted to know if she could ask you a few questions about the night Edith Penn died."

"Just some anonymous background information for the Gazette," Rebecca put in. "You won't have to worry about being quoted or anything."

"Oh, a reporter, huh?" Tyler asked. The grin grew wider, but no less inhuman. "What do you want to know?"

"The article's about what happens after a person dies without any next of kin. The responsibilities that fall on the county. Like Edith Penn's cats, you took possession of them after she died, correct?"

Tyler waved his hand dismissively. "That had nothing to do with nobody to claim an inheritance. Those cats *ate* her. They were bound for the crisper no matter what."

"And that was done the same night? Or the next day?"

"Something like that," Tyler allowed. "But it was a few months ago. I'd have to check the records."

"There are records?" Rebecca asked. Practiced calm allowed her to conceal how eager she really was.

"Of course," Tyler said. "Come on. Let's take a look." He set the clipboard down on a shelf with a loud smack.

Brian and Rebecca followed him out of the supply closet. Tyler didn't take them far, just a few doors down to a room he opened with a swipe of a keycard. He beckoned them inside with a tilt of his head and closed the door behind them.

It was not a records room. It was a narrow, claustrophobic chamber with ceramic tile walls, powerful overhead lights, and dominated by a gleaming steel machine that took up an entire quarter of the room with its dominating bulk.

The sterile cleanliness of the machine made the back of Rebecca's neck hair shudder. It felt like overkill, like a conscious attempt to ward off something best left forgotten. The machine was nearly as tall as the ceiling and twice as wide as a person. A square cabinet with a roll up door took up the majority of the front panel. A few buttons and dials, along with a temperature gauge, were mounted to one side.

A rolling cart sat in the center of the room with a white cloth draped over it. Contoured bulges rose up from beneath the fabric. They looked like pieces of patio furniture left out after a snowfall.

Tyler's grin was at last fully human. No animal could take such relish in the confusion of others. He went to the machine and thumbed a large red button. There was a brief hiss of gas, followed by a short spark and then the dull rumble of a fire roaring to life.

"Tyler, what is this?" Brian asked. Without realizing it, his hands had crawled into fists at his side.

"Just a little stop," Tyler said. He went back to the rolling cart. "Hope you guys don't mind. You know how it is- the schedule is the schedule."

He yanked back the sheet with obscene pride. Rebecca gasped, even though she'd already guessed the punchline to this twisted joke. Brian had seen too much in his line of work to be repulsed, but the petty cruelty of the reveal made anger pound at his temples.

Dead animals littered the top of the cart. Possums with their torsos crunched by truck tires. Raccoons with the eyes bulging out of their heads from poisoned bait. And the unmoving, unmarked bodies of a couple dogs and cats. Victims of lethal injection after their time at the local kill shelter had run out. The domestic animals were curled up peacefully, like they belonged on a hallmark card instead of this hellish tableau.

Tyler casually wheeled the cart towards the steel machine and pulled up the roll up door. A row of low, blue flames flickered inside the empty chamber.

Rebecca thought back to what Tyler had said to them in the other room. The crisper. Here it was.

Tyler slid a long, gleaming tray out from the belly of the incinerator and began to toss the animal carcasses onto it.

Each one landed with an ugly clatter that settled in Brian and Rebecca's bones.

"You wanted background, right?" Tyler asked with mocking ignorance.

Clang.

"I got your background right here. This is where kitties go when they don't have a litter box to call home. Much more interesting than a stack of paperwork."

Clang.

Rebecca found her voice. "But-"

Tyler shoved hard, sending the loaded tray and its mangled passengers clattering into the inferno. He cranked a dial and the flames inside the incinerator ratched up into a constant thunder.

Rebecca continued, forcing herself to speak normally even though her throat had suddenly gone dry. "But you said there *was* paperwork," she continued.

"Sure. And I can get it for you. I might even be inclined to make a correction or two so it's accurate. But I'm not doing anything until you quit peddling this bullshit about 'background' for some toilet paper story that doesn't exist."

Brian tried to protest. "Listen, we told you why we're here. There's no-"

Rebecca cut him off. "Fine," she said to Tyler. "You're right. I'm not just looking for background."

"Thank you," he said with fawning magnanimity."Now that we're being honest with each other, I'm sure we can make a deal."

"Who said we were dealing?" Brian asked.

"I did. And it's funny you mention dealing, because ketamine is so cheap these days, it's barely worth stealing. Opioids on the other hand? Opioids fetch a good number. You want to know about the cats, right? That's what we're tip-toeing around?"

Guardedly, Rebecca nodded.

"Okay, so thirteen cats. I'd say that two pills per cat sounds like a fair number. So that's 26 doses. What do you say, Bri? Oxy, percs. Whatever you can get your hands on."

"You're a fucking lowlife," Brian said.

Tyler shrugged the insult off. "You're here with a lady, aren't you? Seems to me the gentlemanly thing would be for you to pay the bill for this little outing. I'll tell you about Edith Penn's cats. I'll tell you all about them, but I'm not doing it for free."

Rebecca shook her head. "To hell with this. Come on, Brian."

But Brian stayed where he was, carefully surveying Tyler's shit-eating smirk.

"You've really got something to tell her?" he asked. "You're not just bullshitting us?"

"Kid, I don't just have something to tell your girlfriend. I've got everything."

"Brian, forget it," Rebecca said.

"I mean it," Brian said to Tyler. "If you're lying, I'll come back here and I'll beat the living shit out of you."

Tyler rolled his eyes. The paramedic was big, but Tyler knew the type of guy who could fly off the handle and he knew the kind that couldn't. This kid didn't have it in him. "You saw me leave with the cats," Tyler reminded him. "I know what I did with them. I just need a little incentive to remember is all."

Brian gritted his teeth, physically hauling the word out of his throat one letter at a time.

"I'll deal," he said.

"Brian!" Rebecca cried. "I'm not asking you to do that."

"You need to know what happened," he said.

"You could lose your job. You could lose your license. No."

"Rebecca, let me worry about it."

His face was set. He'd made a decision and he was sticking to it. Rebecca bit her lip, torn between loving him and wanting to knock his macho head in.

She turned to Tyler instead. "Three hundred dollars cash. Right now."

He chortled. "This is the most romantic shakedown I've ever seen. And darlin', I've seen a few."

Rebecca scowled at him.

Brian seethed.

Something inside the incinerator slammed hard against the door.

They all jumped. Rebecca couldn't stop a small shout from escaping her lips.

"Son of a bitch," Tyler muttered. "Somebody was just playing dead." He went to the dial on the incinerator and cranked the flames to their highest setting. "So you said three hundred?" He had to shout to be heard. The flames roared like a jet engine, and the thing inside the incinerator continued to thrash and rail against the steel door.

Rebecca suddenly stepped backwards, away from the hellish drum solo emanating from the crematory machine.

"Brian, let's get out of here," she said.

Brian grabbed her arm. "Rebecca."

"Something's wrong!" she shouted at him. She felt it in her gut. Felt phantom mud clinging to her wrists.

Tyler laughed, even as whatever was in the incinerator dragged its claws against the metal.

"Settle down, PETA. If you want a pet, I'll let it out right now. But if you're looking for take-out, we should probably wait a few minutes for that extra crispy skin."

There was no waiting. The incinerator door blew open from the inside. Flames belched out. Embers of burnt hair swirled through the air. Tyler had time to scream once before the flaming shape leapt out of the fire and fastened onto his forearm.

He screamed again. Pain this time. Tyler whipped his arm through the air, but the creature held on implacably.

It was a opossum. Its back legs, charred black, dangled uselessly. The thing's tail was aflame, and it trailed behind it like a sputtering flag.

That it was dead was beyond question. It had died on the highway, and the asphalt had peeled the animal's head down to yellow bone. But the creature bit deeper into flesh regardless. Blood ran down to Tyler's elbow.

Rebecca screamed. She didn't waste time disbelieving what she saw, not after the hands of earth, but that was no comfort. She did not have even the distraction of trying to reckon with what was happening. Her terror was sharpened by her perfect clarity.

She fled for the door and yanked at the handle until the veins stood up in her skin. She pulled with every ounce of strength she had, and gained absolutely nothing for her effort. The door remained frozen in the frame.

"Let us out!" she howled. She slammed her fists against the metal door. *"Let us out!"*

Brian simply stared, agog, as Tyler battled the dead thing attacking him.

More came crawling out of the incinerator. A racoon, cinders for fur, limping out on three legs. A mongrel dog, unmarked except for the flames that had burned its flesh black. Another opossum, this one trailing burnt intestines behind it as it clamored free.

Tyler never saw it coming. He was too focused on the fucker ripping his arm to the bone. Some freak who wasn't dead and got lucky with the cheap latch on the door. He didn't realize the danger he was in until the sharp pain bloomed in his calf.

Tyler whipped around and finally saw the creatures coming at him. The smoldering things left pawprints of charred flesh as they shambled closer. One of the cats, its eyes burnt from its head, was already clawing its way up his body.

"Jesus fucking Christ!"

He bent to pry the cat from his leg and that was when the dog leapt on his back, hitting him like a wet sack of trash and driving Tyler face first into the floor. He rolled over just in time to see the dog's blackened fangs plunging for his throat.

"NO!" Tyler screamed. Those were his last words before fangs broke skin and blood flooded into his mouth.

Still, the other animals lurched forward.

Rebecca pounded at the door. "Help us!" she shrieked. "Please help us!"

Tyler tried to grab the dog's fur and wound up peeling away a section of flesh instead. It didn't matter, the dead mutt would not be denied. It bit down harder and ripped into arteries. Tyler's eyes rolled back in his head. Blood spread around him in a growing aura like a rising sun.

The flaming revenants marched through the blood, step by sizzling step.

Tyler still fought weakly. He was dying, but not so quickly that he wasn't aware as more of the creatures ripped into his body. The burning creatures swarmed him. Teeth and claws scoured his flesh. He gurgled a scream through the blood flooding his throat.

Brian had joined Rebecca at the door. There was no lock. The handle turned freely in his hand. The door simply refused to open, no matter how hard Brian hauled at it with all of his strength. Rebecca slammed at it.

"Oh God! Oh God let us out!"

Behind them, Tyler shuddered for the final time. His hand dropped slackly away from the mongrel's pelt. He was more dead than the dead things savaging his flesh.

And then they fell too. At Tyler's last death throes, whatever energy was powering the smoldering carcasses fled, and the creatures fell like castoffs.

The door flew open at the same moment that the creatures fell still. Brian and Rebecca didn't look back. By then, people had begun to filter out of their offices, drawn into the hallway by the commotion and the stench of burning flesh, but Brian and Rebecca kept running. He was no longer a paramedic who'd borne witness to the dead and dying. She was not a reporter with the easy ability to disconnect herself from any situation. They were frightened children cast adrift in a nightmare without rhyme or reason.

Some of the staff tried to stop them. Others simply watched the horrified pair run by. The only one who never even glanced their way as Brian and Rebecca passed was the receptionist who'd greeted them at the door.

The woman never even looked up from her phone. She'd recently installed a wireless camera in her home, the better to look in on her new cat while she worked. Glover was in the living room now, staring up at the camera as if she knew that Mommy was watching her.

Such a smart kitty cat.

Chapter 22

BRIAN SKIDDED DIAGONALLY INTO two parking spots in front of the first liquor store they came across. He staggered inside and came back a moment later with something clutched to his chest in a paper bag. He got back into the car and managed to get the pint of whiskey open with fingers that refused to stop jittering. He took a deep draught and passed it to Rebecca. Between them, three quarters of the bottle was already gone. If a cop showed up, fuck 'em.

"That really happened," Brian said out loud. "It wasn't a trick or a mistake, or..."

Rebecca shook her head. "It happened. Just like what happened to me at the farm."

Brian took another swig of the whiskey. They were going to need more. "He was going to talk. Tyler. He knew something about the cats... somebody didn't want him to talk."

"I don't know if that was the message," Rebecca said.

"What do you mean?"

"Killing him like.... that. Even if we don't know how it happened, now we know for sure that something unnatural is going on, and Edith Penn's cats are part of it."

"Then why do it?" Brian asked.

"I think," Rebecca said slowly, "I think it was a warning. Something is telling us to stay out of this."

They sat in silence outside of the liquor store for a long time. Finally, Brian spoke up hesitantly. "There's no shame if you don't want to push this," he said. "It's all right if you want to let it go."

"Not for me it's not," Rebecca said. No hesitation. There was a story here, one like nothing she'd ever experienced before, and Rebecca felt the familiar tingling in her wrists. The urge to get her hands dirty. She was in this until the end.

She felt something else as well though. A new urge that diluted her normally pure drive to chase a story, no matter the cost.

"But that's me," she told Brian. "You didn't sign up for this."

A smile formed on his face. Shaky but genuine. He grabbed a pen and scribbled his signature on the paper bag. "Now I did. So what's our next move?"

Rebecca finished the last of the whiskey. "Get us back to my apartment. I need a minute to think."

***

Rebecca had an idea in my mind by the time they made it back. It was a start at least. She got her laptop out, logged into her VPN, and brought up a search engine. She began to type.

Sitting beside her on the couch, Brian watched the letters form in the search bar.

"Witches?" Brian asked.

"This all comes back to Edith Penn and her cats," Rebecca said. She pressed enter and watched the list of results appear on the screen. "We've both heard the stories about her. Edith Penn- town witch. Where else can we start?"

Rebecca set her phone to speaker and dialed the first number that came up. Somebody answered after the second ring.

"Coreolis Crystals, the focal point of spiritual forces in this latitude" a dreamy voice answered. The call was to Salem, but the answer seemed to be from somewhere beyond Jupiter. "How may I help you?"

"Yes. Hi." Rebecca said. "I don't mean to be rude, but time is a factor here. Am I speaking to the owner?"

"Yes, this is she."

"And, again, I'm sorry to be so blunt, but you are an actual witch?" Rebecca confirmed.

The voice on the other end of the phone sharpened slightly. "The proper term is Wiccan; but, yes, I'm a genuine practitioner. What can I help you with?"

"It's actually 'who.' I'm calling from Rhode Island and I'm looking for some information about a local Wiccan. Do you know or could you refer me to somebody who might be able to tell me anything about a Miss Edith Penn?"

"I don't know that name." The woman replied. There was nothing dreamy in her terse, clipped words now. "I've never heard of anyone named Edith Penn."

"Miss-" was all Rebecca could say before the woman hung up. Rebecca traded an ominous look with Brian before pulling up a second number.

The response was the same. "We have *nothing* to do with Edith Penn," the leader of a Coven in Connecticut hissed. "Do you understand me? Nothing!"

A spiritualist in Edmonton hung up at the very mention of Edith's name.

"You can almost feel them forking the evil eye at you," Rebecca muttered after a fourth call ended with yet another vehement denial of anything to do with Edith Penn.

Rebecca decided to try outside of New England. She got through to a botanica in Louisiana and was received by a woman speaking in a thick, Creole accent. "Laveau Botanica. Blessings, and how may I help you find the answers ye seek?"

"Edith Penn," Rebecca said, deciding to cut to the chase. "Do you know who she is?"

The woman on the other end practically spat all the way from Louisiana to Rhode Island. "That *moun sal*! Don't you dare mention her name to me!"

"But why?!" Rebecca implored. "Please, things are happening here and I'm just trying to understand-"

"Understand that she's a *butcher*," the woman cried. "You want no business with Edith Penn."

She hung up.

"Jesus," Rebecca muttered.

"We have to keep trying," Brian pressed. "Somebody will talk."

Rebecca ran a hand through her hair. "Maybe. But I don't think we're going to have any luck over the phone." She stood up and grabbed her coat. "I need to show my face at the office anyway. Jerry has every old-timer and local historian in town on speed dial. If anyone knows somebody willing to talk about Edith Penn, it's him."

She kissed Brian. "Wait for me here. I'll be back in a few hours."

Brian nearly let her leave. He almost kept it to himself.

"Rebecca!" he called, moments before she would have been out the door.

Rebecca spun around at his call. He was surprised to see a broad, effortless grin across her face. For a moment, it was as if everything they'd gone through was completely forgotten.

"I love you too, Brian," she said to him.

Her declaration hit his brain like a massive short circuit. The words enveloped him in his own personal sunbeam, and he wished for nothing more than to luxuriate in their warmth.

"It's about Tituba," he blurted.

Rebecca blinked. "....What?" she said.

The cat was there, in the living room with them. She lazed on the top floor of her cat tower, seemingly indifferent to the scene before her.

"I've been waiting for you to bring it up," Brian pressed. "But if you're not, then I have to say it. The black cats, Edith Penn's black cats, they're at the center of this."

"Brian-"

"That's what you told me, Rebecca. And you found Tituba right around the same time Edith Penn died. That doesn't worry you? Whatever's going on, what if she's part of it?" He gestured to the cat, who responded to Brian's accusation by leisurely licking one forepaw.

Rebecca went back to him. She cupped his elbows. "Brian, I'm freaked out too, but we can't just assume that every black cat in the world has something to do with Edith Penn."

"I know that. But-"

"You've been closer to me than anyone the last few weeks. Have you seen me acting strange?"

"No. But that doesn't mean-"

"Have I done anything supernatural? Made the earth move? Raise anything from the dead?"

"Rebecca, I don't-"

She kissed him hard. Grabbed the back of his head. Let her taste linger on his tongue.

"Don't get paranoid on me. We've got enough real insanity to deal with without inventing more. When I get home, we'll figure out what to do next."

She turned and went back to the door.

"I love you too!" Brian shouted as she was leaving. Rebecca didn't reply, but the way she paused before she left told Brian that she'd heard him.

But I still don't like that cat, he brooded.

For her part, Tituba stretched and hopped off the top of the cat tower, graceful as a falling feather. The cat sauntered into the kitchen without so much as a glance at Brian.

Brian dropped dejectedly onto the couch. He considered turning on the TV but decided against it. HIs gaze fell onto Rebecca's laptop, still open onto the listing for Laveau Botanica in Louisiana. He realized that their mission hadn't been a complete failure. They had managed to learn one fact about Edith Penn after all.

She was a butcher.

Chapter 23

1956

"MMISS EDITH!" CATARINA GREETED her.

Edith smiled warmly as she entered the shop. "Good day, Miss Catarina. You're well, I trust? The Loas still watching over you?"

Catarina wiped sweat from her brow. There was still no air conditioning here in the Treme, and the ceiling fan stirring overhead was no match for the thick, humid Louisiana summer.

"The Loas do their part," Catarina said. "'Wish payin' the rent t'were their part. No such luck yet, but that don' stop me askin'."

Edith went to the shelves lining the walls of the botanica. "In that case, I'm happy to do whatever I can through my own province." She moved along the walls, only occasionally glancing at the scrawled list in her hand as she took a pouch of this and a vial of that. She sniffed at a dried stick of some withered meat and turned questioningly towards the shop keep. "Dried alligator heartstrings really work as well as fresh?" she asked.

"Dey do if you soak 'em in swamp water for an hour," Catarina said.

Edith nodded approvingly. "I hadn't thought of that." She added five to her clutch of purchases and brought everything to the counter.

Catarina rang up Edith's purchases. After accepting the white woman's wrinkled bills, Catarina added a cheesecloth pouch to the rest of Edith's purchases. "Dat's powdered cave mushrooms from Leesville. Not sure what kind but supposedly picked under a new moon. I can't seem to get anytin' out of 'dem, but maybe you'll have better luck."

Edith bowed her head gratefully. "If anything works you'll be the first to know. I'll see you tonight?"

Catarina raised her arms in a flourish. "*Men nan kou!*" she replied.

Edith smiled. *"Jiska aswe'a, zanmi mwen a,"* she answered in Creole.

"And if you see me brother first," Catarina called, "Tell 'im to make sure the food is *spiced* dis time!"

Edith rolled her eyes and waved, the bell over the door marking her departure.

Catarina watched her friend go. *"If anything works,"* Edith had said when she accepted the powdered mushrooms. Catarina rolled her eyes, certain that Edith would find a use for them. And she did trust Edith would come to her first with whatever she brewed up. Several of Edith's potions and powders lined the special shelves behind the counter. They all fetched an exorbitant price for the shop, which was no small thing, but Catarina would have shared ingredients and information with Edith even if she never saw anything from it in return.

White women were viewed as suspicious in the Treme. White witches, even more so. The Voodoo Queens of New Orleans did not divulge their secrets lightly.

Edith Penn was an exception. A witch that powerful was *yon pati nan tout.* A Part of All.

It would be an insult against magic to hold anything back from a witch like Edith Penn.

Edith strolled through the bustling Saturday afternoon streets, marveling once again at how different this city was from anywhere in New England. The volume, the brightly painted buildings, and the vibrant, pulsating life everywhere you looked. The merchants overflowed onto the sidewalks. Men and women freely passed flasks and amber jugs back and forth. She passed an impromptu parade of trombone players marching up Canal Street.

There were spellcasters in every society on earth. Different practices, different languages, but they were always there. Some places scorned this truth, others barely tolerated it. But New Orleans...

This is the difference in a city that embraces magic, she thought. Not for the first time. She'd felt it the moment she stepped off the train in Union Station.

And, also not for the first time, she swore that she was never going back to New Birmingham.

Edith rented a small house in the Sixth Ward. It was a simple, three-room dwelling with a postage stamp front yard. There was no lawn, only native grasses and a thriving patch of purple phlox. The smell of it greeted Edith as she returned with her shopping.

It was cool inside Edith's house. Far cooler than Catarina's shop, and fresher smelling than the air-conditioned department store in the heart of the city. Edith kept several blocks of dry ice around her home. She'd devised a simple *Semper Prunis* incantation that allowed the blocks to linger for months without melting, keeping the small dwelling refreshingly dry and temperate, no matter how the heat raged outside. She would have happily taught the spell to Catarina and the others, but none of them possessed the *mana* needed to give the words weight.

Not yet, anyway, Edith thought to herself.

The cats came slinking out at the sound of the door. She never returned home to find them on the couch or lazing in a sunny spot on the floor. They always came pouring out like spilled oil, slinking from the dark corners and under furniture.

But they always came; all thirteen of them meowing gently and milling about as they waited their turn to wind around her ankles in welcome.

Edith set her canvas bags down and removed a package wrapped in brown paper. The chorus of feline chirps and rumbles intensified at the sight of it.

"Yes, yes. Patience," she chided them. Edith went to the trough in the kitchen and upended the two pounds of raw shrimp into the long tray.

Despite their eager hunger, the other cats lingered in place, coming to feed only after Tituba prowled forward and selected the choice first morsel for herself. Edith shook her head at the unmistakable pride in the big Maine Coon's eyes.

With Tituba's permission, the others finally came forward. The dark cloud of cats shouldered and jostled, pushing each other aside for prime position.

"Pss," Edith hissed. Sears, the runty Tabby, looked up from her usual position at the far edge of the trough. Edith discreetly flipped a chunk of raw salmon at her. Just as neat, Sears gobbled up the slice of fish before the others could snatch it from her.

"Big plans tonight," she told her Familiars as she pulled her own lunch of red beans and rice from the ice box. A few choice words in Nepalese quickly brought the meal to a pleasantly warm temperature. Steam and the delicious aroma rose to greet her nostrils. "I don't think you'll see me back before sunrise. I'll leave the TV on for you, shall I?" She chuckled to herself as she fetched a spoon.

She never got a chance to actually sample her meal. The knock at her door came first.

Edith didn't mind. She knew who was calling, and he was much more satisfying than any meal.

He had flowers for her. He always came bearing some small gift, as if he still had something to prove to her. He didn't, and she proved it once again by flinging the bouquet carelessly across the room before pulling him inside.

Marcus barely got the door closed behind him before Edith's lips were on his. She was tall for a woman, and he was short for a man. They met perfectly on the same level. He moved from her lips to the curve of her chin, and then down to her neck.

"Propei," Edith groaned, and the drapes pulled themselves shut with a brisk snap. Marcus murmured and bit down on her neck. He loved it when she used spellcraft. He said he could feel it tingling off of her. Edith believed him.

"Where are dey?" he murmured. His voice was low, but not as low as his hands. Down at her hips but slowly working their way between her thighs. Edith sighed. His accent always kindled in her ears like lighting fire. "Not getting stage fright, are we?" she asked.

"Look who closed the drapes, cher."

She pulled him towards the bedroom. "You don't have to worry about them, they're busy with dinner. No need for a show." It didn't bother her that Marcus didn't like her cats. He wasn't the first lover to be uncomfortable around them.

Besides, she had much more important things to think about.

He didn't say it until afterwards, but Edith felt the words brewing inside of him. She felt them even while he was looming over her from behind and panting in her ear.

"Your sister said to remember the spices this time," Edith said as she nestled against him, hoping to forestall what was coming for as long as she could.

Marcus scoffed. "Catarina not happy if dere's an inch of skin left on her tongue. One day I'll skip the shrimp all together and stick her in a feed bag filled wit' cayenne powder."

Edith laughed, but he lapsed back into a contemplative silence just as quickly.

"...My sister, she like you, ya know." he said.

"I like her too," Edith said. "She's been a good friend."

"And the others," he continued, stroking her hair as her pale cheek lay against his brown chest. "They don't care, you know. If you wanted to stay, I mean."

Edith raised her head so she could look into his eyes. Aura-sight was something she'd had since birth, but she'd spent six months honing the skill with a Datuk in Malaysia and she now saw them as easily as fresh paint. Marcus' aura was always a beautiful, compassionate green that flared around him now like spring in full bloom. He was kind and sincere, and always completely unashamed to show it.

She prayed she wouldn't hurt him too deeply.

"It's not about that, Marcus. There's too much to learn and there's no one place to learn it all. There's no one place for me. There never was."

"That's what you said when you came here, but that was then. You know us now. You know.... Me. You're happy here, aren't you?"

"I am," she said. "But do you remember when we went to the zoo?"

"I do," he said, already sensing where she was going with this.

"We saw the tigers. And they were happy. Fed, sheltered, taken care of... but they were caged. All of that power and nothing to do but let it go to waste. Is that what you want for me?"

"What I want is to take care of you," Marcus said, laying himself bare. "Seems to me like there's worse places to be than surrounded by people that love you."

Melancholy blue had already creeped in around the edges of his aura. It broke Edith's heart, but it didn't change her mind.

"It's not my path, Marcus." She took his hand. Kissed his knuckles. "If that means you can't come to call on me anymore, I understand."

He brushed a stray strand of brown hair away from her face. "I t'ink that a conversation for another time."

He rose from her and began to dress all too quickly. "I have to be ready for tonight. I'll see you 'dere."

"Of course," Edith said. She wrapped herself in a sheet to see him to the door. They kissed, but it was as shallow and fleeting as a puddle baking in the sun after a short rain. Edith watched him from the corner of the window as he made his way down the walk and around the corner.

"A conversation for another time." That's what he said, but Edith knew better.

His aura, drenched in midnight blue, told her it was so.

Edith could have inspected her own aura, but there was no reason to. She could already feel everything she needed to know. She felt it churning in her stomach like too much fried dough.

It would be so easy, the easiest thing in the world, to run after him. To talk to Catarina about becoming a partner at the shop. To...

No. Edith pushed those distractions aside. Marcus had his preparations for tonight and so did she.

She let the sheet fall away. Ribs and clavicles visible on her slight form, she went back to the kitchen. The red beans and rice had gone cold, and she suddenly didn't have the energy to heat it again. She morosely ate a few bites to replenish her strength and then set to work.

She spread her purchases from Catarina's on the table along with the rest of her makings. Her Familiars were still at the trough, gnawing the last bits of meat from the shrimp shells. "Enjoy it while it lasts," Edith told them with forced casualness as she prepared her things. "Another week or so and I think we're heading north. The constellations are turning over Manitoba. It might be time to finally take the Sisters of Azeroth up on their letters. Though the salmon should be good, I suppose."

Edith breathed. She set aside rocks suddenly hardening in her belly. Set aside the lingering memory of Marcus sweeping her away with his gentle caressing. She waited for the tingling eagerness to assert itself in her wrists. Her talent, begging to be let off the leash.

Edith eagerly let herself loose.

She started with the pouches. Red leather. Edith inspected each one for imperfections before adding the ingredients. Powdered rose quartz, a dash more than the usually prescribed sprinkle. A gator tooth in this one. Some chopped Ashwagandha root in the next. She kept count as she added the array of ingredients to each pouch. Any odd number was prescribed, but Edith always had the most success with nine.

There was nothing written down. Edith had no spellbook to refer to. No list of ingredients to consult. She had read the books, and she'd taken everything she needed from them in order to set them aside and chart her own path. What drove her forward now was her own intuition. Edith's every move was certain. Her every choice of ingredient was totally assured. A person who didn't know any better would have been awed at Edith's seeming mastery of spellcraft, but the witch herself knew better. There was more, so much more for her to learn. Edith had only scratched the surface of what she could become.

"Tituba," she called once all of the other ingredients were in place. "Come up."

The Familiar approached willingly. The big cat hopped first onto an empty chair and then up onto the table. Edith picked up the small stone bowl and then, after a moment's hesitation, the bone knife. There were no words spoken between them, but Edith's blue eyes met the feline's yellow orbs and held there for the length of a slow, measured breath.

Edith made no secret of the bone knife in her hand. The blade was never hidden from the animal's sharp gaze. It was a crude tool. A wood handle with a length of raven's bone wedged into it and the far end cut at an angle to make a sharpened point.

Unprompted, Tituba raised a paw to her mistress. She *mrowed* gently.

Edith regarded the proffered paw with solemn respect. "You're very good to me, Tituba." She looked around the table. The other cats had formed a circle around her, bearing solemn witness to the ceremony with their mistress. "All of you are," she told them.

Edith took the spike and pierced Tituba's paw. The black cat did not flinch. She did not hiss. She held utterly still while Edith collected her blood until the red pool nearly overflowed from the stone bowl.

"That's enough," Edith finally said. It was only at her command that Tituba retreated to the floor, leaving a spit spot trail of red in her wake.

Edith took the bowl of (not quite) cat's blood. Using the tip of her finger she carefully flicked three splashes into each leather pouch. As she did, she repeated a Gaelic invocation before cinching each one closed.

To an outsider, they wouldn't seem like much. A dozen red pouches, too small to hold anything more than a handful of children's marbles.

Edith Penn knew better. She decided to take a short nap while she had the time.

It was going to be a long evening.

Chapter 24

REBECCA STEPPED INTO THE normal bustle of the newsroom. Clattering keys. Ringing phones.

"I'm looking for a quick statement-"

"Sure. I'll shoot you an email."

"I like him, but I'm tired of going out to the same damn bar every time he calls me."

So comforting. So mundane. The regular world where mud didn't claw at you and roadkill didn't rise back to squirming life.

At the desk by the door with a phone tucked under his shoulder, Tom Senzer saw her and waved briefly before somebody answered his call.

"Bill, it's Tom. What can you tell me about some kind of rabid dog attack at the shelter this morning?"

Rebecca shuddered and forced herself forward. She saw Jerry through the glass, jawing at somebody in his office, and sat down at her desk while she waited for him to become available. She traded a few anxious smiles with her coworkers as they passed. Marge Thompson inquired if she was feeling all right. Rebecca forced a shaky smile. "Yeah, just a long morning. You know how it gets."

Her chirping cellphone spared her the agony of any more small talk. Rebecca mimed, "I have to take this," and grabbed the phone. She recognized the Boston area code, but the number was otherwise unrecognizable. It didn't matter. Rebecca would listen to a spiel about her car warranty if it meant a distraction.

"Hello?"

"Yes, is this Rebecca Spencer?" a semi-familiar voice queried.

"Speaking."

"Ms. Spencer, this is Alicia Garza with customs. I have the information about that shipment you requested."

Shipment? It took Rebecca to dig through the wreckage of the last twenty-four hours and muddle that statement into something that made sense. Boston. Customs. A shipment.

Hyde.

Rebecca sat up straight in her chair, her world clear and concise for the first time in days.

"Ma'am, are you there?"

"Yes," Rebecca said. "I'm here. I can hear you. Please, what did the shipment contain?"

"The shipment was 100 ccs of Veratridine. The extra paperwork was required because it's a class 1A toxic material."

Rebecca's fingers were already blurring across her keyboard, bringing up the safety data sheet in Google.

...Toxic was an understatement. Veratridine was colorless, odorless, and tasteless. And just a few drops was enough to send a person into cardiac arrest. You could be totally healthy and then just-

A connection fell into place and sent a two hundred volt charge up her back. A story from the same day that Hyde's "special assistant" had retrieved the package of deadly poison. One of Hyde's political rivals- Coffer, Cooper, something like that. His son had died suddenly. No pre-existing conditions, no family history, just a teenager, and one night he dropped dead of...

Rebecca's hands were suddenly very cold. Her chest was burning.

"Ma'am? Ms. Spencer? Will that be all?"

Rebecca forced herself back forward. "Yes," she said. "That's it. Thank you."

"Anything at all, mistress."

The woman hung up.

"Mistress?" Rebecca thought. That was weird. Weirder still, it felt... *right.* Of course she would think of Rebecca as her mistress. After all, she was...

She was what?

Rebecca thought back to her initial phone call with the customs agent. The bureaucratic stonewalling, the agent's utter apathy to her plight. Rebecca's own furious desire to throttle the woman on the other end of the phone. Doodling to distract herself.

Then I pricked my finger with the staple remover. And I needed something to stop the bleeding so I grabbed the closest thing I could...

Rebecca plunged into the trash can under her desk. Budget cuts had them down to once a week cleaning, and her trash from the other day was still there. Rebecca plunged past yesterday's sandwich wrapper and some torn envelopes, and uncovered the crumpled sheet with telltale signs of rusty blood.

She smoothed the paper out with hands that had grown preternaturally calm, the ripped paper unfolded like a flower opening up, practically sighing with relief as it took on its natural form.

The paper was almost totally black with pen marks. Rebecca had drawn much more elaborately than she'd realized.

Really? Is that all you didn't realize?

....No. No, that wasn't the only thing at all.

The drawing was a chaotic scrawl, but only at first glance. A more diligent eye would see the deliberate path of every winding line, note the careful pattern amongst the short hash marks and the way the drawing seemed to coalesce around the bloody smear in the center of the page. There was a cohesion to the piece that became clear if you stared at it long enough.

More than just clear, the drawing was *powerful*. There was an ominous strength in the contrast between the swirl of blank ink and the single, stark splotch of red blood at the center- the eye amidst the storm Rebecca had conjured.

The blood was the core that gave the drawing its power, but the ink was what gave it direction. Rebecca couldn't explain how she knew that. For the first time, she didn't have the words for what she knew. She couldn't tell you the language of what she'd drawn, and she couldn't recognize the culture that it had come from, but she knew exactly what it was that she had done. She knew it with a primal confidence deep within her blood.

Rebecca pushed hard away from her desk. Cold sweat dampened her hairline. Her body no longer felt like it was her own.

Tituba. The cat *was* like the others. Somehow, she'd... done something to Rebecca. Changed her.

Christ, Rebecca chastised herself. *How could you have missed this? Brian laid it right out for you and you still didn't see it.*

But the blindspot must have been part of the effect. Part of the spell or whatever Tituba had done to her. Or was it still doing it to her? That cat needed to get out of her apartment. Or maybe it was Rebecca that needed to be gone. Her and Brian somewhere on a long vacation.

Her keys. She needed her keys. Where the hell were her keys? They weren't in her pocket. They weren't in her purse.

Tituba knows. She won't let me get away.

Rebecca's keys were on her desk. Exactly where they always were.

No. Come on, stop acting like you don't know how to think, she cautioned.

Rebecca sucked in a shaky breath. Then another. She sat back down in front of her computer and forced herself to scroll through bullshit on Twitter until her mind settled down into something less frenzied than a wasp's net stirred up with a stick. She couldn't afford to lose her shit now. Her shit was just about the only thing she could rely on.

In another minute, she had some semblance of a plan. Get Brian. Get away from Tituba. She wouldn't even go into the apartment, she'd call him from the car and tell him to come down. She considered calling him first, warning him to get away from the apartment and meet her some place, but decided against it. Brian was alone with the cat, and Tituba was now dangerous. Best to let him stay ignorant. Let the cat believe he wasn't a threat.

She probably already thinks he's a threat.

Rebecca stowed that shit down and locked it away. Get home. Call Brian. Tell him she had something heavy in the car and ask him to come down and help her carry it.

And then drive. Get the hell out of town and regroup. Maybe just never come back. New Birmingham suddenly didn't seem to matter so much anymore.

If she were still panicking, that would have been the end of it. Rebecca would have been halfway across town by now.

But Rebecca had settled, and she recognized that there was still one other thing that mattered.

The story.

Jerry was alone when she came into his office. There was none of her usual bravado. She came forward as meekly as any intern on their first day, and yet she pushed forward with an urgency that wouldn't be delayed. She had a few printed pages clutched in her hands. The edges were wrinkled and damp with sweat.

"Rebecca," the editor greeted with his usual dry cheer, primarily focused on an array of bills spread out before him. "Tell me, my employee. What great good can I do for you today?"

She tried to smile back. "Some time off, actually, if you can manage it, Jerry."

His eyes sprang upwards, focusing on Rebecca with total attention. "Time off? Now? Rebecca, the Hyde vote is in *two days.*"

She winced. "I know. But this is serious, Jerry. I need to get out of here, *right now.*"

He stood up. "Rebecca, has anyone threatened you? Someone from the Senator's office?"

If you only knew, she thought. "No. It's not that."

"Because I've been there," he said. "And it is scary, but you can't fold to pressure like that. You'll regret it-"

"*Jerry.* I can't explain. I just need you to listen."

He sighed. "All right. Fine. But there's enough story here that I need to keep chasing it. I'll leave you on the byline, you've done enough work to earn that, but you're going to have to share the credit."

"I know." She handed the papers to Jerry. Everything she had on Senator William Hyde, offered up with only a minimum of rending pain like a mother giving up her only child.

"Give it to Tom if you can. His nuts-and-bolts prose is best, and that's most of the work now."

Jerry reviewed the printouts. The shipping manifest. The paper trail tying Hyde to it. The photos of his assistant with the package. Matt Cooper's obituary and the M.E's report. Everything.

Jerry had to sit down. "Rebecca," he said. "This is..."

"Just make sure it gets out. Okay, Jerry? Nail the bastard to the wall."

Then she was gone. Out the door before he could say another word. Jerry reviewed the documents one more time,

He was worried about her, but there was no time for that now. Jerry heaved himself up from behind the desk and pushed open the door. Luckily, nobody was passing by or they would have been flattened as he swept out of his office.

"Everyone on me!" the editor bellowed, bringing the small newsroom to a halt.

Jerry spent ten minutes getting the ball rolling. Tommy Senzer, indeed, got the nod for the front page piece, but Jill Childs had to stop what she was doing and start a background piece on Hyde's legislative career. Kyle needed to pull pictures.

"I'll handle the layout," he shouted over his shoulder, already barreling back towards his office. He had a friend at the Providence Journal to call. Jerry wouldn't give him the whole story, but if he gave the guy a head start, he could guarantee a favorable shoutout for the Gazette.

And Rebecca, he remembered. She deserved the spotlight, even if she'd fled it at the last second.

Under other circumstances, he might have noticed that the blinds to his office were closed, even though he always left them open, but there was too much else to think about. Jerry got back into his office and didn't realize he had company until the door was already closed.

There was a man sitting at his desk. A man Jerry instantly recognized from the photos Rebecca had given him.

"Mr. Williams," Duncan greeted him from Jerry's chair. "It's a pleasure to meet you. I've been an avid reader ever since that series on local veterans and their struggles with the VA. Has veteran's issues always been a passion of yours, or did the story just present itself?"

"What the hell are you doing in my office?" Jerry demanded.

Duncan shook his head, sorry to move so quickly onto business. "I've had your office bugged ever since Miss Spencer first accosted Senator Hyde. It seemed like a wise investment, and clearly it was since here we are."

"Get the fuck out," Jerry said.

Hyde continued as if the other man had never spoke. "As I said, here we are. You have a story to print. I represent someone who doesn't want that to happen. My hope is that we can work something out."

Jerry laughed. "You think you're the first thug to come in here and threaten me if I run a story their boss didn't like?" He did his best to straighten up a spine curved by decades hunched over a keyboard. "The story runs because it's the truth. End of discussion."

Duncan laughed and spread his sausage fingers. "I thought we might have this misunderstanding. Yes, of course powerful men have threatened you before. However, I assure you that this is very much your first experience dealing with someone like *me*. I, as they say, am cut from a different cloth. I've arranged a presentation to clear up any confusion about this point."

The fat man sat back in Jerry's chair. The oil glistened on his face beneath the cheap lights. The only sound between them was the police scanner on the back cabinet.

"Get on with it and get out," Jerry said.

"Just another moment," Duncan assured him. "I already placed an anonymous call to precinct 19. Somebody should be- Ah," Duncan broke off. He raised a finger as the normally placid clatter from the police scanner suddenly ratcheted up to a frantic cacophony. "Perfect timing," he said. He spun around in Jerry's chair and raised the volume.

"Jesus Christ!" a voice shouted in horror. *"We've got a 187 here at All American. She... Christ!"*

All American was the dry cleaner next door. It was a small shop run by a solo woman named Kira Albreck. The two of them had a standing tradition to pass a cup of coffee together every Friday afternoon.

...A 187 was the police code for murder.

A sweeping rush of unreality hit Jerry like a shot of novocaine. It kept the fear at bay as he grappled with the sheer impossibility of the panicked shouting coming over the radio.

"One shot in the back of the head," the voice on the radio continued. *"But her eye... Morgan, do you see her fucking eye!?"*

Jerry saw it. Duncan's hand went into his coat pocket and came out with a human eyeball. The white orb stained pink with fresh blood. The pupil stared blankly into the void.

The unreality was gone. And the most pristine terror he'd ever known flooded through his body. Jerry's heels rattled. He was actually shaking in his boots.

"Don't worry," Duncan assured him. He shuffled the eyeball idly across his knuckles as if it were a ping pong ball. "We've done polling and crime really isn't the priority with local voters that you'd expect. The more important question, the only question really, is are you going to stop the presses on this libelous, thinly sourced hit piece you're putting together... or am I going to kill your daughter next? I realize I'm here with you and Dartmouth is forty minutes away, but before you answer you should consider if I'm resourceful enough to already have somebody in place to put an icepick in Mary's neck."

The newsroom hummed behind him while Jerry faced down a challenge he always dreamed of. How many times in the last thirty years had he reported on some tragedy or scandal and thought to himself that it all could have been averted if someone, in a critical moment, had the willpower to do what was right?

Here was that moment. All these years, and it had been waiting for Jerry Williams in his tiny office in a town of twenty thousand people.

And while Jerry waited for the strength of his convictions to surge through his spine, Duncan had picked up the photo of Mary from his desk and idly turned it over in his hand. He left a small smear of blood on the frame.

Jerry's shoulders slumped. He looked down at the scratched, dull floorboards.

"I'm not convinced the sourcing is sound," he whispered. "I'll need to delay the story until we get more information."

"Excellent," Duncan said with chilling casualness. "That's all we're asking for."

He heaved himself out of the chair. Jerry saw his daughter's photo clutched in the intruder's sweaty grasp, but said nothing.

Duncan brushed past him on his way out of the office. "I'll leave you to your business. I can only imagine how much work goes into keeping a paper going these days."

He paused with his hand on the door. "If I may," Duncan said, "I suggest drafting a job posting for a new staff reporter. I understand Miss Spencer is about to accept a new position as an obituary writer... or something like that."

Jerry whimpered, but he did nothing except loathe the pathetic sound of his own voice.

Duncan left, taking everything that mattered along with him. Jerry had nothing to do but move on legs that had aged about thirty years in the last five minutes. He sat behind his desk and waited for someone to burst through the door. Someone to tell him that he didn't belong here and to get the hell out.

Nobody did.

Chapter 25

1956

EDITH MET CATARINA AT the final trolley station, just outside the city limits. They walked together in companionable silence as the trees grew taller, the mosquitos got bigger, and the paved road transitioned to hard packed dirt. It was a clear, cloudless night, and the full moon overhead provided ample light to guide their way.

"My brother come to see you?" Catarina asked, her wry grin saying she already knew the answer.

Edith's good-natured scowl did not quite hide the melancholy underneath. "Yes. He came."

"He'll be grey for a while after you leave," Catarina assessed. "But him solid underneath. He'll brighten back up eventually. Me? If I could do half of what you can, I wouldn't stop either."

Edith patted her friend's hand. "Is the shop really in trouble, Catarina?"

Catarina shrugged in a way that wasn't completely honest. "We always pull through. Lately not quite so many people looking to cure their ills with poultices and gris gris. As if aspirin and rosaries solved everything. We'll get 'dem back. The world never stays still, Edith."

They were getting close now. They felt it before they saw the firelights flickering through the Spanish moss. The energy built in the air. A pleasant chill, like slipping into a soothing pond after a hot day, swept over them. The fireflies were gathering in greater numbers. They twinkled together, strong enough to cast Edith and Catarina in their own pulsing field of starlight.

The two women couldn't help but trade barely suppressed grins. It was never routine, this walk. Edith still felt the same giddy rush as the first time she'd been invited. She knew it was the same for Catarina.

Edith heard them now. Laughter and music mingling together in a beautiful mess of noises. A curtain of Spanish moss hung in their path, obscuring their view of the gathering, but not for long. Catarina did the honors, she swept the hanging moss aside to unveil the gathered figures cavorting in the light from the torches gathered in a wide circle.

There were twenty people all told. Voodoo Queens, Priests, and some select worshippers. The spell practitioners of the Treme. They'd come together to praise Bondye and the Loas, to curry favor and to practice their abilities.

And they came to celebrate their community.

The men wore top hats and brightly colored coats with fraying threads at the hem. The women wore head scarves and diaphanous dresses that swirled at their ankles. Some had painted faces. They all came with charms and gris gris bags around their necks and dangling at their wrists.

The band had already started. Horns and drums blended together in a cocoon of sound that insulated them from the outside world. The music was accompanied by a chorus of sizzling and bubbling. The fires were already roaring. A massive cauldron hissed with boiling crawdads. Gator meat crackled on the iron grill. The smell was enticing enough to raise the dead.

"Shall we?" Catarina asked, nodding towards the crowd of revelers.

"One thing first," Edith said. She produced the first of the red pouches and offered it out to her. "This is for you," Edith said. "For focus. And fortune."

Catarina took the bag with gentle reverence. She recognized it immediately for what it was. A gris gris bag handcrafted by the most talented witch she'd ever known... and also a parting gift from a dear friend.

"Bondye bless you, Edith Penn."

"And you, Catarina Laveau."

They joined the revelers. Edith Penn, the outsider from the North, was greeted with a full chalice of Sangria and more kisses and embraces than she could count.

Since leaving New Birmingham, she'd lived and studied with Druids, monks, and practitioners of a dozen different spellcrafts. The voodoo community of the Treme was the only place where she'd felt like part of a family, and she hoped that her gift would tell them all how much that meant to her.

She drank. She sang the praises of the Loa. She brought water and bourbon to the grateful musicians. She flitted with easy familiarity amongst the revelers.

And at every stop. At the end of every conversation. In the lull between the last laugh and the next joke, Edith said her goodbyes. Person after person, friend after friend, Edith reached out with a gentle touch and then bequeathed another gris gris bag. She wove through the gathering in this manner, handing out charm bags one by one.

Last of all, she went to Marcus.

Edith found him at the fires, stripped to the waist, gleaming with sweat, and dancing between the grill and the jambalaya cauldron. He tried to pretend he didn't see her coming, but it was a poor showing.

"How are you doing?" she shouted over the music.

Marcus shrugged. "Happy as a tiger."

"Marcus," she said quietly, willing him to hear her despite the clamor around them. Marcus recognized the spellcraft tingling in his ear and reluctantly gave her his attention.

He was intoxicating. Edith took in the sight of him, his slender body gleaming like a bronze idol in the firelight. His deep set eyes enveloped her body in a way that Marcus would not allow his arms to do.

Edith wished that he would. And if he wouldn't, she wished that she could throw caution to the wind and claim him instead. She remembered how his lips felt only a few hours ago and wished desperately to ask him for one last kiss. One last time in the comfort of his touch.

Instead, she held out the last gris gris by its drawstring.

"I made you something. Will you take it?"

Marcus hesitated, as if refusing might make her stay. But in the end, he knew better and accepted her offering. He wrapped the bag around his wrist and wordlessly returned to the pot, pushing the wooden spoon through the thick mixture of rice, sausage, and shrimp.

Edith waited, but Marcus remained gamely focused on his chef's duties. He would not meet her gaze. She sighed.

"Goodbye, Marcus."

She was about to turn away when she heard his voice, low but distinct from the festival around them.

"I'll keep it forever, Edie."

He grabbed a carved wooden bowl and filled it with jambalaya. "Eat up, yeah?"

Edith took the bowl gratefully, but decided not to torment him with her presence any longer. She retreated to a wooden stump at the edge of the revelery and sat down for the first time all night.

She savored the first spicy spoonful. Not just because Marcus was a tremendous cook, and not only because the next place she called home likely wouldn't offer jambalaya this good. Edith Penn relished her meal with the same deep satisfaction that any craftsman would after a job well done.

Edith looked out over the dancers and musicians and saw her red gris gris bags everywhere, hanging from a sash or a wrist, or draped across a neck. Tonight, they were laughing and merry. Tomorrow, they would continue to battle poverty and discrimination against their faith and their skin. Good, loving people who had to sweat and struggle just to live in peace with full bellies. People who understood the forces that ordered the universe, but with the bad luck not to be born with the same talent as Edith Penn.

And luck was all it was. All of Edith's studies and travel wouldn't have amounted to anything were it not for the sheer ability that had kindled within her at birth. That gift of fate was what set Edith apart from her friends.

Until now.

"Ay! Ay look 'ere!"

Eating her dinner, Edith saw the first small manifestations of her gift start to spark. Eziekiel Johnson laughed in amazed delight as he finally conjured a successful flame sprite from one of the torches. The tiny ballerina with a body of fire and hair of sparks danced in his hand, rolling its hips and pirouetting gracefully on one foot. The small group around him hooted and clapped as the small figure of fire finished its performance and took a deep bow.

Malia Rambeau danced by herself at the edge of the swamp, far beyond the glow of the torches. Edith watched blue light like cotton candy weave its way across her skin. The girl swirled her arms through the air, leaving glowing trails of fae light in her wake.

And there were still others. The amazed murmurs and newfound feats rippled through the congregation. Josephine dispensed with her tarot cards and told Frederick Facile's fortune by casting the chicken bones off of his plate. That was a Scapulimancy skill. Nothing that she could have possibly learned by herself.

Edith silently clenched her fists. Elated chills ran up and down her back. *It's working,* she thrilled.

Of course it was working. Edith would never have played games with her friends' lives, but she also hadn't really permitted herself to believe the charms would work *this* well. Sharper divination skills, a little extra potency in Catarina's potion making. Maybe a warding charm to keep the worst of the city's bigots from the Treme. That was what Edith had hoped to achieve. But this... Edith ducked as a massive shadow swooped low over her head. She looked up in time to see a Great Horned Owl perch on Benji L'Fontaint's arm. The owl turned its head 360 degrees to meet Edith's gaze, its eyes flared with unnatural orange light and shadowy smoke rose from the owl's outline. *A summoning!* Edith realized.

It was the gris gris bags Edith Penn had made. They seized on the latent abilities in her friends and amplified them. And the bags would continue to do so for years, long after Edith had taken her leave of them. They weren't as strong as Edith, no charm could do that, but her companions were now strong enough to make their lives more prosperous. Of that, there was no doubt.

Edith was grateful they were all too focused on their burgeoning gifts to notice her watching from the fringes. She didn't want anyone to see her as joyful tears turned the firelight into sparkling diamonds.

You deserve it, she willed out to them. *All of you.*

She set her bowl aside and sought out her beloved. Marcus was no longer by the grill, and Edith didn't see him clapping by the drums where he sometimes liked to sit. She tried to key in on his aura and... yes, there. She spied his unique green hunkered down at the water's edge.

Edith drew closer. They were outside the light from the torches now, but the moon did her part. Edith saw him clearly- crouched down with his back to her, the ridges of his vertebrate outlined by silvery lunar light.

He was talking to something. Edith brightened. Was he exhibiting Druid skills? Beast tongue? Marcus would love that. Edith drew closer. She crept carefully through the grass, fearful of breaking him from his revelry.

It was a bullfrog Marcus was talking to. A real humdinger, almost the size of a football. Marcus was crouched down in almost the same posture as the frog; leaning down, utterly transfixed, so they were practically eye to eye. If he was aware of Edith hovering in his periphery, he gave no indication. He and the bullfrog had each other's undivided attention.

The frog croaked.

Eyes swollen in his head, Marcus croaked back. The sound rumbled from deep within his throat.

His pronunciation is excellent, Edith marveled. She could follow their conversation perfectly.

"You know me?" the frog queried.

"I do, little brother," Marcus responded.

"Then what am I?"

"You are mud and water," Marcus croaked. *"You are blood and bone."*

The Louisiana summer disappeared. Marcus' words unleashed a Rhode Island blizzard in Edith's chest. She shook her head. "Marcus!" she screamed. "Marcus get away!"

Edith broke into a run. Wet grass slid under her feet, but she caught her balance and staggered forward. "Marcus, listen to me!" she shrieked.

"You are life."

Edith was wrong. Not Druid magic.

This was an invocation of the Carcass God.

"You are sacrifice."

Marcus unhinged his jaw. It yawed impossibly wide as he seized the bullfrog with fingers suddenly gnarled and twice as long as normal.

"Marcus, stop!" Edith shrieked one final time, but it was too late. Far too late. Marcus stuffed the thrashing body of the bullfrog into his distended jaws and bit down. The amphibian squealed like a leaky balloon before the sound was lost in the gutsy *crack* of its bones breaking between Marcus' teeth. Its body burst like an overstuffed pastry. Blood and tangled organ meat ran down Marcus' face as he stuffed the twitching limbs into his mouth.

Edith skidded in the grass and fell onto her behind. She covered her own mouth in revolted terror.

Edith's first instinct was to grope for a spell. Something to turn this back and wipe the slate of time clean, but she knew better than most that there was no such thing. There was only Marcus' throat, bulging like a tumor as he forced the frog carcass down his gullet. A choked, hitching breath burst from his lips in staccato chunks.

Laughter.

A scream erupted behind Edith. Terror and a sudden flare of orange light, bathing the edge of the swamp in noonday sun.

Ezekiel's flame sprite was no longer graceful and it no longer fit in the palm of his hand. The conjured creation was now a brutish flame golem towering so high that the low canopy of branches above it caught fire. The effigy roared and hurled fireballs from the ends of its massive swinging fists. A blast caught the bass player and incinerated his instrument before melting a slag hole into the center of the musician's chest.

Ezekiel ran towards Edith, fleeing an out of control creation he couldn't rein in. Edith glimpsed his terror, his confusion, before a bolt of fire rendered him instantly into charred, smoking meat.

The flame golem vanished, blown out of existence with the soul of its conjurer, but the screaming still rang out unabated into the night... and there were more horrors to behold.

Malia was no longer swaying dreamily. The phosphorous blue under her skin had swollen into growths of glowing fungus spreading all over her body. They sprouted beneath her dress, bonding her to the swamp. More massive, luminous swellings of blue obscured her face and turned her body into a misshapen statue.

There were still others. Josephine gouged her eyes out with a chicken bone, trying to blot out the stream of futures assailing her senses. Benji's owl sunk its talons into his throat.

"Take them off!" Edith screamed. "It's the gris gris! You have to take them off!"

The warning was too late. Josiah Moraeu had tried to shift into a wolf and lay on the floor, emitting some horrid combination of screams and howls as morphing bones pierced through his skin in a dozen places. Some of the other revelers simply convulsed, the magic thrumming in their veins simply too much power for their bodies to contain. Their skin split and blood ran down their bodies. They bit down until their teeth exploded and fell writhing in the grass.

Catarina laughed in the open field. She spread her fingers before her face and marveled as lightning crackled between her fingertips. Her eyes met Edith's.

She knows, Edith realized. *She's the only one that understands.*

"Catarina, you have to take it off!" Edith cried.

The lightning only arced further, fountaining from one palm to the other. Catarina's pupils swelled, covering her eyes in black oil. "Is this what it's like, Edith?" she asked.

Rain began to pour from the clear sky. "How is it you can walk around every day without going insane?"

Edith staggered through the downpour. The torches guttered to death, leaving the two women bathed in shadows. There were other things around them. Unmoving mounds of darkness, some of them with contorted fingers still reaching up to the sky. Edith didn't allow herself to think about those. It was Catarina, only Catarina that she focused on.

"I made a mistake," Edith begged. "But I can fix it if you'll let me. There has to be- if I can just... I can help you."

Catarina tilted her head quizzically to the side. The rain fell harder. Catarina might not even hear her over the downpour, but Edith didn't want to risk magically amplifying her voice. Not with Catarina like this. Edith inched closer.

"Catarina, do you remember that night we tried to make a sleeping potion?" she asked. She forced herself to laugh, like they were still in Catarina's bungalow, laughing over wine and bowls of dried herbs. "Remember how the brew curdled? I thought we used too much Witch Hazel, but you taught me it was because the snake venom had gone bad." Closer still. Catarina's eyes had begun to throb with pulsing white light. " It's just like that, Catarina. The gris gris has gone bad. Can we take it off?"

"Off?" Catarina questioned. That queer disconnect again.

"That's right," Edith nodded. Lightning broke overhead, briefly lighting the field and its still inhabitants with its stark flashbulb, The thunder rumbled shortly after, but not so loud it could drown out Edith's heart pounding in her ears. The lightning flash had shown too much.

Dead. All of them dead.

Except Catarina. Edith focused on the charm dangling at her friend's wrist. "Give me your hand, Catarina."

Catarina lifted her hand up to her own face. She examined it as if the limb were barely connected to her being.

"Catarina. Please." Edith reached out, but not for her friend's hand. She reached for the charm.

Lightning struck Catarina in the chest then. Edith recoiled, but it didn't make a difference. There was no heat to be felt. The lightning didn't burn Catarina. It unmade her. The bolt ran through her and Catarina disassembled like a sugar cube dropped into a cup of tea. She was scattered on the gusts left behind by the lightning bolt. Dust in the wind.

Edith sobbed from deep within her core. She clawed frantically for a handful of ash and felt nothing but grit slipping between her fingers.

The rain stopped. It had killed the torches. Killed the cooking fire. Left Edith alone with nothing but the darkness and her toxic ego. She buried her face in the sodden grass and wished she could never raise it again. It was not just dead friends and a dead lover that awaited her. Edith was dead too. Everything she knew about herself... everything she believed for her own future... one witch had gone into the swamp this evening. Edith had no idea who would be walking back out.

It was better this way. Better to weep into the grass and be alone with her grief than to find out what awaited after.

Fingers like talons grabbed Edith's hair and yanked her head back.

"Mine nowww," Marcus croaked. He pulled harder, lifting Edith up off her feet, and then flung her out on her back. She struck her head hard against the earth. A dozen sun flares went off in front of her eyes.

Marcus sprung on top of her before her vision could clear. Edith only had the briefest glimpse of what the spell had made him. His back rose in a hunch. His legs were elongated and bent at the knee in a warped, inhuman angle.

His aura was midnight black.

Marcus sat on her chest before Edith could gather herself. He pinned her down, the bony mass of his torso pressed painfully under her ribcage. Hands clutching at her wrist oozed with slime. His eyes, eyes that had turned decaying black, devoured the sight of her sprawled beneath him.

"My Looovvleey." His throat bulged hideously at the words. Marcus' tongue unfurled; a hideous, three-foot long dead fish. He dragged the slimy end of it across her face, down her neck, and into the nest of her cleavage. Edith moaned and tried to squirm free,but the hands at her wrist only squeezed tighter.

"I'm sttrroonng now, Edittthhh. Strong enough to keep you with me."

The tongue slid back into his mouth, but the weight holding Edith down stayed firmly planted on her chest. There was nothing of Marcus in this creature. Not in his eyes. Certainly not his heart. The thing above her was a predator, relishing the prey trapped in his grasp.

"Exintero," Edith whispered.

Marcus ripped apart. Not like Caterina did; Marcus went off like he was smashed by an invisible trolley. His head and half of his limbs splashed into the water. The rest of him landed in the trees. A bathtub of blood and viscera splattered over Edith, drenching her head from head to toe in gruesome consequences.

In the silence that followed... Edith Penn stood up. She walked, step by squelching step, across the grass and into the murky water. The first step took her in up to her knees. Then her waist. Edith Penn marched deeper and deeper until the water swept over her bloody features and she sank into the swamp.

It was impossible to know how long Edith stayed submerged. Longer than a normal person could hold their breath to be sure, but that wasn't an issue. She was still Edith Penn after all.

And Edith Penn was strong.

Chapter 26

CONTROL.

Everything in Duncan's business came down to control. Men in his profession didn't get far without self-restraint. You couldn't get flustered. You couldn't let your frustrations goad you into acting impulsively.

Like that embarrassing situation with the shipping company. Duncan still vividly recalled the anger he'd felt when he'd reviewed the recordings from the editor's office and learned that he'd been caught up in the reporter's little surveillance operation.

The young man in the silver SUV. Looking back, that was probably the one recruited for the stakeout. Clean cut looking white kid. A little anxious, but Duncan had pegged him for some frat boy waiting on a drug dealer and dismissed him as a nonentity.

An amateur's mistake. Sloppy. Inexcusable. A lesser operative might have let that embarrassment drive him to do something stupid. He might have been goaded into some impulsive act of retribution. Not Duncan. Duncan just excised his frustrations on a prostitute, one who would never look the same again, and remained calm. The package by itself meant nothing, and supposedly there was some other story taking up the girl's time lately. There was no reason to act rashly. Duncan could continue to monitor the situation and act on any of his contingency plans as needed.

And now here they were. The reporter had come back around to Senator Hyde, just as Duncan anticipated she eventually would, and he had been lying in wait just as he'd prepared to be.

It all came down to control. Control was what separated the professionals from the pretenders.

And when you were a professional, you were rewarded with opportunities that pretenders could never even dream of.

Opportunities like Rebecca Spencer's tiny sedan looming ahead of him on an empty road.

Deciding to chance that she might recognize him, Duncan goosed the pedal a little more and brought his car up for a closer look. One tail light was smashed, a recent development, but the Honda in front of him was definitely the reporter's model and license plate. Despite the headstart she'd gotten while Duncan was "discussing" things with her editor, he had managed to catch up with the reporter before she'd reached her apartment on the outskirts of town.

Kill her where she lived. That had been Duncan's plan-some elaborate charade designed to look like a fall in the kitchen or maybe a hair dryer in the bathtub. To catch up with her on the road like this was an unexpected development.

Unexpected, but not unwelcome.

Not trusting the rearview mirror, Duncan looked over his shoulder. He saw nothing behind him except empty asphalt. Ahead of him, no other cars except for the girl's. It was just the two of them as they approached the bridge over Booth River.

It was the perfect opportunity, especially if you were the kind of person who had spent time considering just what to do if such an opening presented itself.

Duncan set his milkshake in the cup holder and withdrew his silenced Sig Sauer pistol from the glove box. He rolled down the window and took casual aim at the blue Honda in front of him. After years of experience, a quick glance down the barrel of the gun was all he needed. Duncan fired, and the single hollow point round destroyed the car's left rear tire and then exploded against the asphalt in a dozen unrecognizable fragments.

Duncan eased on the brake as the car in front of him sluiced wildly out of control. By the time he came to a gentle stop, the reporter's Honda was already careening uncontrollably towards the guardrail. Stashing his gun under the seat, Duncan missed the moment where the car actually smashed through the railing. He heard the ugly sound as the metal came loose, but by the time he looked up again there was only empty roadway in front of him.

Duncan got out of the car and approached the railing with a rubber mallet dangling loosely from one hand as an insurance policy. He made it to the edge of the bridge just in time to see the Honda's back end disappear under the water with a parting kiss of bubbles.

There was still no traffic on the bridge. Duncan was willing to improvise if he had to, but it would be best if his luck would hold for another moment or two. He leaned against the railing, a respectful distance from the gaping gash Rebecca had driven through, and settled in with his gaze fixed on the murky water.

He waited.

No head broke the surface. Nobody paddled, gasping, onto the river bank. Duncan gripped the mallet tighter. He was willing to improvise.

If he had to.

Another two minutes passed. Satisfied, Duncan walked back to his car and swung into a U-turn back towards town. Senator Hyde would want to hear the good news.

Rebecca Spencer was dead.

Chapter 27

DUNCAN SHOULD HAVE WAITED another two minutes.

Rebecca had been a mess leaving the newspaper. She smashed into a delivery truck backing out of her parking spot and wasted precious minutes convincing the fuming, cursing delivery driver to accept her insurance card, plus whatever cash she had in her wallet, to let her out of her parking spot.

She could barely make it out of downtown. A drive she'd made like clockwork for three years was suddenly a foreign country. She made wrong turns twice. Once, she had to pull a U-turn in the middle of Main Street.

Too much. Just too damn much on her mind. *I have no clue what this cat has done to me,* she fixated. *No fucking clue. Brian was right. Goddamnit. I should have listened. And Brian. Jesus, Brian. He hated me so much that night at the bar. Why would he have dinner with me? What if I did something to his mind? What if he doesn't even actually love me?*

As she reached the Booth River Bridge, Rebecca was utterly unaware that she was being followed. She was too fixated on the cat in her apartment and the unwelcome knowledge lurking in the back of her mind to pay any attention to the black Chevy Cruze hovering in her rearview mirror.

She did notice when the gun came out. Even through all the chaos, some things were too uncanny for her reporter's instincts to ignore. She looked in the rearview mirror and her eye immediately honed in on the grey blob dangling out the car window behind her.

...Is that a fucking gun?

Then her tire exploded. The back of the car dropped like a chair with a leg cut out from under it. Rebecca screamed. She grappled with the steering wheel, but too much was happening too fast. The familiar asphalt road was gone. The guardrail, and the grey river beyond it, suddenly filled her windshield.

She hit the metal barricade. The airbag went off with concussive force, striking Rebecca in the face and bouncing her skull off the headrest behind her. Her nose broke. She greyed out, so dazed that she didn't even realize that her car was off the bridge and plunging headfirst into the rushing water below.

Somewhere, dimly, she heard something splash. *Bad*, she thought, without exactly understanding why. Rebecca barely knew where she was, but she understood she was in trouble. Something very wrong had happened to her.

It was the frigid water lapping around her ankles that finally brought her around, but by then it was too late. Rebecca's vision came back into focus just in time to see her car submerge completely under the river. The water inside the car was already higher, clawing at her knees. Her feet were turning numb.

Rebecca screamed then. She looked out the window and saw nothing but murky grey water all around her. The roar of the rushing river overhead pounded in her ears.

Frantic, she fumbled her seatbelt off. She clawed for the door handle and threw her shoulder against it with all her weight. She managed to force the door open a crack, and succeeded only in letting water in up to her waist. The weight of the river was too great to force the door open any further. Rebecca was sobbing now-

I'm going to die.

But she tried to break through the driver's side window. She braced herself and kicked at the glass, gasping with exertion. Rebecca's foot thudded into the window again and again but her body, sapped of heat and strength, didn't have the power to even crack the glass.

Rebecca fell back, panting and shuddering. Her lips were turning blue and the water was climbing up towards her chest. She swung her head around desperately in the gloomy interior of the car. She needed something to try and smash the window with. She plunged her hands into the icy water, groping for something heavy enough to break the glass.

What she felt instead was something slimy. Something that squirmed beneath her touch and turned its head until glowing yellow eyes stared back at Rebecca from beneath the water.

Rebecca gasped. She recoiled as something small and dark rose up from the water with scarcely a ripple.

Pointed ears broke the surface first, followed by yellow eyes swirling dusky light.Then the beginnings of a limber back and swishing tail. Soaking wet black fur, clinging to a skeletal frame.

It was Tituba. The cat rose higher. Not swimming, she levitated out of the freezing water until her dainty paws rested atop the churning surface. She *meowed* gently, utterly unbothered by the freezing water.

There was a dull thud as the car settled to the bottom of the river, but Rebecca barely felt it. She was held firmly in Tituba's gaze. She felt something primal radiating from deep within the cat. Something dark and immensely vast, asking to make itself known.

Like a phantom limb come back to life, it was a presence Rebecca recognized from her deepest sleep. Except this time, she was awake and able to take hold of it for herself.

If she chose to.

She did. Rebecca reached out with desperate urgency. She opened herself up willingly, and gasped as the black depths of Tituba's snake slit pupils opened up and washed over Rebecca in a torrent of knowledge.

The force hit her with a current even more powerful than the river thundering overhead. There was nothing for Rebecca to hold onto. Nothing to do but give herself over completely to the neverending rush of secrets pouring into her. Tituba filled Rebecca up to overflowing and then swept her away completely.

...At last, Rebecca returned to herself. There was no longer any cold now. No fear. Rebecca held her hand out toward Tituba's maw without hesitation, and the cat willingly opened her mouth and punctured Rebecca's fingertip, just enough for the wound to bleed freely.

Rebecca dipped her hand into the water. Blood and river water, a powerful combination. Especially in the twilight before a new moon.

The windshield was fogged over with condensation. Rebecca drew on it with her wet, bleeding hand. She traced shapes and letters in a forgotten language from the Himalayas, muttering words in Ancient Persian as she did. Rebecca's pronunciation was flawless. She didn't garble a single syllable or make a single conjugation error.

The spell took time to finish. Rebecca had to cover the windshield from corner to corner with a collage of markings and invocations. The water was up over Rebecca's head by the time she finished.

...It didn't matter.

Duncan should have waited two more minutes. He would have heard a dull *thump* like an explosion underwater. He would have seen corresponding bubbles rise up to the surface.

But he would not have seen Rebecca Spencer. Rebecca came ashore a couple hundred feet downriver. Not swimming, not gasping for air. She strode up out of the water and onto the river bank as easily as if she were stepping out of the bathtub in her apartment.

Tituba rode perched on her shoulder. Neither of them shivered from the cold. Neither gasped for air after four minutes submerged in the water. Wet hair was plastered to the sides of Rebbeca's head and hung over her eyes. Streaming rivulets of water drizzled off of her and the cat and ran back into the river from whence they came.

The sun had just about set. Rebecca and Tituba's breath hissed out white in the frigid air. Rebecca pushed lank hair away from her face. She held her hands up and flexed them experimentally, as if seeing them for the first time.

In a way, she was.

Tituba nuzzled the side of her head, and Rebecca responded by reaching up to rub the cat's neck.

"You know what to do," she said.

Titutba did. From her perch on her mistresses' shoulder, the black cat tilted her head back and yowled long and loud. The mournful cry echoed off of the water. It bristled in the trees and hummed in the metal of the bridge.

For those who knew how to listen, the call reverberated deep into the heart of New Birmingham.

...And was answered in kind.

Chapter 28

THE UNRULY CLAMOR FROM outside sounded again, much louder this time, and Ward finally accepted that he couldn't ignore it anymore. Apparently, a peaceful evening watching *Jack Ryan* just wasn't in the cards.

A little easier than it used to be, though. Yes, Ward could acknowledge that much. There was no pausing a TV program back in the early days. Time was, it didn't matter if it was the bottom of the 9th in game seven of the World Series. When the farm called, you had to get up and get to work and then whatever you missed, you missed. At least these days you were able to make a show work around your own schedule.

Ward lumbered towards the back door, wincing slightly. His bad hip was acting up again. He considered calling Maura down and making her deal with whatever burr the animals had up their collective ass, but decided against it. The girl had been out of sorts ever since the food poisoning incident at her school. Not that Ward understood why she would be upset, it wasn't like Maura had any friends in the hospital.

But that's its own problem, isn't it? Ward wasn't completely ignorant of his daughter's woes at school. He just didn't have much in the way of solutions for it. For lack of a better option, all he could do was hope that it sorted itself out.

The sounds grew louder as he reached the backdoor. It wasn't just any one animal, Ward could hear the hogs shrieking and the goats bleating, underlined by the distressed bass of the two cows. They were butting into the pen, adding a hollow rattle of wood to the cacophony.

Reluctantly, Ward reached into the broom closet and came out with his .22 rifle. Coyotes and wolves were rare, but not unheard of. The old farmer kept the gun at about waist level as he stepped out the door. Not quite high enough for serious business, but not dangling at ease either.

He stepped outside onto the back steps and saw no shadows nipping at the edges of the fence. No snarling or barking. The animal pens seemed as undisturbed as ever.

But the agitation inside the enclosures was only growing more frantic. Ward's assortment of normally docile petting zoo animals rumbled within the fencing like a growing thunderstorm.

Ward peered into the darkness, but he saw nothing in the pen except for his animals. It was too cold for snakes. What the hell was going on?

The first set of red eyes kindled in the hog's pen then, bright enough that Ward could see the outline of the hog's snout and ears in the fiery glow. He gasped. "What in the-"

One of the cows turned next, and the animal's eyes lit up like twin matchsticks.

A third set of eyes like embers flared in the goat pen.

And then a fourth.

A fifth.

Ward clutched the gun together, even though he had no clue what to do with it. His fields burned with dozens of fiery flickers as the eyes of his animals turned one after another.

Did it hurt? The animals certainly screamed like it hurt, there was no other way to describe the sound. The goats churned in the mud. The cows ran into the posts. The hogs reared up and thudded back down.

And then it all stopped. The field grew silent as a graveyard.

In perfect unison, every creature in the field swiveled towards Ward. A field of red lights stared into his soul, making his knees go weak. "Jesus, fucking..." Never taking his eyes from the hellish herd, Ward groped blindly for the door.

His hands closed around clammy fingers instead of the doorknob.

"Get out of the way, Daddy."

Ward screamed. He spun towards what should have been the safety of his home and instead stared into the vacant eyes of his daughter. The cat was there too, curled around the back of Maura's neck like a fur stole. Eastern, Eastey- whatever she called it.

"Maura, stay back. Get your momma-"

His daughter brushed past without waiting for him to move. Ward pinwheeled his arms and nearly tumbled off the steps.

Maura descended. She wore nothing but the long t-shirt she slept in. Her bare feet squelched in the cold mud.

The red-eyed animals watched her. As she drew closer, the chorus of snorts and bleats began again. One of the cows reared up on the fence, making the wood beam groan in protest.

"Maura, get away!" her father cried.

Maura ignored him. She went to the fence. The animals began to gather there, bleating excitedly. Their smoldering eyes burned brighter still.

Ward hustled after her, ignoring the pain in his bad hip. His fear of the creatures had not gone, but it was overwhelmed by fear for his daughter.

"Resero," the girl muttered, and the latch for the hog pen slid open without anyone so much as touching it.

The gate swung open by itself. Ward didn't have the bandwidth to even try and process that. He just saw his daughter, his *daughter* for god's sake, alone against a sea of glowing red eyes.

Coming forward was Ward's mistake. If he had stayed by the house, they may never have even noticed him. The animals would have passed him without incident.

But it was his kid. His goddamn kid! Ward lunged forward. He reached for Maura's arm to pull her away.

The hog rose up first. It was a bruiser, jet black and heavy as a wheelbarrow full of cement. The boar snapped forward and caught Ward's fingers in its snout. Pain hit him in a blinding, inarticulate burst. Ward fell, moaning, to his knees. Three of his fingers were gone, down the pig's gullet, leaving only ragged, bloody stumps behind.

More hogs fell on him. Smoldering red eyes beset him from every side. Ward shrieked. Grinding molars smashed through bone and ripped away misshapen hunks of flesh. He tried to raise the gun, but another hog came forward. *Big Chief*, Ward recognized. Missing an ear. Born that way. A favorite with the kids. The 300 pound hog raised a hoof and stomped on his gun hand, smashing the bones to broken glass. A single shot fired harmlessly across the field.

The bullet didn't so much as graze a single pig as the drove descended on the farmer.

Ward's wife, Kelly, was taking a bath when the screaming began. She'd had her eyes closed, adamant that she wouldn't doze, because people drowned that way. Then her husband shrieked, so loud that it rattled the glass shower door on the second floor. Kelly ran out of the bath, hastily tying a towel around herself. Thinking of his bad hip. Fearful of an accident.

"Ward!?' she called. "Ward, where are you?!"

He wasn't in the kitchen or in front of the paused TV. The screaming had stopped by then, but Kelly's dread only rooted deeper. She ran outside, still wearing nothing but a towel. She made it as far as the back steps, and then shrieked.

She plunged down the steps. The towel slipped away and she didn't care. Her own screams filled the void in the night as she plunged into the churned mud and cradled what was left of her husband.

"Ward!" She howled. "Oh, Ward!"

Her focus was on her husband's mangled body. She saw nothing else of what was around her. Not the empty pens, not the sturdy churn of hoofprints leading away from the farm and marching towards town.

She certainly didn't peer closer to examine the mass of prints in the mud. But if Kelly had, then she may have been able to notice the trail of small, human footprints tailed by the dainty, padded prints of a house cat.

***

Closer to the center of town, Tom sat in the car while the pizza cooled in the passenger seat.

He had to go inside. He had dinner, and his family was waiting for him. They were hungry.

His whole family.

His miracle family.

You've been blessed. He remembered being in the hospital after Martha's stroke. The ICU ward around them was filled with accident victims riding out their last moments wrapped in a blanket of painkillers. The bed next to Martha's hosted a burn victim surrounded by his sobbing wife and kids. Any one of them would have given everything they had, signed it over without a second thought, for just five minutes of what Tom had been given.

But they don't know the fine print.

Tom laughed. It echoed in the confines of the car like a madman laughing in a coffin. It was like the setup of a bad joke. *My wife was supposed to be a vegetable for life. I prayed and prayed and prayed for her to come back to me... and she did! Best of all, she came back as a raging nymphomaniac. Now, here's the punchline..."*

He fought back a sob. Instead of going inside, he took a slice out of the box and bit into it. The pizza was already cooling, but at least he was guaranteed a slice. These days, Martha could get through four slices before he even finished one.

She'd become ravenous. Martha ate the cupboards bare every day and fucked him every night until his lips throbbed and his torso burned from the half dozen tic-tac-toe boards she'd scoured into his chest with her nails. She'd made him take a shower with her once, and the water was cranked all the way to scalding.

She still wasn't herself. That's what it really boiled down to. Something had come back from the stroke, but Tom still missed his wife just as badly as when she'd been trapped in that chair.

Maybe there's another support group, he wondered. *One for ungrateful-*

The front door opened. Tom hastily swallowed his mouthful of pizza and put the rest back. He tried to wipe the guilty sheen from his eyes before rushing out of the car with the pizza box as Martha and Ginny came down the front steps.

"I'm back, I'm back." he said. He tried to force a smile. These days, it made the corners of his eyes ache.

Martha knocked the pizza box from his hands. The box tumbled open, staining the melting snow in orange and red. Martha crowded into his personal space. Her lips were pressed together, as straight and unyielding as railroad tracks.

"I'm sorry, Martha," Tom babbled. "I was just-"

She pushed him. Tom skidded backwards, insubstantial as dandelion fluff, and slammed into the car. Martha was on him just as fast. One hand clasped his arm. The other closed around his throat. Tom outweighed her by forty pounds, but trying to push her off was like trying to push a school bus.

Their eyes met, but not really. Tom saw nothing of Martha there, he only saw what had probably been there all along. Something with a hungry, malicious gaze and clenched teeth. *I don't think she sees me either. I think she- it, I think it just sees meat.* It squeezed tighter on his larynx. Tom gurgled for a breath that didn't come. Dark spots already gathered at the corners of his vision, but not yet so thick that he couldn't see Ginny step up alongside her mother.

Not in front of Ginny, he tried to beg.

But their daughter didn't seem distressed at the intertwined bodies of her parents. Her lips were moving. The blood pounding in his ears blotted out most of the sound, but Tom thought that she was saying, "Sorry, Daddy."

It was the last time he saw her. What was left of his wife forced his head backwards. He stared up at the night sky as the pain began to build in his neck.

Tom focused on the sky as the agony only bit harder. It was a clear night; he and Martha used to come out with a bottle of wine and a baby monitor on nights like this after Ginny went to bed. The light pollution had gotten a little worse in the last decade, but the view was still better than the city.

So many stars...

Then his neck snapped. New stars exploded in his eyes, the most beautiful he'd ever seen, before darkness claimed him.

Tom's body went limp. The thing that had once been his wife held his slack body up by his grotesquely stretched neck. The thing that had once been his daughter produced a small paring knife.

"Hold his mouth open," the girl commanded.

Martha obeyed. It let Tom's body slump into a sitting position and then forced his jaws apart. Ginny came forward. Her nimble fingers pulled the pliant slug of his tongue out from between his teeth.

From a comfortable distance, Hobbs watched with approval as the girl made a confident, precise cut and removed Thomas' tongue from his mouth.

***

There were others. Alice Lowry carried Bethiah and a carefully curated bouquet of rat's tails and Aster through the glass doors of the bank. At the vault, she swiped her executive keycard and the heavy steel door granted her access with a thumping *clunk*.

Alice surveyed the neatly stacked rows of bills, twenties, fifties, and hundred dollar bills...but it was Bethiah who purred with delight.

Elaine Benson, widow of choking Peter, left her children watching TV without saying a word of goodbye. Morey was the only one she took out with her through the backdoor and into the cool evening air. The cat bounded down the steps and stalked ahead of her, delicate pink nose sniffing for that which they sought. It would not do to arrive empty handed.

Mike stood outside Joy's apartment, trying to look relaxed and doing a terrible job of it.

It was different between them this time. Mike felt it and he knew Joy did too. Neither of them was a twenty-year-old idiot this time, neither of them was tied up in a bad marriage or coming off a bad divorce.

Sixty-five was too old to get your shit together. That was what Mike always believed. But ever since that night with Joy at the bar... suddenly he wasn't so sure.

He knocked on her door again. "Joy, you awake?" She had told him to come over at six, but she also enjoyed a late afternoon nap on days she didn't have to work at the bar. He checked the doorknob, just because that was what you did. If somebody didn't answer, you tried the knob just to know that the door wouldn't budge.

Joy's apartment apparently hadn't gotten the memo. What happened to Mike was the doorknob turned effortlessly under his head. Cautiously, he pushed the door open a crack, revealing a gloomy stripe of the kitchen. "Joy, I'm coming in, okay?"

The hair stood up on his arms the second he stepped inside. The silence in the apartment was wrong, he sensed it immediately. It was the silence of overdoses and bathtub water tinted red from slit wrists.

No. Please God, no.

He lied to himself, even as he eased further inside. *Maybe she's out. Maybe she got called into work at the last minute.*

The paramedic knew better. The silence was too full for an empty apartment. A dead body had a way of announcing itself. Eventually, you learned to hear it. And Mike knew how to listen, even if he was deliberately pretending that he wasn't. He pushed open the door to her bedroom, where he would surely find Joy dozing after her nap had stretched too long.

Mike found her on the bed all right. She was under the covers, still wearing her nightgown.

That fucking cat was nestled over her face.

Deliverance, she called it. A big, black hairball with a thick mass of fur that was always wild. Joy's features were completely obscured by the body nestled over her face.

"Joy!" he cried. He lunged for the cat, fearful of suffocation and, on a level that even he didn't realize, thinking of Edith Penn. He seized the cat by the collar and flung it to the foot of the bed, heedless of Deliverance's outraged wail.

Joy's eyes snapped open at the cat's cry. They boiled in the wrinkled nest of her brow. Her brown eyes had turned verdant green, vibrant with new energy.

Mike saw the change, but he had no time to even say "shit!" The thing that Joy had become reacted on instinct at Deliverance's call. There was no Mike. There was only the call of the Familiar.

"Turbinem metent!" Joy howled.

The windows were closed, but a storm erupted in the room. The blankets flapped like bat wings. Pillows flew. Joy and Deliverance were safe in the eye of the whirlwind. Everything else was at the mercy of the chilled, supernatural wind. It pulled drawers from the dresser. It dashed her TV against the wall. And the razor-edged wind peeled Mike's skin from the bone and left him on the carpet in an oozing heap.

Joy left his body to stain the carpet. Like the others, Joy had heard the call. There were places that she and Deliverance needed to be, and time was short.

Chapter 29

TWO HOUSE CALLS IN the same month was two too many but, with the vote only a week away, Hyde was relieved to see Duncan and his extra large soda at his door once again. They faced each other in the living room, a mirror image of their last meeting.

"Roads were wet tonight," Duncan opined.

"That's too bad," William said. "I hope you didn't have any trouble getting here."

"I managed fine," Duncan assured him.

Senator Hyde felt fifty pounds of stress unshackle from his spine. He tried not to let it show in his face. "How do you think conditions will be for the rest of the week? I'd hate to run into trouble on my way to the state house."

Duncan slurped until ice cubes rattled at the bottom of the cup. "The forecast looks good, but you know me. If anyone starts calling for a storm, I'll make sure you know about it."

Hyde squeezed his arm, and then just as quickly pulled it away. Duncan didn't like to be touched. "Thank you for your hard work, Duncan. I don't know what I'd do without you."

"Crash," Duncan said. He didn't smile. William honestly thought it would be worse if he did.

"Daddy."

William instinctively twisted, placing himself between his daughter and Duncan.

Lexie stood on the steps with her hands folded behind her back. The fucking cat winding between her legs.

"Daddy, I understand what Oyer's been saying to me."

"Lexie, go back to bed, honey."

Lexie came down the stairs instead. She opened her mouth and rasped at him like a seventy-year-old who smoked four packs a day.

"Oyer told me what you've done, Daddy." The little girl's face was rigid. Chubby cheeks set in stone. Eyes unblinking. Skin taut with an unnatural sheen like botox. Her jaw seemed to move like a doll's, independent of the rest of her face. The relief Hyde had felt over the reporter's demise evaporated as quickly as it had come, drowned by the all consuming dread flooding through him as his daughter came down the steps on rigid legs.

"You've been bad, Daddy. But you can't get spanked. Oyer says you like it too much. We'll have to find another way to punish you."

Hyde sensed movement behind him. Duncan reaching slowly into his coat. "Don't you fucking dare," he snarled.

Duncan stilled, but his hand lingered over his heart like a devotee saying the pledge of allegiance... a devotee with his hand on the handle of a Sig Sauer.

William slowly approached his daughter. "Lex, we're going to take a drive to Doctor Donovan. Okay?"

He cautiously reached for her wrist and pulled his hand back just as quickly as a black shadow blurred back at him. Swiping claws still nicked his fingertips. The cat hissed at him from Lexie's side. Daring him to try again.

"Duncan," Hyde said. His eyes never left his daughter. "If you shoot anything, shoot that fucking cat."

"Daaddyyy," Lexie sang. *"Don't hurt, Oyer. You're in enough trouble already."* She rocked back and forth on the bottom step, her hands were still folded behind her back. Despite whatever was wrong with her, Hyde recognized these mannerisms. It was a trick Lexie was fond of when she brought home a new project from school, or when she'd baked cupcakes with her mother and wanted to give him one.

His daughter had a surprise for him.

"Baby, what's going on?"

The girl took her hands out from behind her back and held them out in front of her. They were clenched into tight fists the size of clementines.

"Pick a hand, Daddy."

William leaned back, edging away from the four year old he took down to the pier on summer Saturdays. "Alexa, I want you to stop this. Right now." He tried to put some authority behind his quavering voice. "Where's your mother?"

The answer was a scream. Torrie's scream. The agonized shriek echoed all around them with an unearthly timbre. The sound rattled the china in the cabinets. It made William's teeth ache in their sockets...

And there was no doubt that the scream originated from within Lexie's clenched right hand.

"I ate Mommy up." The child made an obscene slurping sound. "*Oyer told me Mommy would make me big and strong. She was right. Now, no more dilly dallying, Daddy. Pick a hand."*

"Sir..." Duncan warned.

Hyde cut him off. Sweat glistening, heart pounding, he slapped at his daughter's fist because he feared what would happen if he didn't. He picked her left hand. The one his wife wasn't screaming from.

The lights went out.

All light. Every light in the house. Every light in the street.

The moon.

The stars.

Pure darkness swallowed Hyde up. He couldn't see Lexie. He couldn't see Duncan. He screamed, and the sound was the only thing that told him he even still existed at all. He staggered backwards, groping for the couch, the table...*anything*, but he only clutched at empty blackness.

"Duncan!" he screamed, and there wasn't even an echo to answer him. He was alone. Utterly knee-shaking, blood-curdlingly alone.

"I'm not afraid of the dark anymore, Daddy," Lexie whispered. Right in his ear, so close that her lips sent shivers across his skin. *"...But you will be."*

William staggered blindly. He felt something furry and sinuous wind its way around his calf.

"Everyone's going to be afraid. This whole town... you're all going in the dark."

Light erupted then. A bright flash of white exploded through the darkness. The gunshot shattered the silence with the same brute force.

Hyde blinked rapidly, trying to banish dazzling spots of color from his eyes. The lights had come back on, revealing the same couch. The same house. All was as it was. Duncan still stood behind him, slightly to the side. Lexie and Oyer were still on the bottom step. The only difference was a hole, the size of a marker cap, oozing black ichor from Lexie's shoulder.

Smoke rising from the barrel, Duncan adjusted his aim.

"Radharc Stiall," Lexie snarled.

Duncan's eyes turned white. His pupils drowned in a blank sea before he pulled the trigger. The second shot went wild, brushing Lexie' hair as it sailed past her ear.

Duncan fell to his knees, making the floorboards rattle. He shrieked and clutched his eyes.

Lexie came off the steps towards Duncan, unperturbed by the bullethole in her shoulder. Her head tilted slowly to the side, as she observed the killer's agony. He was whimpering now.

"Do you want to be blind, Daddy?" she asked. *"Would that make it easier?"*

Hyde didn't respond. Fear. That was what Lexie and Oyer assumed. He was too scared to even speak.

A draft of cold air told her differently. Lexie turned and saw the open front door swinging in the winter wind. Oyer voiced her displeasure with a low yowl.

He'd ran. Such a small moment, the bullet and the spell, but it had been time enough for her father to go fleeing into the streets. Lexie sighed.

But Duncan was still there. Still moaning, but now clawing fruitlessly at the air in front of him, as if his vision could be physically clawed back. "Please," he begged. "I'm sorry. I'm so sorry. Just please let me see again."

Oyer padded cautiously behind him as he clawed at the air. The cat circled around to his back and leapt up. She couldn't have weighed more than twelve pounds, but Oyer hit between his shoulders like a sack of fertilizer. The cat's mass drove Duncan headfirst into the floor and kept him there.

"You're a dog," Lexie said with easy calm. The decayed croak was gone from her voice. She walked closer, the pads of her pajama feet hissing along the floor. "We prefer cats, but that's okay. Sometimes dogs have their uses."

"Yes," Duncan blubbered. "I'll be your dog. I'll do anything you want."

Lexie knelt beside him. He felt her cold breath on his neck, and the colder patter of her blood on his leg.

"Go fetch my daddy," she whispered in his ear.

And then she whispered something else, something in an uneven tongue full of harsh consonants. Duncan didn't recognize the language but, to be fair, very few people spoke Medieval German.

Regardless, he understood Lexie's commands with perfect clarity.

Chapter 30

1957

EDITH CAME INSIDE, GRUNTING as she battled against the screeching wind to force the door closed behind her. She stomped grey snow off her boots and began the laborious process of removing article after article of clothing. Hat. Gloves. Scarf. Coat. Sweater. Then, last, the protracted battle of removing her boots. Edith groaned when she was finally free and could at last slump into the kitchen.

She set the paper bag of groceries onto the counter. The contents clattered together in a rattling of aluminum cans, but nobody came to answer the call.

Their business, Edith decided. She removed her own dinner first. The can opener had made half a rotation around the can of tomato soup before the first set of guarded yellow eyes came out from under the couch. It was Tituba, of course. She approached the table with the other Familiars trailing cautiously behind her.

"You'll have to wait now," Edith told them. Only when her soup was heating on the stove did Edith begin methodically opening the cans of cat food from the grocery store. The cats watched her plop can after can of Spratt's cat food into the faded wooden trough. The packaged fish product fell from the can in a stiff, oval-shaped mold. It landed in the basin as a stiff, oval-shaped mound. And it remained a stiff, oval-shaped mound as Edith set the trough before them.

Tituba was again the first to come forward. She sniffed at the unyielding mass of fish and then cast her eyes upward. The cat's flat, dismissive gaze made her feelings about the cuisine perfectly clear.

Edith threw her hands up. "It's life, Tituba."

It's life now, she did not add, removing her own meal from the stove. She wished they would just accept it. Even now, Eastey cast a baleful eye in her direction as the Familiar dug into her rations with clear distaste.

But Edith knew they couldn't accept it. It wasn't just about the food. It wasn't just about slinking back to New Birmingham and the dilapidated rental they now called home. The cats were her Familiars. Their role was to help focus and amplify her natural abilities. If Edith refused to practice witchcraft, then what purpose did they have?

"I'll let you go." That was what Edith had told them months ago, slurring her words in a fleabag motel somewhere in West Virginia as they made their slow trek home.Word had spread, and there were no covens willing to offer Edith shelter. Neither warm bed nor fellowship to be had for the butcher of the Treme. Edith had been halfway through a bottle of bourbon and finally unable to take anymore resentful scowls from the gathered cats around her. "This is what's left," she told them, sweeping the bottle around the small room and not caring what she spilled. "I'm not telling you to take it. I'm telling you to leave it."

That was what Edith said, and she truly meant it, but she knew better in the hungover light of day. The cats were bound to Edith by a pact of the soul. There was no freeing them.

So Edith took care of them as best she could. And they stayed with her, even as every day that passed made a mockery of the bond they were supposed to share.

Outside, the wind wailed and rattled the cheap windows in their frames. The snow was already a foot deep. Edith was thankful she'd managed to get to the store and make it home before the weather got any worse. She already dreaded the idea of battling her way to work the next day, but knew better than to hope the car dealership would close over a blizzard. "Always someone looking for a deal." That was Ed Hyde's credo, and that meant there was always a desk girl to answer the phone.

Edith considered asking the cats what they thought, but none of them wanted to chat with her anymore. Not when all she had to talk about was the mundanity of New

Birmingham. Edith sighed around her first spoonful of watery, canned soup.

The knocking came. Edith mistook it for the windows rattling again, but it was the urgency of the noise that eventually set it apart. The wind did not need to be heard as desperately as whoever was at her front step.

Cautiously, Edith went to the door.

A woman waited outside. Slightly older than Edith herself, freshly rinsed blonde curls overflowed from outside her knitted cap. Her coat was neatly stitched. Manufactured, not homespun. Almost everything about her spoke to a level of material comfort not found in the Greenville region of town.

Her eyes were the only thing that made her look like she belonged. Her gaze greeted Edith with a desperation that was all too familiar here.

"Are you Edith Penn?" she asked. She reached out and clutched Edith's sleeve. Edith felt the chill soaking through the wool. This woman had been in the cold for a very long time.

"Are you?!" she asked. "I haven't lived here long, I only know stories. But my friends, they said your mother lived here. They said she was... they said she could help people."

Grand oversimplification, Edith thought. Edith's mother was the town witch. Genevieve Penn didn't help people, she just took their money. There was no shame in it, it kept her daughter fed, but no. Edith shook her head.

"I'm not what you think I am."

And yet, she was. Edith had returned to New Birmingham a few months ago. There hadn't been any fanfare, no grand announcement. Edith had simply slinked back into town. She got a quiet job. She kept to herself. She never talked about her mother or her family history with anyone.

It didn't matter. "Pretenders and connivers hang a sign in the window," that was what her mother had always said. "Reputation is the only advertisement a true witch requires." And Genevieve Penn's reputation lingered, even years after a Ford truck with faulty brakes claimed her life in '54. Edith had been in the lowlands of Sri Lanka at the time, meditating beneath a waterfall when the impact of her mother's death went off in her head like breaking glass. She'd taught herself astral projection to attend the funeral.

The hand tightened at Edith's wrist, bringing her back to the present. "It's the heat," the woman babbled. "Our furbs- furnace. Whatever it's called- it's gone out. My husband's not home, Sears won't send someone during the storm, and I have four children at home!"

Edith peered over the woman's shoulder. She didn't see a car. All she saw was an ugly, solitary gash carved in the snow. Edith tried to see where it began, but the woman's lonely path was lost in the swirling storm.

"You walked here?" Edith asked.

"I've got the boys wrapped in a blanket together, but it's so *cold.* We don't even have any firewood. You can do something, can't you? That's what they said."

"Those are just stories. There's nothing I can do." That was what Edith told this desperate woman. As if there weren't already three spells buzzing at the back of her tongue.

"I have money," the woman insisted. "Money's not the problem. I just can't find anyone who's able to help me!"

...It *was* bitterly cold. Especially with children to look after.

No. Edith closed the door. "I'm sorry, I can't help you."

"Wait!"

Edith ignored her. She latched the door and turned the deadbolt.

Now comes the banging at the door, she thought. Edith waited.

...Nothing. Good. Edith went back to the table, pointedly ignoring the yellow eyes evaluating her from the food trough. Her soup was still hot. If the reception wasn't completely shot, maybe she could watch *I Love Lucy* after dinner.

Another night watching TV. Just like everybody else.

Edith put the spoon down and stood up. She went back to the door and pulled it open. The blonde woman had barely made it to the bottom of the front steps. She turned warily as light from inside spilled over her.

"Give me ten minutes," Edith told her, barely audible over the howling storm.

Thankfully, she wasn't much of a housekeeper. Edith opened the oven and stretched far back into the deepest corner. She used a butter knife to scrape up some charred remnants from her woeful attempt at a lasagna.

She didn't have much in the way of supplies. No potions, herbs, or animal parts. Edith had taken nothing when she fled New Orleans. But she could make do.

"Come inside," she said to the woman, still lingering outside the door. "Warm up."

"I- I'm fine here," the woman called from where snow pelted her head.

"Of course," Edith thought sourly. She went to the garbage and rooted down until she scavenged a few shards of egg shell. Chicken was a poor substitute for raven's eggs, but it would manage. Edith ripped off a square of a tinfoil and crafted a small bowl. She placed the burnt scrapings and the egg shards into the tin foil nest.

Next, the flame. Edith got out the box of kitchen matches. She took out a single match, but stopped just short of striking the spark.

She remembered the swamp. The death. The screaming. She remembered Marcus and the twisted abomination her power had turned him into.

And she remembered the tingling in her fingers. The way it felt to know that the rules that governed the lives of most people just simply Did Not Apply.

"Schwlen," Edith said. She lit the match and dropped it into her makings before crumpling the tinfoil and its contents into a packet the size of a tennis ball.

"Yata Aendum," she intoned.

Edith brought the packet to the door. The blonde woman regarded Edith and the foil package with skepticism. Some rationality had reasserted itself as she watched this threadbare, gawkish woman set garbage on fire and bring it to her.

"Take it," Edith told her.

Uncertainly, the woman held her hand out. Edith passed the tinfoil ball to her with as little ceremony as a passed cup of coffee.

"Oh," the woman said softly. The heat from the small bundle seeped through her gloves, raced up her arms, and nestled deep in the core of her stomach.

"It spreads," Edith told her. "Keep your family together in one room. That should last you twenty-four hours. Hopefully you can get someone to come out by then."

Numbly, the woman nodded. The reality of what had happened to her was still floating out somewhere where it didn't seem to quite register.

"Good night," Edith told her. She closed the door without waiting for a response.

She hadn't even thought about payment until she saw the smattering of bills on the credenza by the door. The woman had left them there while Edith worked.

Edith counted out tens and twenties, realizing that she didn't have to trek through the snow to the dealership tomorrow if she didn't want to. She didn't need to work at all for two whole weeks if she didn't want to.

And what did you have to do? She asked herself. *A simple charm you conjured from the trash? Was that so dangerous?*

The cats had gathered. Her Familiars stood around her in the foyer, all eyes fixed upon Edith Penn.

"Is it enough?" she asked them.

Tituba answered first. She prowled towards Edith and wound her body around their mistress' leg, purring deeply.

The others followed.

Chapter 31

HE WAS STILL IN his office.

The lights in the bullpen were all dark. His desk lamp cast the newsroom in barely tamed gloom, like the last light left on at a funeral home.

She saw him clearly in the dim light. The bottle of Cutty was up on his desk. He looked well on his way to finishing it.

She drew closer, leaving wet footprints behind her as she crossed the newsroom.

As was her way, Rebecca entered his office without knocking.

Jerry looked up from his personal hell of scotch. There was a moment's elation at the sight of her alive, then reality reasserted itself and he sank back into his morose stupor.

"I suppose I don't have the right to say that I'm glad you're okay," he said.

Soaking wet, hair frozen in wild tendrils, Rebecca sat in the chair opposite his desk. A huge black cat hopped onto the corner of his desk and surveyed him with snake slit pupils as the pile of bills and articles on his desk turned gray and damp from the cat's drenched fur.

"How did you know?" Jerry asked her.

"You told me."

She had heard it humming in the air, all the way at the river bank. And she saw it now in his aura. Deep, throbbing blue.

Jerry drank deeply, inhaling half of the glass of scotch. "He took Mary's photo. Hyde's 'special assistant' from your article. I suppose taking it was his way of making sure I stayed in line.."

"And I guess it worked," Rebecca stated.

He shrugged. "Some choices aren't really choices." Jerry stared her down over the expanse of the desk. "And if you feel like whatever you have to do now isn't a choice... I'm hardly one to judge. Go ahead, kid."

Rebecca and Tituba took the measure of him. A tired old man in a small town. A man with the intelligence to probably have gone further. A man that had gone through most of his life with integrity and knew what he'd lost when he threw it away.

Rebecca reached across the table. She took his glass and tossed the remainder of scotch down her own throat.

Then she refilled the glass with what she'd brought with her.

She'd carried it in an empty Pepsi bottle from the side of the road, the label faded after months in the sun. Rebecca had filled the bottle with river water and Quillwort. Tituba had sniffed out a garter snake to provide the serpent's blood.

And then spit from the wronged... Rebecca had plenty of that.

She filled his glass to the brim and then pushed it back across the desktop. Jerry watched it rumble towards him; grey, murky water lapping at the edges of the glass but never quite spilling. His eyes flicked from the glass up towards his favorite reporter. For the first time, he truly saw her washed-out pallor. The eerie way she didn't seem to blink. The black cat sitting at the edge of his desk, perched like a judge at a trial.

Suddenly, he suspected that she really was dead after all.

"Drink it, Jerry," Rebecca pressed. "You owe me that much."

He did. God help him, he did. Jerry raised the full glass to his lips and slammed it back. The smell of aquarium water filled his nostrils. The taste of iron and late winter rain flooded his mouth.

He'd drank worse.

Jerry slumped back in his chair, the empty glass clutched loosely in his hand. "Is that it?" he asked.

"Not quite," she said.

Something surged in his throat then. Jerry lunged forward, certain he was about to throw up. The familiar sensation of something vulgar-tasting and urgent propelled up over his tongue. He opened his mouth, expecting to see grey puke filling his lap.

Instead, a snake unfurled from between his open lips.

Jerry tried to scream, but the sound was muffled by the thick, muscular body slithering out of his throat. This was no small garter snake, the serpent was as thick around as a spraypaint can. Its back was a never-ending pattern of flowing green diamonds as it stretched on and on.

The snake twisted, spinning with muscular grace until its narrow, triangular head could look into the face it had crawled out of. Jerry recoiled back in his chair. His breath burst from his nostrils in frantic, hyperventilating bursts.

The snake's eyes were a perfect duplicate of Jerry's. Bloodshot blue eyes knotted with fury, set above a flitting black tongue.

"It is a shame, Jerry," Rebecca said. "I would have liked for you to have made it through the night. It would have been the story of your career."

The snake opened its mouth. Jerry barely saw the fangs before they were buried in his face.

Once.

Twice.

Three bites.

The poison burned through his system as if his veins were full of natural gas, scorching away the alcoholic haze that had numbed him through this surreal interview. There was no curtain between him and the terror now. Or the suffering. The poison ripped through him like wildfire. Jerry was already dying even as he clutched at his heart. His eyes sought Rebecca's looking for mercy. Or maybe forgiveness.

Whatever he sought, it wasn't to be had. Rebecca and Tituba impassively watched him slouch in the chair. His chin drooped gently into his chest. He fought to keep Rebecca in his gaze, but his eyes inevitably drifted closed.

The snake faded with Jerry's life, dropping limply into his lap and turning from green to black, and then from black to ash.

Inside Jerry's chest, his heart underwent a similar season of decay. Rebecca left him there, slumped among the ashes of the serpent.

Back in the newsroom, there were several favored front pages hung on the walls in frames. The opening of The Badger's Den. The year the first baby born in the entire country was a boy in New Birmingham. The 2010 election of favored son William Hyde to the State Senate.

Rebecca strolled the perimeter, briefly reviewing each one before Tituba meowed gently at her. A courteous reminder.

"I know," what was left of Rebecca Spencer said. "You're right."

She closed her eyes. Her breathing fell into a deep, steady pattern. She listened to her own heartbeat, mentally timing every pulse.

There were no ingredients here, just focus. This was the rawest kind of magic- nothing but the natural ability of a witch refined and directed at will. She sensed Tituba's presence with her, stoking the energy brewing within.

The papers on the desk were already beginning to crackle. Smoke hissed out of the copy machine. Tituba purred with satisfaction at the rising heat.

Rebecca opened her eyes. The whites had turned blood red. Her pupils were ragged gashes of yellow.

"Le Bruler Au Sol."

The building caught fire at a single stroke. Every piece of paper. Every wooden desk. Every chair. The spreading flames, inky black, spread in the blink of an eye.

De la Barre flames. Rebecca and Tituba took a moment to enjoy the flickering shadow flames, but they didn't linger long.

There was much more to be done.

Chapter 32

SOME OF THE PATRONS at Lisa Lee's thought it was a joke at first.

The eight o'clock reservations had just sat down. It was a good crowd for a Thursday. The tables were completely filled, and there was a healthy jostling of people around the bar.

The first pig pushed its way through the door to high-pitched shrieks, but also some delighted hoots and hollers. Particularly from next to the bar. Even the screams came with a note of amusement behind their distress.

Then a second pig came inside. And a third. Patrons cried with more genuine alarm and scrambled away from the entryway. The manager discreetly told a waiter to call 911.

One fellow stayed on his stool near the door. He finished his third gin and tonic and set it down on the bar.

"Hey! Who ordered the extra bacon!?" he called out.

He was the first. A black hog surged forward and clamped its teeth down around the drinker's thigh. The pig chewed off a steak-sized hunk of flesh and broke his leg for good measure. Another pig reared up and slammed a waiter through a table for two. The diners shrieked as entrees and blood splattered their laps. A woman wearing open-toed sandals lost three little piggies to another of the surging hogs.

The blood washed away the humor. The screaming was raw now. A tide of bodies scrambled away from the hogs, fighting each other to get as far back as possible.

A would-be hero sprang up from his table. The ink on his concealed carry permit was barely dry.

His first wild shot struck the bartender in the gut, knocking him back against the array of liquor bottles on the shelf behind him, but the second two struck the large, black hog savaging his victim at the bar. One bullet buried itself in the animal's throat. The next broke off half of its jaw.

The pig merely swung toward the man and his gun and lurched towards him, trailing blood as it shambled forward.

The man screamed. He managed another two shots before the hog was on him.

Across the street, one of the cows interrupted a painting and wine party.

The goats entered the grocery store.

Screaming followed.

***

At the Badger's Den, all of the vodka turned black and gave off a smell of burning feces. The beer turned into blood as it poured from the taps. A bartender screamed and dropped the bottle of Jim Beam she'd been about to pour.

The whiskey inside had turned into a writhing mass of worms.

It was the same all around. Every drop of alcohol inside the bar had transfigured into something noxious and vile to the human body.

The same transformation happened to the alcohol already inside the customer's stomachs as well.

***

On Craft street, a night jogger stopped and pulled out her phone to record a livestream.

"I don't know if you guys can see this," she narrated. She pressed the camera up to the glass front of the New Birmingham Bank. Inside, the air was thick with thousands of flying shapes flapping back and forth. The combined racket of their wings could be heard, even from outside.

"It's not birds. Or bats.... I think it's money. I swear to God, I think it is."

It was. Millions of dollars. Everything from George Washington to Ben Franklin had taken flight, bent into an approximation of a bird and fluttering back and forth like a penned aviary.

As the woman kept recording, the flying bills suddenly took a coordinated, banking turn. The accumulated net worth of New Birmingham Bank turned in a unified flank and slammed into the glass.

The jogger gasped and jumped back. Her phone slipped from her hand.

The money fell to the floor in a pile that could pay off three block's worth of mortgages. The bills quickly shook off the impact and took flight again. The jogger watched them build up steam and do it again, hitting the glass with a thump like a clenched fist. *It's just paper,* she thought. *They can't break the glass.*

Thud. The glass rattled in the frame.

Just paper, but so many. And a bundle of hundreds had to weigh at least a few pounds.

Thud.

They took flight again. There had to be thousands of bills. Maybe together-

The glass shattered. The woman dove back, shielding her face as shards of glass flew across the sidewalk. She raised her head just in time to catch the last glimpse of the money. Millions of dollars set against the moon like a departing colony of bats.

***

A miracle was underway at the Calla Valley Senior Living Complex.

The entire Dementia Wing had risen up in a paradigm of perfect health. The eldery patients laughed, but with a coherence some of them hadn't exhibited for years. They danced with delighted staffers. Those with phone access called children and grandchildren.

"Mary," Ethel Warner sobbed into a cell phone. "Your daughters are so beautiful. I've been trying to tell you for five years!"

In the excitement and, yes, anxiety among the staff, nobody noticed Melissa Adisson and her cat slip into the bedroom of Kelly Torrice.

The old woman, ninety-five and clinging to life on a ventilator, was the only one that Melissa and Sears had not revitalized with the Invocation of Hebe. She served a different purpose this night, one that was a better fit for the ice cream scooper that Melissa had surreptitiously smuggled from the kitchen while the nurses and aides were distracted by the spontaneous regeneration of a dozen eldery invalids.

But there were none more invalid than Kelly Torrice.

She didn't even struggle when Melissa scooped the eyeballs out of her head.

Chapter 33

"I HAD SOMEONE PASS by the paper, Brian. I'm not sure what else you want me to do."

"Yeah, and she wasn't there, Jeff," Brian said. "I asked you to help me find her. Put out an APB on her plates."

Brian heard Officer Jeffrey Murray sigh. "I did that too," he said. "Plus her description. Listen, man. Her boss said she left work like normal. I'm sorry you're worried, but you're not giving me anything to push this higher up the chain."

Brian tried to keep his own aggravation penned in. His fear made it hard. "She just said she'd be back," he pressed. He heard for himself how insufficient it sounded.

"I need her missing more than an hour, Brian. We've got shit going on tonight. I'm sorry, but it's the best I can do."

His friend hung up.

"Fuck!" Brian shouted into the empty apartment. He called Rebecca's phone again.

"Hi, you've reached Rebecca Spencer. I'm not available..."

He listened to the whole message, just to hear her voice, before hanging up. It wasn't just that she wasn't picking up. Her phone didn't even ring.

There was no reason for her not to be back. Not with everything going.

That's not true, a cruel, unfamiliar voice needled at the back of his mind. *There is one reason she might not be back.*

He clamped that shit down. Clamped it down hard. But he was no closer to figuring out what to do. He'd called his friend with the county PD, but he hadn't expected them to do much and he wasn't disappointed.

Brian's phone buzzed in his hand then, and he brought it to his ear without even looking at the caller ID.

"Rebecca?!"

It was not Rebecca. It was Kristy in dispatch.

"Brian, you need to get your ass in here. Right now." Brian sat up straight. The dispatcher's normal, placid poise was twisted with barely restrained panic.

"I'll be there. What's going on?"

"There's no time!" she snapped. "All hell is breaking loose. Report in and suit up."

She slammed the phone down without another word, but Brian got the score for himself by tuning into the emergency frequency scanner as he sped to the station.

"I DID shoot the fucking thing. It wouldn't stay down!"

"Poison control at Saint Aidan's isn't having any success. Divert any new cases coming from the Badger's Den to Columbus General!"

"I've got no clue what the fuck is fueling this fire. We're going to fall back and try to keep it from spreading to the next block. The paper's a lost cause."

The paper. For about five minutes, he'd been too distracted to worry about Rebecca. But news of the Gazette pushed her back to the front of his mind and kept her there. Before putting on his uniform, he took two seconds to text her-

Rebecca. PLEASE call me.

-before jumping into an ambulance.

"Where are we going?" he asked his partner in the passenger seat.

"Residential," Tino answered. "Shots fired. Screams. Cops already en route. If they have any to spare."

Brian shifted the wagon into gear and the two spoke no more. There was no rapport between them. They didn't usually ride together, but Mike hadn't answered his phone. There could be a million reasons why not, but Brian couldn't shake the sense that something bad had happened to the tough old bastard.

Then again, it was all too easy to feel pessimistic. The radio on the dash blared incessantly with grim updates from greater New Birmingham. Two more poisoning victims from The Badger's Den had died. Along with another animal attack victim from downtown.

And then there was the horizon as they drove. The night was dark, but the pulsing light from the horizon was somehow darker. It was a contradiction in terms that made Brian's brain ache, but there was no other way to describe the black fire set against the night sky. A glowing dark.

"The fire's moving up the block!" a voice screamed on the radio. *"It doesn't react to water or CO2, and the Cesium didn't do shit! We need the feds on the phone. We're going to lose the whole town if we don't find a way to stop this!"*

Brian risked taking out his phone as they sped through the side streets, flashing lights and sirens slashing through the night. Rebecca still hadn't answered him.

"Your irony detector broke?" Tino asked, noticing what his partner was doing while he drove.

"Right. You're right." Brian acknowledged. But just one more text....

"Brian, look at the road!" Tino screamed.

Brain looked up. A man stood in the spotlight of his headlights, waving frantically, oblivious to the fact that he was about to get run down like a stray cat.

Brian slammed on the brakes and jerked the wheel hard to the right. The ambulance missed the idiot in the street by a hair on God's ass, but there was no avoiding the Ford F-250. The ambulance smashed into the rear of the pickup truck. The airbag went off, smacking Brian in the face with the equivalent of a 200-pound sack of flour. He might have blacked out, except the guy was immediately at the driver's side window, slamming the glass with both hands.

"Hey! Help me! You've got to fucking help me!"

Head swimming, Brian's training took over. He tried to push the door open. "Sir, I need you to step back." The lunatic kept pounding at the glass, completely oblivious to his commands. Brian tried again with more force in his voice. "Sir! Step back!"

"Forget it," Tino said, looking as banged up as Brian felt. He opened his own door. "Come on. This way. I'll get the bag. You deal with this idiot."

Brian followed out the passenger door, shuffling across the bench seat and noting that while he was sore, nothing seemed broken. Tino went around to get the medical bag from the back of the ambulance while Brian went to attend to the victim. He barely rounded the corner of the truck before the guy was in his face, grasping the collar of his uniform.

"Help me!" the man repeated. "Fucking help me!" His cries echoed up and down the dark street. Brain checked the houses to see if anyone was coming out, drawn by the crash or the cries for help. There were cars in the driveways all around him, but the windows were all dark. The shades were pulled. There was nobody standing on their front step to see what had happened. No crowd of neighbors gathered together to rubberneck at the chaotic diorama on their quaint little block. There wasn't even somebody stomping out onto the lawn to ask what the fuck had happened to his truck.

They feel it too, he thought. *All of them*. The air itself had turned foul and bristling, like spiders crawling in your airway. It made you want to curl up wherever you could and hide until the bad wind had blown away.

Brian didn't have the luxury. The man before him wouldn't sit, but Brian got a hand on his shoulder and held him in place.

"Settle down, sir." Brian took out his penlight to check the victim's pupil dilation. The small beam flared to life, giving Brian his first good look at the person he'd nearly run over. Bloodshot eyes, pale cheeks with spittle flicking his lips. The man was almost almost unrecognizable.

Almost.

"You've got a radio, right?" Senator William Hyde pressed. He grabbed Brian's wrist and clung tight to it. "Get the cops here. You've got to get them right now." His carefully blow-dried hair stood out at wild angles. There was mud on his slacks and a rip in his sweater.

Tino arrived with the bag. He got a hypo and a vial of Diazepam, just a mild sedative to calm him down. One more look at the guy made him take out another vial and load up a second dose. *One now,* Tino thought. *And then another on deck in case he needs it. This guy looks like he's gonna need it.*

Brian shook his head and forced himself to focus. Right now, the job was what mattered. He took the stethoscope around his neck and tried to get a bead on Hyde's heart rate.

Hyde kept rambling. "And call a doctor," he babbled, the man's voice and his heartbeat were in a race to reach Brian's ears first, and it was hard to tell which one was faster. "A real doctor. My daughter... something's wrong with her. Shit, maybe you should get a priest too. And a vet."

Suddenly, Brian's own heartbeat was louder in his ears than Hyde's. "...What do you need a vet for?" he asked. His voice was tautly restrained, giving Hyde one chance to clarify what he was saying.

Hyde just laughed. The cackle overflowed from his lips, splashing out in a way that made it clear he wasn't pouring from a full pitcher. " Who else do you call when a cat needs to get put down?"

Brian lunged forward like a sprung trap. He seized Hyde by the shoulders and squeezed until his thumbs were buried up to the knuckle in the senator's flesh. "What cat?" he demanded. "Did you see a woman tonight? My age. Curly hair. Rebecca Spencer. Did you see her?"

Hyde shook his head. One eye twitched. "I never saw her," he mumbled. "I wasn't there."

Something different twitched in Brian's eye. A switch flipped and a connection fired inside of his head. Rebecca would have recognized it as an intuitive leap. She would have praised him for it if she was there.

But she wasn't there, was she?

Brain's hands migrated from Hyde's shoulders to his collar and locked in tight. He was three inches taller than the Senator. Twenty pounds heavier. He lifted Hyde off the ground with ease. "What do you mean you weren't there?" Brain demanded. "You weren't *where*?"

"Davis, what the fuck are you doing?" Tino shouted. "Put him down!"

Brian ignored him. He slammed Hyde hard against the side of the smashed pickup. He was barely aware that he'd even done it. He'd caught a glimpse of something in Hyde's gaze, like the barest hint of a worm burrowed in the corner of the Senator's pupil. And he was determined to pull it out.

"I will beat the fucking life out of you," Brian snarled. "What happened to Rebecca?! Tell me!"

From the darkness on the far side of the street, something else snarled back in response. The new sound, nails and razor blades in a blender, made Brian sound like a kitten.

"Oh, noo," Hyde moaned. He tried to worm out of Brian's grasp. "Come on, we've got to get the fuck out of here," he begged.

Brian kept him in place, but his grip on the Senator's collar loosened as another malicious sound rumbled from the darkness.

"Brian, I think we ought to get back in the ambulance," Tino said.

"Too late!" a voice rasped out at them. Hyde whimpered at the sound of it, and Brian's fingers suddenly went numb.

The caller came out of the shrubs by the house across the street, sniffing the air to be sure it was on the right track. Its legs were broken so that it walked on knees bent backwards like an ostrich's. Its lips were peeled away, permanently exposing bare gums and teeth sharpened into fangs. Jagged edges of bone stuck out through the sheared edges of its fingers. The thing's newly molded claws twitched constantly as it stalked forward on its bastard bird's legs. Its stretched, wasted belly swayed down by its knees with every step.

Even though Brian had met him before, he never once recognized this misbegotten thing for what it was- the twisted remnants of Special Assistant Duncan Carter.

William tried to edge away. Scared as he was, Brian noticed and pressed him against the truck.

"You stay right there," he said.

"Hyyyddeee," the Duncan-thing called out in a wretched sing-song voice. Like a wind chime made out of broken glass. "Hyyydddeee." It came close on its twisted legs, remarkably well-balanced for something that looked so broken.

Tino keyed his radio. "I think we need police presence at Proctor & Miller. We've got a 10-8 here and a possible 10-66." The paramedic cautiously stepped towards the... no, Brian couldn't quite think of it as a man. Not with the slime running down its chin. "Sir, this is an emergency situation. I need you to step back."

The radio crackled on Brian's shoulder. Dispatch came back with the answer Brian expected to hear. It was a little more technical, but what it boiled down to was this: they were on their own.

William Hyde squeaked at his side. Brian took his eyes off Duncan, only for a second, just to make sure that Hyde wasn't running.

That was when the Duncan-thing moved. It covered the length of a front yard in three vaulting steps and swung at Tino before the paramedic could even stagger back. The bone claws dug into flesh, ripping his throat open with gruesome ease.

Tino fell backwards onto the street, blood jetting across the creature's face from his ruined jugular. The Duncan-thing pounced on his chest with its prehistoric legs, grinning with a terrible intelligence. It tilted its head with gruesome delight, and that grin kept getting wider... wider and wider until the creature roared and plunged down like a rain of razor blades.

Tino saw the fangs rushing at his face. As a medical professional, he knew exactly what had been done to him- massive tracheal trauma and uncontrolled hemorrhaging. He was already dying, and his only hope as the fangs fell was that it would happen faster. He didn't need to be alive for what was going to happen next.

...On a night where there was precious little mercy to go around, at least one request was granted.

"Oh, Jesus," Hyde retched, barely audible over the creature's snarls and the crunching surrender of Tino's skull.

The Duncan-thing lifted its head at the sound of the Senator's voice. "Why did you leave us, Senator?" it asked. Tino's gushing blood had turned the thing's face red all the way up to its thinning hair. It rose back to its horrible feet. "I know how much you love to be recognized, and we have such an honor waiting for you..."

The thing came forward again, bounding towards them at a speed too fast to run from. Hyde watched it barrel towards him like a weasel who knew that the fox had finally cornered it. There was nowhere to run.

Brian threw the paramedic bag at it. The fifty-pound canvas sack struck the creature high in the shoulder and sent it sprawling off balance. The Duncan-thing still slammed into Hyde, but it hit in a sprawling stagger that saw the two of them fall in an uncoordinated tangle of limbs.

Brian moved quickly, with no fear of the thing's gnashing frenzy of claws and teeth. He took a glancing slash to the forearm and ignored it. His calculus was simple. Hyde knew something about where Rebecca was, so Brian had to get him out. Simple as that. He grabbed Hyde by the collar and hauled him free of the whirlwind of thrashing teeth and claws. "Come on!" he roared, pulling the Senator down the street on wobbly legs. To where, he didn't know. But they needed distance before-

The creature lashed out without even getting up. A long claw caught Brian in the calf and dropped him to the asphalt alongside the smashed pickup truck. Blood gushed into his shoe. He heard the creature snarl somewhere, but panic had narrowed his perception. The thing could have been right over his shoulder or a hundred yards away. Brian crawled towards the underbelly of the smashed F-250, seeking out the blind animal comfort of the shadowy hollow underneath the smashed truck.

He barely got his shoulders under the chassis before he felt rough fingers, sticky with blood, grasp his ankles and haul him back under the streetlights. The Duncan-thing flipped him over. It reared back and roared to the cold sky before plunging its fangs down toward his throat.

Brian stabbed it first. He took the broken length of axle he'd grabbed from under the smashed truck and drove the jagged metal shaft deep into the creature's torso, not even realizing that he was unintentionally angling the weapon up under the ribs and into the monstrosity's lungs.

The thing's roar turned into a shriek. Its wretched breath washed over Brian. He sat up and pushed on the makeshift spear, pushed until he was up on his knees and the thrashing creature was spasming like a marionette. It still refused to die, slashing through the air between them with its ragged claws.

Brian yanked the axle back out and choked up in the same motion. He swung the metal rod overhand. The Duncan-thing's skull *squelched* under the force. He put a dent the size of a cereal bowl into the creature's skull. A bowl that quickly filled with blood from its split skull.

Brian didn't wait to see if it went down. He brought the axle around like a baseball bat, screaming as he did, and this time the creature's head cracked open completely. It crumpled over, spilling rancid, black brain pulp over the street.

Killed it, Brian realized. No question this time. No chance of this... whatever coming back off the asphalt. He'd killed it.

He hit it again anyway. The ugly squelching sound of the metal rod striking against mashed bone echoed down the street. Panting, Brian let the axle slip out of his hands. Killer's hands.

Behind him, Hyde groaned. He was still down where he'd been tackled. Brian retrieved the medical bag and crouched beside him.

"Don't move," Brian cautioned.

"My ankle," Hyde groaned. "Something's wrong with my ankle."

"You tore something." Brian could tell by the way it was already swelling. "Hold still." He dug around in the bag for a roll of medical wrap.

And a scalpel.

"I can get you help," Brian told him. His hand came out of the bag with the scalpel glinting in his tightly clenched fist.

Hyde saw the blade, and his eyes bulged in his waxy face. "Hold on now, buddy..."

Brian's hand was shaking, but his voice was absolutely steady. "Rebecca Spencer. Start talking."

"Not now, please," William begged. He was sweating, but not just from the pain. "Come on. Just help me."

Brian's grip on the scalpel burned all the way to his elbow. He still wasn't sure what he was willing to do with it, but he kept seeing Rebecca's face and suddenly everything was on the table.

"Tell me where she is," Brian warned.

"Please," Hyde blubbered. "I don't know what you're talking about."

Brian's free hand came up. All on its own, almost like... like magic, it grabbed Hyde under the chin, squeezing the Senator's face and bringing him closer. Brian felt the man's tears and saliva soaking his hand as he squeezed tighter.

Brian's other hand got into the act. The scalpel came up to William Hyde's eyes.

"Where's Rebecca?!" he yelled. He pushed the scalpel closer, and this time it was all him. All choice. "Where is she!?"

"I told you!" Hyde screamed. "I don't know!"

"But I dooo," the Duncan-thing crooned. It's ruined corpse rose back up, swaying like a cobra. One ruined eye bulged out of its mutilated face. The sight of it dunked Brian's spine in ice water. He might have run, were it not for-

"I can tell you where Rebecca is," it croaked.

Brian fought back the urge to vomit. He made himself stare into the dead face, even as fresh ichor oozed from the dead thing's broken skull.

"Tell me," Brian said, but the dead thing only twitched its head from side to side. Broken teeth rattled from its jaw. It raised one rictus finger and leveled it at Senator Hyde. *"Bring him to us,"* it cackled. *"Bring us Hyde and we'll tell you where she lies."*

William Hyde clutched his arm. "You can't listen to it. For Christ's sake, look at it!"

Brian answered by letting the scalpel slip from his hand. Hyde breathed a sigh of relief.

And then Brian stabbed Senator Hyde in the thigh.

William didn't scream. Hissing, high-pitched breath escaped from between his teeth. He looked from Brian's iron glare... and then down to the hypodermic needed sticking out of his thigh.

Brian depressed the plunger on the syringe Tino had loaded with a double dose of sedative. He looked Hyde right in the face as the Senator's eyes glazed over, but it was the dead, broken thing he spoke to.

"Tell me where."

Chapter 34

ONE BY ONE, THE thirteen black cats of Edith Penn arrived in the graveyard.

They came through the night. Untouched by the moonlight, darker than the shadows around them. They came with their human companions following close behind. They came with their heads held high and their tails held higher, and with good reason. None had failed in their task this night.

Eastey came first with Maura in tow. The girl still reeked gloriously of the herd running rampant through the streets.

Hobbs was next, along with Ginny, Martha, and the dripping length of tongue needed for the spell. The girl still carried the paring knife used to do the deed.

The others followed. Some bore signs of their revenge upon the town. Others came with the ingredients they'd been tasked with for the spell. Elaine, Morey's companion, came bearing a bundle of holly branches. Deliverance came with an infant's pinkie finger cradled in her jaws.

The black cats and their companions formed an arch as they gathered, but it was not an orderly arrangement. Sears and Dorcas stood side by side, but Bethiah ambled to the opposite side from the other two. The gaps filled as the others arrived, the cats picking their spots by attuning their energy along the compatible ley lines. Each Familiar that fell into place was like another circuit kicking on in a series. The air thrummed with their gathering power.

Rebecca and Tituba were the last to arrive. The big Maine Coone had the freedom to prowl further from Rebecca's side than any of the others. She sprinted to her gathered sisters and stalked the perimeter of their gathering. Her yellow eyes surveyed every whisker around her. Every branch. Every drop of blood.

"Is it enough?" Rebecca asked as she drew closer.

Tituba answered by striding to the space reserved for her and Rebecca- the focal point at the top of the arch. Rebecca moved to stand beside her.

At their arrival, the thirteen black cats of Edith Penn let loose in an atonal celebration of yowls and shrieks. The terrible joyfulness of their cries echoed through the cemetery- rebounding off the headstones, rushing past the wrought iron gates, and echoing to the full moon above.

It was almost upon them. Every moment, every spell, everything they'd done had been done with this moment in mind. And the cat's finely tuned ears heard the last piece coming closer. It came on the sound of a choppy, struggling hemi engine.

Brian dragged the ambulance into the parking lot at the base of the hill. The battered truck wheezed, and something inside the engine was screeching, but it had gotten them there. That was all Brian cared about.

Holy Slumber Cemetery. That was where the undead thing told him to go. That, and no other instructions. The thing simply shuddered and slumped back down into true death.

Now that he had arrived, Brian saw that that instruction would be enough.

They were up there on the hill, a circle of figures, little more than shadows.

Waiting for him to arrive.

Hyde groaned in the seat beside him. The dose had not been enough to put him to sleep, but Hyde had spent the entire drive staring blearly out the window. The black firelight at the horizon seemed to hold a special fascination for him. One glance told Brian that he would likely have to carry the Senator up the hill. So be it.

He got out of the ambulance. Brian meant to go straight around to get Hyde, but he was distracted as his gaze continuously drifted up towards the gathered figures on the hill. Did Brian hear a rhythmic purring drift down on the breeze?

Yes, he thought that he did.

Brian opened the passenger door. The rush of cold air made Senator Hyde simultaneously shiver and giggle.

Brian sighed and didn't bother trying to get him to stand. He heaved Hyde up on his shoulders, like the horizontal bar of a cross, and set up the hill.

He marched up, one squelching step at a time. Headstones loomed around him on every side, some of them topped with statues of somber angels that bore mute witness as Brian trudged higher with his burden.

The Senator's weight was actually a blessing. It forced Brian to focus on not slipping in the wet grass or dropping the Senator on his head. It distracted him from what awaited them at the end of this climb and let him pretend that his pounding heart was just exertion and not terror.

It seemed to take hours, but it was only minutes later that the ground beneath him began to level, and Brian was forced to look up and see what awaited him.

But there was no time for fear then.

"Rebecca," he said.

The figures weren't shadows anymore. They were women. Once mothers, friends, children, but no longer. They weren't even women, truly.

They were witches.

Brian almost wished they were still shadows. Rebecca was a damp, sodden wraith. The others were spotted with dirt or bloody splotches. The youngest among them was only a child. The oldest was a shriveled relic in what looked like a hospital gown with dark stains. Brian recognized Joy among them. The bartender who'd once poured him a shot of whiskey now regarded him with a cold, predatory mirth that he saw reflected in the other women with their eyes upon him.

And then there were the cats. At the feet of the women, the felines regarded him with a knowing that was too focused to be animal. They were waiting for him too.

It was a headstone that served as the focal point of their gathering. Witches and cats, they stood in a curved line with the grave marker as their central point. Rebecca and Tituba flanked the stone on either side.

Here Lies Edith Penn. God Grant She Lie Still.

"Put him down," Rebecca told him. Her voice smacked him like a piece of roadkill. No warmth. No recognition. Tituba regarded Brian from the other flank of the grave, and Brian *felt* the contempt radiating from the black animal.

"Rebecca," he tried. "It's Brian. It's me."

"It's not me," Rebecca responded. But not Rebecca. Not really. "Put him down on the grass," her lips said. "We've fulfilled our end. We brought you to her. Now give us what's ours."

Hyde stirred over his shoulder. "Please," he slurred. "Please don't."

Brian sucked in a breath. He stood in the cemetery and realized that there was no good end for Hyde in this. Brian had brought the man to his death.

The youngest witch broke the chain and stepped closer, a black cat trailing behind her. Brian saw Senator Hyde's cheekbones and chin helping to form the child's features.

"Give him to us," the girl said. "Give him to us before we take him."

Brian warred with himself. He'd taken an oath to act only for the benefit of the sick and the injured. To abstain from neglect and maliciousness. Handing Hyde over spat in the face of everything he valued in himself.

Against that, he weighed the slenderest of hopes that maybe, just maybe, he might still pull Rebecca out of this and get her back.

Brian knelt down. He shifted the bulk of William Hyde and gently laid him down in the cold grass. The Senator groaned, and Brian did his best not to hear him.

He stood back up and faced the gathered coven. "I want to speak to Rebecca. The real Rebecca."

The thirteen witches laughed. The scale ranged from the child's giggles to the old woman's hoarse cackle. The cats added their own throaty huffing to the chorus.

Brian forced himself to stand his ground, even as his stomach twisted with knots of dread. "You're in there," he said to Rebecca. "I know you are."

Rebecca made a single, graceful flip of her wrist, a gesture mirrored as Tituba raised a paw. On cue, the young child and her cat stepped back and Rebecca and the big Maine Coon came forward. The cat and the woman regarded him with chilling playfulness.

Brian only saw Rebecca, achingly beautiful, even like this. But it was Tituba he spoke to.

"I don't know what's going on here," he said. "Hyde. The town. I don't know what the hell any of it means. But you don't need Rebecca. Please, let me take her and we'll get out of your way. That's the end of it."

The others spoke by the grave in a single, unified voice.

"As if you could stand in our way."

"That's right," he said quickly. "I can't. And I don't want to... but I love her. I'm not telling you, I'm asking. Please let her go."

Rebecca's flesh considered. Her brow furrowed with a familiarity that made Brian ache.

"You did bring Hyde to us," she acknowledged.

"That's right. I did," Brian pressed.

"So we'll make this painless for you," Rebecca said. *"Ba li dòmi kavo a."*

She killed him with the swiftness of anesthesia. Brian was simply there one moment, listening to Rebecca promising him a quick death, and then the next he was nothing. His brain turned blank, and his eyes switched to the same blank channel. Brian's strong body slumped to its knees and pitched backwards next to Hyde. The only difference between them was the shallow rise and fall of Hyde's chest as he sucked in air.

Brian's chest was utterly flat, never to rise again.

The witches began their final preparations. The death of Brian Davis passed without remark. Elaine set the birch branches into a sturdy pile and instantly set them alight with an utterance of *"Shaoshang."* Alice provided a battered, seasoned cast iron pot and held it over the flame as the other women gathered.

Osborne's chosen, a podiatrist in her life before the coven, poured in rain water that she'd had the undeniable urge to gather a month ago. As it boiled, Joy dropped in the severed baby finger.

The flesh of birth.

Wildes' caretaker threw in a fistful of graveyard dirt.

The prison of earth.

Melissa added the eyeballs scavenged from the old woman's head.

The memories of life lived.

The fire was unnatural, quickly heating the murky brew to a simmering boil. Noxious, crimson smoke began to rise from the pot. Maura came forward with a long, crooked tree branch and began to stir.

The witches without ingredients went to Edith's grave. They knelt in the grass and began to pull up chunks of earth and sod with their bare hands.

Rebecca and Tituba sauntered to where William Hyde was trying to grope his way back up to his feet. To them fell the most important task of all.

They were to make the murderer of Edith Penn ready for sacrifice.

Chapter 35

2019

EDITH PENN AWOKE BUT did not immediately rise from her bed.

Those days were long behind her. Now were the days when she woke and had to wait for the feeling to creep back into her numb limbs before she could do anything else. Only when she had sensation back in her arms and legs could Edith begin the laborious task of wrestling off the blankets and struggling up into a sitting position.

She was an old woman now. Hair cut short and bristly because it was easier that way. Her scrawny legs protruded like tent poles out from under her faded nightgown. Bony arms with slack skin around the elbows strained to push her weight up onto her legs.

But rise again she did, the same as she managed every morning for the last eighty-five years.

Edith made her way to the bathroom, relying on a cane to help support her meager frame. Her medication awaited in the vanity. Dried Kotu Kola leaves mixed with Horse Chestnut picked on last year's solstice. She gummed it down, already feeling the tingle of additional sensation in her fingers and toes as circulation picked up.

The cats were waiting for her in the kitchen. All thirteen of them were as lithe and inky black as they were in 1944.

By that point, some warmth had kindled in Edith's joints. She could get the first six cans of Fancy Feast open without much difficulty. But by the eighth, her wrists began to ache. And pain gnawed at her forearms as she struggled with the twelfth.

Edith didn't complain. She methodically prepared each cat's bowl before setting her own meager breakfast of oatmeal and tea to cook.

...And then there was nothing to do. Edith sat at the kitchen table and stared blankly into the distance. Like many people of her age, silent moments like this were a time to slip back into a deep pool of memories far more vibrant than anything she experienced now.

Lying at the bank of the Mississippi with Marcus. The stars were clear here, He liked to cradle my hand and point out the constellations. I studied astrology in the Caribbean, I knew all of them, but it was better to pretend ignorance so he wouldn't let go of my hand.

My mother holding those same hands, smaller then, teaching me how to knead dough into bread.

Women in the streets, shuffling their children aside at the farmers' market, lest I turn them into toads.

Crumpled bills passed shamefully across my kitchen table.

Broken windows on Halloween.

That last night with Marcus in the swamp.

The screaming tea kettle brought her back to the present, and Edith returned gratefully.

"Do you think we'll see a thriving trade today, dears?" she asked her cats, her voice a rusty set of gears struggling to turn. The cats didn't answer, but that was fine. Edith already knew the reality- the generation of cellphones and Netflix had precious little use for wards of iron nails and charms of salamander tail and rose thorn.

"The world never stays still." That was what Catarina had told her once. Maybe so, but Edith doubted it would move back towards magic in the few years Edith had left.

That's what you say, Edith cackled bitterly. *And yet, here you are.*

Yes, here she was. Adding Wurt Root into her tea and sprinkling her oatmeal with some Hawthorne berries and a mumbled *"Hayeem ra baera,"* that turned the whole bowl a midnight shade of purple.

And turned it as bland as stale bread. Edith desperately wished she could add even a sprinkle of sugar, but she knew that even a single crystal would spoil the spell's effect. Edith dropped a spoon in the bowl, and was not heartened by the dull thud as the spoon barely even dented the bed of oats. She sighed wearily.

"Mreow," Tituba reproached, staring up from the floor.

"I know," Edith said. "I'll eat it."

She brought the bowl and the tea mug to the table. It took two trips, one hand occupied with the cane while the other ferried the cup and then bowl.

But Edith set both down and then she was out of excuses. There was only nourishment in front of her, and there was nothing to do except take it in. But the idea was suddenly completely unappetizing to Edith, both in body and in soul. The phantom taste of the bland paste was already in her mouth, and she couldn't bring herself to encounter the genuine article.

Somebody knocked at her door. What Edith should have done was ignore it. The power of the Wurt Root and Hawthorne only lasted for a few minutes at most, and she'd dawdled enough already.

But it was likely the Carson boy. One of the few people not scared of Wicked Edith Penn, he stopped by every few days to see if there were any chores he could do for her in exchange for pocket money.

Tituba bared her teeth and hissed as the knock came again.

Edith shushed her. "It will only take a minute," she said. "We have time."

She opened the door. It was not the Carson boy.

It was a man Edith recognized from bus bench advertisements and his god-awful campaign commercials.

"Good morning, Miss Penn. How are you on this brisk morning?" Senator William Hyde asked. He smiled with what he thought was incredible charm.

"Tired," was Edith's one-note response.

"My mother's getting on in years as well," Hyde said, dripping with sympathy. "But do you know what I always tell her, Miss Penn? I tell her that being tired is a yardstick for measuring just how much life you've lived."

Edith chuckled. Her laugh, like ripping paper, told him exactly what she thought about that idea.

Her laughter didn't bother him. He inched a little closer on her doorstep. The kind of man who looked formal and composed, even in jeans and a sweater. "I recognize your time is a precious commodity, ma'am. Might we speak inside? There's a business proposition I have for someone of your... skills."

Reluctantly, she had to admit he'd piqued her interest. Her experience was that men very rarely look to either women or spellcraft to solve their problems.

The cats were against it. All thirteen had stopped eating. The smacking of their teeth was replaced by a silent animosity that rippled in the air around them. Most guests would have picked up on it, but not the guest patiently waiting at her doorstep.

In the end, Edith's curiosity got the better of her.

"Let me start with the good news," Senator Hyde began. He took a seat at her kitchen table without asking. "You don't need to convince me of anything. I believe in the people of this town. My whole life, from my first grade teacher to my housekeeper today, the women of New Birmingham believe in the power of Edith Penn. That's enough of an endorsement for me."

Edith didn't so much as shift a wrinkle. "I'm relieved."

"I should clarify who I am. You maybe recognize me from my ads or, hopefully, from the ballot box."

"Last vote I cast was for Eisenhower, but I know who you are."

Hyde was unperturbed. "Well, we'll see what we can do about changing that come November, but there's something a little more immediate I'd like to discuss with you. I won't bore you with the details about legislative sausage, but I've got a major bill I'm looking to push through this legislative session. I've got most of the 'yes' votes I need already lined up... but there's one pesky little 'nay' that I need out of the way."

"I can't control minds," Edith said.

Not technically true, but people never seemed to take "won't" for an answer. Lying was easier.

"I understand," Senator Hyde nodded along. "We all have our limitations. But let's focus on what you can do. Puppet strings are out, but where do we stand on... poison apples? Voodoo dolls? You know, something in a tragic accident at a not-so tragic time."

Much as it pained her, Edith made her weary spine straighten. "I think you should say what you mean more plainly, Senator," Edith said with careful dignity.

He shook his head playfully. "That's not wise for a man in my position. I've found it better to be more 'presidential' about certain requests. That's why I'd rather engage your services as opposed to more... conventional resources. And I should mention that, if the results are favorable, you could become a full-time staffer, Miss Penn. Benefits. Salary." He turned over his shoulder at the cats pacing behind him. "Pet insurance."

At a loss for words, Edith rapped her knuckles twice against the chipped tabletop. She shook her head in wonderment.

Hyde flushed, though it was typical to tell beneath his ski tan. "Don't think of this as just serving my ambitions.

This is about the good of the town, Edith. There's lots of economic potential-"

Miracle of Miracles, Edith laughed for the third time in the same day.

The edges of Hyde's smile trembled, burdened by a sudden weight. "We all stand to benefit here," he insisted.

Edith's blood was flowing, but there were no potions that had anything to do with it. "A friendly tip from a constituent- No matter how many people benefit, there's always someone who pays. I speak from experience."

"Eight hundred dollars," Hyde said. "Do we have a deal?"

Edith stood up, the cane forgotten. "Get out of my house."

"Five thousand. Final offer."

Edith bared her teeth, wrinkles ringed around her mouth like the inside of a California redwood.

"I have been many things in my life, Senator. A witch. An outcast. A murderer. What I am *not* is an attack dog for some preening little Hitler. I don't care how much money you offer- I wouldn't so much as wipe the clap from your scrawny little pecker."

Hyde had a response. He opened his mouth.

"Abartan," Edith said. Hyde's throat went dry. His voice died between his lips.

"And this town?" Edith went on. "They have come to me with their every cruelty. Their every fear. Everything they were too weak to solve for themselves. They've benefited enough from me. I'll tell you what they deserve now. They deserve to..."

Edith swallowed. Her heart was hammering out of control in her chest. Fury wasn't the only thing raging inside her.

She sat down, what little color remained in her cheeks was totally gone.

My tea, she realized. The effects only lasted so long from day to day, and in her distraction she'd lost track of the time. She reached for the mug, but slowly. Hyde was faster. He had no idea what was in the ceramic cup, but he knew that she wanted it. That was reason enough for him to fling it against the wall as hard as he could, reducing the mug to a wet stain on the wall and ceramic shards on the floor. Edith's cats scattered in a hissing cloud.

For good measure, Hyde flipped the bowl of oatmeal off the table as well. Edith slumped off the chair, her mouth gaping open and closed. Cold sweat drenched her nightgown. She thought to try and scoop some oatmeal off the floor, but her entire body was dead phone lines now. There was no pain, but she felt herself going away. Sight blurring, ears buzzing. She barely heard Senator Hyde as he leaned over her.

He reached into his pocket and flicked a quarter off the back of her head. "There. That's my new offer. Call it a consulting fee, you fucking hag."

William Hyde left without a second look back at the woman on the floor. As far as he was concerned, all he'd lost was fifteen minutes at the gym.

Edith couldn't even hear the door close behind him. All she heard was the roar of her shaky breaths coming in and out. They were to be her last. She understood that.

It wasn't awful, honestly. It put her in the mind of floating along in a small boat drifting down a long river.

She'd considered suicide after what happened in New Orleans but, whatever her despair, Edith was simply not wired that way. That was why she lived to make her way back to Rhode Island. Why she'd brewed her tea and oatmeal every morning the last few years, no matter how weary her bones grew.

But now, lying on the floor and rocking on the gentle waves of death, thinking back over the decades since that night, she wondered why she'd bothered. This wasn't so bad.

Her cats came then. Danvers. Wildes. Oyer. Eastey. Glover. Deliverance. Osborne. Dorcas. Hobbs. Morey. Sears. Bethiah.

Tituba.

They formed a circle around her. To Edith's dying eyes, the cats were almost formless. They looked like little more than shadowy wraiths.

Maybe they always were.

That was Edith Penn's last thought. The low tide of her chest settled and did not rise again. A black curtain fell behind her unblinking eyes.

Edith Penn was dead.

Tituba came first. The black cat nuzzled under Edith's chin in a final show of affection. She purred deep in her throat.

Then, she bit off a sliver of her mistress' bottom lip.

The others joined in, swarming Edith's small, prone body. Deliverance gnawed at the stringy meat of Edith's calves and forearms. Hobbs chewed her earlobes to pulp. Eastey dug bloody divots out of her stomach. Edith's blood ran across the linoleum, and Glover and Osbrone were there to lick it up.

When Edith's body was found, the paramedics took one look at her ravaged carcass and assumed that she had been dead for days. In actuality, it had been little more than a day. The felines gorged, shat, and then gorged themselves again. They ate until they were bursting and then forced themselves to eat more.

They ate of Edith's flesh and soul to prepare for what was to come.

Chapter 36

WILLIAM HYDE ROSE FROM sedation one reluctant degree at a time. At first, it was just his extremities that woke up. His fingers curling and feeling wet grass. Then the seeping cold of the earth through his slacks.

Awareness came back next, but it came like a piece of furniture with some parts missing. He'd left home, Hyde remembered that much. He'd been talking to someone. They'd gone for a drive... but where? Where was he now?

Senator Hyde opened his eyes and was met with a damp, black snout inches above his face. Red eyes peered deep into his soul and made Hyde's blood thunder in his head. He tried to scramble away, but nails like talons gripped his hair and forced his head down.

A woman loomed over him from the other side. Blonde. Probably pretty once, but her unblinking eyes kindled with feral hate. She clutched his head and bared her teeth like a chimpanzee.

The message was clear. Stay.

The hog snorted and trundled to the side. Close enough that it could snap if it wanted to, but far enough back that William had a clear view of exactly where he was.

Hyde whimpered and wished for the pig to block his view again. The scene around him looked like something from a war-torn countryside. Generations of women, the oldest to the youngest, digging fervently in the earth. Mud caked their hands black. Filthy fingers threw slop into an ever growing pile beside the hole. Some of them were up to their waists. The youngest- *not my daughter,* he tried to pretend, was barely visible in the hole.

They went on. Deeper and deeper. Wet squelch after wet squelch, until the women hit something that rang out with a dry *thud.*

Senator Hyde couldn't see inside the hole, but only one thing in the bottom of a grave could make a hollow, wooden *clunk* like that. It was the same kind of thing that cracked open with an ugly screech like he was hearing now.

One by one, the witches crawled out of the grave. Hyde recognized a few. Joy from the Badger's Den. Alice Lowry, just promoted at the bank. The little girl, a stranger now, who had his nose and chin.

They all were, really. Strangers. It was impossible to think of these women as anything they may have been before this night. They crawled out of the earth, covered in graveyard dirt. Midnight wind stirring their sodden hair.

The cats turned towards him first. Thirteen black felines rose from their perches on the headstones and their beds of grass. Yellow eyes like olive oil fixed on him.

The witches followed. They began to lurch towards him, one heavy step after another. The woman with the bared teeth pinned his shoulders before Hyde could even think to run. Warm urine puddled beneath him.

But the witches moved past Hyde without slowing pace. It was another destination, just at the edge of his peripheral vision, where they congregated. A simmering sauce pot over a fire that cast their gathered faces in a murky red glow.

The oldest of them carried the pot back to the edge of the grave. The youngest-

Not Lexie. No. No. Not her.

- went with something grotesquely wet clutched in her hand.

The witches gathered together around the open grave.

"Enlil, Enki," Joy intoned. *"Shamash Sin."*

The sky responded. Low thunder rumbled from somewhere far above. The bartender took the pot from the elderly woman and raised it to her lips. She drank deep.

The new bank president, the one Hyde had congratulated in his official capacity, stepped forward next. *"Gaeryn. Us."*

The earth quivered at her words. Headstones toppled and fell. She took the pot, and her throat bobbed as she brought it to her lips.

It went on. The women all spoke in a different language Hyde didn't recognize. Most drank from the pot. One or two knelt down and chanted while carving shapes and symbols into the earth with a butcher knife.

Then came the one who was *(not)* his daughter. Whatever abomination she held in her hand, she dipped it into the smoking pot and then swung back in his direction. She lurched towards him, and Hyde began to twitch beneath the blond woman's inexorable grasp, trying to get away.

"No. Jesus, no. Baby. Don't," he begged.

The child loomed over him. A severed human tongue dangled from her hand like a paint brush. The ripped out piece of flesh dripped with the fluid from the pot, the stench so caustic that it singed William's nostrils. His-

"Lexie. Don't do this to me, Lex. I love you."

She dragged the limp, slimy tongue across his face. Not randomly, Hyde could tell that much. The trail of viscous slime along his face was too deliberate.

"Interfectores fatum tibi loqueris," Lexie chanted as she finished her markings. Her father's eyes were ringed with scarlet from the painted tongue. She'd marked his cheeks with outward facing arrows. She smeared a second smile across his chin. All according to the spell's direction.

Her work done, she retreated to the gathering of witches. Another child, only slightly older, brought the pot to her, but Lexie did not drink. She took the remainder of the potion and poured it into the open grave. The liquid kindled like embers in the depth of the hole. Murky, red, lava lamp light kindled within the grave, spilling out over the gathered witches.

The last one to come forward was the woman with the thick mane of hair and the largest cat of all trailing at her side. The reporter. The one who was supposed to be at the bottom of the river. But she didn't go to Edith Penn's grave...

She went towards Senator Hyde.

"Wait." He tried to scramble away, but the feral woman held him in place with clamps for hands. "None of this is fair. The old lady had a heart attack, okay? Are you gonna kill me for that? Come on!" He was squirming in the grass. Squirming like a worm. He knew it, but he couldn't stop. The pig rose up and sauntered over.

Rebecca stood at his feet, looming over him. Hyde gulped and tried to hide his dread.

"And you..." he said. "Listen, I don't know exactly what happened to you tonight. But look at you now, you're fine, right?"

The pig answered for Rebecca. It seized Hyde's ankle in its snout at the same moment the woman moved, quick as flipping a switch, and seized his wrists. Together, woman and beast pulled William Hyde forwards.

Towards the glowing grave.

"Hang on!" Hyde screamed. Straining in frantic terror for one final deal. "Hang on!"

He tried to dig into the grass with his free heel, but it was to no avail. The blonde woman and the hog hauled him inexorably towards his final destination. They gang-carried Hyde so he was parallel with the open grave. The woman and the pig rocked him back and forth. Hyde had the briefest sensation of swinging in a hammock at his cottage in Martha's Vineyard. Drinking a beer and reading the latest Lee Child.

And then they threw him into the grave. Hyde screamed. He kicked in the empty. He clutched for handholds that didn't exist. He braced himself for gravity and the earth to claim hin.

But the fall never came. William Hyde floated in the cold, still air; suspended over the grave by invisible strings.

"What... what..."

Hyde's body did a lazy barrel roll in mid-air, spinning so he stared down into the depths of the grave. He saw that Edith Penn's casket had been forced open. Her shriveled, rotting body yawed beneath him. The old bones glowed dull red from whatever brew the witches had poured over her body. The gaping eye holes seemed to be reaching out for him.

Hyde screamed. The witches watched him kick futilely while he hovered in the air.

"Get me out of here!" he pleaded. "Please, please, please just get me away!"

The witches answered his plea in one voice:

"Pluet Eam."

And then the thirteen cats came. Tituba led the column through the grass to the edge of the grave. She quietly took in the tempo of Hyde's thrashing limbs, and then leapt across the void with perfect precision. The cat bounced off his whipsawing leg and landed easily on the small of his back.

The others followed in short order, evading Hyde's kicking legs with graceful ease until the felines crowded along Hyde's back like commuters on a train platform.

Hyde felt each cat land. Their weight settled on him one after another and he twisted and writhed in a vain attempt to dislodge the invaders. "Get off of me!" he screamed. "Get off!"

They spread across his back like a blanket of taunting, scrambling legs. There was nothing he could do except endure the sensation of the cats creeping along his body. Whiskers brushed at his ears. A furry paw wormed under the waistband of his pants. Hyde shrieked again.

Then the first bite came, piercing the flesh of his earlobe. Claws raked against his waist.

And then more followed.

For the average life, the thing about pain is that it ends. Most people are able to endure a single injury, even a grievous one like catching their hand in the garbage disposal, because it is just a single moment. It's devastating. It's agonizing. But, eventually, it ends.

This did not end. The cats ripped William Hyde's flesh to tatters. They flayed him mercilessly with teeth and claws. For the first time, William Hyde truly lost control. He descended into blind panic as his blood welled up from the devastation the cats had wrought upon his body.

The witches watched the blood flow. It coursed over William's suspended form, down his sides and over his shoulders and, finally, began to rain down over the body of Edith Penn.

"Der Regen Fallt!" Rebecca cried out.

The witches chanted, speaking loudly to drown out Hyde's screams.

"Dia Bangkit!" They cried.

"Dia Bangkit!"

"Dia Bangkit!"

"Dia Bangkit!"

Their words echoed over the hills. Storm clouds fell over the moon like a cloak. The potion within Edith's grave began to froth furiously. The corpse writhed with the motion as more fresh blood fell upon its parchment skin.

Tituba leapt off of Hyde's body with the same easy grace she'd boarded. The other cats followed her cue. They lined up alongside the grave, standing alongside their mistresses.

Tituba landed at Rebecca's side, standing with her mistress at the head of the grave. They stood together over the bubbling hole in the earth, bathed in the red glow of the spell's rising power. Rebecca raised her hands high.

"Revendecati Carnea!"

"Revendecati Carnea!"

Rebecca howled. Tituba shrieked. The cats around them joined in, screeching horribly.

"ADEST THURIBULUM!"

The potion rose in a geyser and flash-boiled into a pillar of crimson steam. Hyde screamed as the cloud rushed over him. He braced to be scalded, but the eruption of vapor was *frigid.* His screams were cut silent as the icy torrent temporarily plunged him into shock.

Rebecca inhaled, and the eight foot column of red bent to her will, twisting towards her in a swirling cyclone. She breathed deep through her mouth and her nostrils, taking in the storm as it descended. The cloud filled her, icy ecstasy in her veins. Taking her higher. Higher.

And then Rebecca fell into blackness.

Chapter 37

AND AWOKE INTO SUNLIGHT.

Rebecca sat up with a gasp. She patted her legs and shoulders. Felt her hair.

Her body was bone dry.

She felt cool linoleum beneath her jeans. The tile floor was an aquamarine floral pattern last popular sometime in the seventies. She looked around and the appliances were similar. A refrigerator shaped like a tic tac. A microwave the size of a buick.

She rose unsteadily to her feet and took another deep breath. There was no water in her lungs.

What the fuck is going on?

Where was her car? Where was Tituba? Nothing was how she left it. No accident. No bridge.

"Get me a Tab," a voice called from beyond the kitchen.

Rebecca swiveled towards the voice. She didn't hear it again, but she was aware of other sounds now. Murmured voices and a steady squeaking sound.

She followed the noises through a single doorway. Rebecca wished she could think this was a dream, but she knew better.

The sounds led her out into a small living room with shag carpeting. Sunlight poured in from a large bay window. Rebecca saw that the voices were a bantering guest and host on Jeopardy. The rhythmic squeaking sound was an easy chair rocking back and forth.

There was a middle-aged woman in the chair. She rocked back and forth with a shawl around her slender shoulders and a cigarette dangling from her fingers. Her features seemed hollow, as if whatever life lurked inside of her had been sucked out long ago, leaving her face to dry out and settle into permanent displeasure at the world around her.

The woman, sitting in her chair while *Jeopardy* played low, regarded Rebecca with casual criticism. "No respect for directions... you and I would have liked each other."

It took Rebecca a moment to prod her mouth into gear. She groped over the words. "I'm sorry, I don't... I don't understand where I am. Who are you?"

The woman hacked up a lung. She ground out the cigarette in a nearby ashtray.

"I'm Edith Penn," she said. "Would you like something to drink? You and I still have a few minutes to pass before your death."

Chapter 38

"A TAB, IF YOU don't mind," Edith repeated. "And then whatever you want for yourself."

In a daze, Rebecca complied. She made the short walk back to the fridge, trying to make some sense of the swirling chaos inside her head. She wasn't thinking about what she would like to drink in this surreal, extremely fucked up moment in time, but she opened the fridge and there was a Starbucks Frappuccino waiting for her next to a six pack of Tab. "Rubbaca" was written on the side of it in the familiar handwriting of her favorite Barista.

Edith Penn nodded her thanks upon Rebecca's return. She opened the can with a hearty *crack* and took a long sip. The Final Jeopardy tune played on the TV between them.

"That's going to get warm," Edith cautioned as Rebecca just stood there, blankly staring with the drink clenched in her hand.

"You're dead," Rebecca said.

"And taken so young," Edith said in mock mourning.

"But... then where are we?"

"The Christian term is 'Limbo.' The Buddhists call it 'Bardo,' which I think is more accurate."

"How did I die?" Rebecca asked. "The river?"

"Not the river," Edith said. "You're not dead. I believe I was very clear about that."

"None of this is clear!" Rebecca screamed, her confusion finally snapping into panic. "You said we're waiting for my death. What's going on? Where the *fuck* am I?" She flung the Frappuccino across the room, splattering chocolate drink over Edith's white drapes. "What the fuck did you do to me!?"

Edith Penn raised an eyebrow. "I've been dead," she reminded Rebecca calmly. "The only thing I've done is try to get invested in *Bowling for Dollars* but I'm sorry, it is just a terrible program."

Rebecca shook her head. There was too much there. Keeping it in order was like trying to untangle a colander of dry spaghetti.

"Your cats. They did this. You started it."

"Oh, my cats," Edith said in a way that seemed totally insufficient. "They are a handful." She set the can down on an end table. "The people of New Birmingham say that I'm a witch. That's like if I were Mozart and they told you I could play a little piano. I am not just a witch. I am the most powerful witch to walk the earth in centuries. I could make Booth River run red with blood. I could turn your insides to sludge. I knew how to do things in my twenties that most witches could never learn in a lifetime."

"And was it the power that fucked you up?" Rebecca challenged. "Or were you just always a butcher?"

Edith shook her head ruefully. "I'll never know. I'm just trying to make you understand that the creatures you're calling cats are really just fur coats for a gathering of witch's Familiars. Do you understand what that means?"

To her own surprise, she did. A day ago, Rebecca wouldn't have had the first idea what a witch's Familiar was. But the definition was there now. It sprang fully formed into her mind.

"A Familiar is a spirit from another realm that helps a witch to focus her power," she said.

Edith nodded. "That's right. Anyone can try to summon a Familiar, but the spirit won't come unless the summoner has enough natural talent to make it worth the effort. Most witches are lucky if they're strong enough to attract one Familiar. I had thirteen. Do you understand?"

Cautiously, Rebecca nodded. There were facts in Rebecca's head, information that she'd never known in her life, enough to fill an encyclopedia, but Edith Penn had more than information. Edith Penn had knowledge.

"It was my power that drew them," Edith went on. "It's a mutually beneficial relationship, witch and Familiar. The Familiars make a witch stronger, and the witch uses that strength to make more magic. The spirits are slavishly devoted to the use of magic in our world. It's the witch's power that they serve. Not the witch herself."

"And Edith Penn is strong," Rebecca muttered.

Edith clapped. "Very good!" she said. "That's right, I am powerful. And my Familiars don't want to see a once-in-a-century power disappear just because an old woman happened to forget her heart medicine and lose her temper. My cats are the ones trying to bring me back. I had nothing to do with it."

Edith raised a clunky TV remote and changed the channel. Rebecca recoiled instinctively from what came on the screen. Her skin clutched at her bones.

It was her own bedroom. The small tube screen showed a fuzzy picture of Rebecca sleeping with Tituba curled up on top of her face. On the TV, the cat was overlaid with a hazy aura of green energy. With every breath of her slumbering form, Rebecca watched that green mist seep into her own body. A growing knot of that green haze nestled in her chest like a tumor.

"It can't usually be done," Edith went on. "The resurrection spell will only work on a tremendously powerful enough witch. One killed by a furious soul."

Edith flipped the channel again. It turned to the same kitchen where Rebecca had woken up, only now the room was dulled by several decades of use and neglect.

Senator Hyde was there, flinging a bowl of oatmeal off the same table while Edith grew pale and clutched at her flat breast.

Edith's mouth curled in a skeptical frown as she watched herself die on the television. "I was already having a heart attack. To say that he killed me seems like a technicality. Then again, what is magic if not the exploitation of loopholes? Anyway- a murdered witch. Then enough time for her Familiars to absorb the witch's Sarx."

"Your flesh," Rebecca said, not realizing she'd never heard that term before in her life. "That's why they ate your body. They did it to safeguard your power."

Edith allowed herself a small smile, one that Rebecca didn't notice, before continuing. "What they needed was a coven. Thirteen witches powerful enough to cast the spell. Not an easy group to find... unless you had the power to share."

She flipped through a series of channels. Maura summoning hands from the earth. A young girl pouring some noxious concoction down the throat of a woman in a wheelchair. And still others, too quickly and too many for Rebecca to keep track.

Women.

Cats.

"They groomed you for this. All of you," Edith said. "They gave you my power and they gave you the time to grow until you were all ready to cast the resurrection spell."

"But why us?" Rebecca asked. "What made Tituba choose me?"

"They can sense talent. The thirteen of you clearly had natural ability for the Familiars to enhance." Edith held one hand out, palm up. "May I?" she asked.

Tentatively, Rebecca held her hand out. She was braced for an electric shock, or a sudden snap of clutching fingers. What she didn't expect was Edith's sudden, sharp intake of breath.

"Oh my," Edith said softly. "The things I could have taught you when I still believed I had anything worth teaching. You'd make a wonderful *Cappotto Strega*."

"Cappotto Strega." The phrase translated itself in Rebecca's mind of its own accord. *A Witch's Coat.* Edith watched as Rebecca came to the only conclusion there was to make.

"It was you," Edith confirmed. "Your body was the one chosen for me to inhabit."

Rebecca did snatch her hand back then, pulling it quickly as if Edith's gentle hands would snap shut like a bear trap.

She knew everything. Again, the information was hers for the taking.

The point of the spell. The potion...

"It's already been done," Edith said. "That's what you and I are doing here, our spirits passing the time in this place between the beginning and the end. My soul is supposed to enter your body. And your spirit...:"

Edith made a flapping gesture out the window

The walls suddenly closed around Rebecca. She recoiled away from Edith. The temporary comfort she'd felt in this bizarre holding cell had blown away like sand. A door. She searched frantically for a door.

"Easy," Edith said. The witch remained comfortably nestled in the confines of her chair. "It's not going to happen," she said. Her flat assertiveness, her clear contempt for the idea, made it impossible to think she was lying.

"Wait. What does that-" Rebecca began.

"I'm going to refuse to accept the spell. The Familiars can come to collect my spirit, but they can't force me to cross back into your body."

"Why not?"

"The spell requires my willing consent. There's no transfer if I don't agree to it."

"No," Rebecca said. "I mean, why don't you want to come back?"

"I died in February," Edith said. "What month is it now?"

"March."

Edith shook her head. "Only a month. Time moves so differently here." She looked around her meager living room and shook loose another cigarette. "It's felt like years to me. In all the time I've been here, I haven't cast a single spell. Not because I didn't want to, or I was afraid to, but because I couldn't. My power was out walking the earth with the thirteen of you." Edith stuck the cigarette into the corner of her mouth. She snapped her fingers, and the tip of her thumb kindled with a low blue fame. Edith watched the azure flame dance for a moment, before banishing the fire as quickly as she'd summoned it. She lit the cigarette with a silver lighter.

"I've lived my entire time here as if I were a normal flesh and blood creature," Edith said. "I had no magic at all until you brought it back here with you. Do you know what that taught me?" She didn't wait for an answer. "Magic is a cheat. I look back at my life, Rebecca. Every spell I cast. All this power. I believed I could fix things that were never meant to be fixed, and I was a plague on this earth because of it. Let me and everything I know turn to dust. I'm done."

She flipped the channel again. *Jeopardy* had ended, and *Wheel of Fortune* had begun. Rebecca stood to the side, sucking breath in and out, fighting back the fury pulsing inside of her.

"So what happens to me?" Rebecca asked

"Are you safe?" Edith asked. "That's what you really want to ask me, even though you already know the answer."

"That's right, but I want to hear it from you" Rebecca shot back. "You want to call this off, but then what? What happens to those kids on the other side? What happens to all of us because of you and your fucking cats?"

Edith delivered the verdict without mercy or maliciousness. "You all die. All of our life forces are entwined now. When I refuse to return to the realm of the living, the Familiars will kill me, and that will kill all of you."

"So we just get tossed in the trash?"

"I told you magic wasn't fair," Edith said. "Neither is life. Everything goes bad eventually."

"Horseshit!" Rebecca yelled. "We're not your fucking collateral damage! I've got a life. A family."

"And a boyfriend?" Edith added. "Someone you love?"

"That's right," Rebecca declared. "I do love him."

"I'll save you some trouble. Your boyfriend is dead."

And to prove it, she changed the channel once again.

Chapter 39

IT WAS A LIE.

It was bullshit.

It was a trick by a literal fucking witch.

And then Rebecca watched it all play out on the grainy TV. She saw her hand raised. She saw Brian fall.

She moaned at the sight. Brian's body, robbed of its strength and assuredness, fell with such hideous disarray. Everything he was, everything Rebecca had kissed, loved, and trusted, was gone in an instant.

It left Rebecca on her hands and knees, her face buried in Edith Penn's ancient carpeting.

The witch watched her grieve. The howling cry hadn't come yet, but Edith saw it brewing. She saw it in the spasms of her shoulders and the knots of muscle sticking out in her forearms. The girl wanted to scream, but the body took time to learn how to express pain that all consuming. It didn't happen all at once.

But it had happened once for Edith Penn in a Louisiana Swamp, and it would happen for this girl now.

When it finally hit, Rebecca reared back with her eyes clenched shut. She screamed loud enough to rattle the windows and sank back down with her face in her hands.

Outside the bay window, the eternal afternoon abruptly swept into moonless midnight. Edith sighed and stubbed out her cigarette. She knew what this meant. The Familiars were coming for them. The time to complete the spell was at hand.

"It won't feel like this for much longer," Edith told Rebecca. "And it's better this way. You don't want to carry that pain with you for sixty years."

"What do you know about it?" Rebecca whispered from between her palms.

"Enough not to wish it on you." Edith interlaced her fingers. Not quite the gnarled branches they would become with age, but they were on their way. "They're coming now. Tituba and the others. It's not going to hurt," she promised. "Just keep your eyes closed."

The witch took her own advice. She settled back in the chair and let her eyes close. In the darkness behind her eyelids, all Edith Penn felt was quiet acceptance.

I refuse, she rehearsed quietly. *I refuse your invitation. Ana arhab biwaqfa.* Just thinking the words induced a beautiful numbness in Edith's bones. The end couldn't come soon enough.

Crumpled on the floor, Rebecca Spencer heaved a deep, shuddering breath... and then she didn't keep her eyes closed. She opened them and pushed herself back to her feet. She made her way to the kitchen and found what she was looking for in the first drawer she opened.

Edith heard her rustling in the next room. She cracked one eye open."What are you doing?" she called out.

"Nothing for you to worry about," Rebecca answered from the kitchen. "But let's be clear about something. I don't know what you did, but you're the one who fucked up and spent the rest of your life wallowing in self-pity. All I did wrong was take in a stray goddamn cat."

Rebecca came back into the living room. She came with a massive butcher knife clenched in one fist. "And if a bunch of fleabags want to end my life, they better be willing to leave some blood on the table."

Edith wasn't impressed. "They're not cats. Not on this side of the veil. They'll rip you to pieces."

"They'll try."

Edith sighed. "That painless death I promised you? I assumed you weren't going to make a fuss. If you give them half a reason, these creatures will make you suffer. They might even keep your soul. That's not the afterlife you want. Just let this happen."

Rebecca ignored her. She paced anxiously back and forth by the window. Red lighting broke the black sky, followed by booming thunder so close it rattled the ceramic plates in the kitchen. Rebecca only tightened her grip on the knife.

Edith watched her. The young woman's aura was yellow tinged with red. Fear shot through with threads of anger. The Familiars were going to pick her out of their teeth.

Edith sighed and closed her eyes. She hoped the Familiars would settle with her first. It would be better not to hear Rebecca's screams.

At the window, Rebecca waited. There was nothing to see yet, but she felt something coming. It hummed in her teeth and wound like razor wire in her belly.

Something was coming.

"What is this for?" Edith questioned. "Your pride? So you can tell yourself you didn't quit? Your pride is the first thing they'll cut out of you."

Something echoed down the empty street. It was like a cat's cry, but lower. Murkier. At the very bottom, it was the wet, deathly curdle of something not from this existence.

And it was getting closer.

"Right on time," Edith said. "Make sure you show them your knife. I'm sure they'll be very intimidated."

Already, the girl's aura was shifting. More yellow. Less red.

But Rebecca still held firm.

"Brian died trying to get to me," she said. "You showed me that. I can't do any less for him. I'm going to try and get back to him. Even if it's only to bury him."

Rebecca waited. Her hands were not shaking right now. They were not.

The horrible shuddering cry sounded again. Then, just as quickly as the sound reached her ears, they were in front of her.

Tituba. Sears. Deliverance. The others.

The Familiars.

The thirteen of them swept across the street, over the lawn, and then they swarmed the picture window. They were not solid things here, not cats. They were formless creatures except for their pointed ears, and malignant, glowing yellow eyes. They were crude sheets of shadow sliding along the glass. Their hissing made Rebecca's ears ache.

There was no fighting them, Rebecca realized. The skin-crawling reality of the Familiars made the idea a joke. It was more than the sight. It was the thudding resonance of what lurked inside of them. Power, in its purest, darkest form. The magic inside of them pulsed like a nuclear core.

Too much. Just... too much. There were no shackles on these creatures. Anything they wanted, they could do. Rebecca's hands fell to her side.

"Just let this happen." Edith's voice in her head. Reminding Rebecca of what the information in her head already told her. Explicit detail of what these creatures would do to her. The brutality of it. The savagery.

The Familiars began to press themselves against the glass with more force. Their shadowy forms may have looked insubstantial, but the glass creaked with their weight. The corners of their ragged forms lifted like fists and beat at the glass.

They shrieked again. The sound penetrated Rebecca's ears and made her spine shudder. She let the knife dangle by her hip. Her grip on the handle began to uncoil. Just a little more and the blade would fall entirely from her hands.

"Let me do this."

The memory flooded back to Rebecca. Another voice with her now.

"Let me do this." That's what Brian had said when he'd offered to go run surveillance on Duncan in Boston.

"Let me do this."

She remembered how she'd felt when he said it. The sense that he was there for her, and always would be. It had been early in their relationship, but she had been right. Brian was there for her. Until the very end.

Her hand stopped shaking. Rebecca stepped up to the window, meeting the Familiars and their crawling yellow eyes, but it was Brian she saw. His body discarded in the graveyard. Forgotten. Abandoned.

But not by Rebecca.

Edith watched the girl grit her teeth and set her feet. Rebecca's aura was green now. A rich, beautiful emerald that took root in Edith's memories and sprouted to life fully grown. She recognized that green with aching familiarity. It made her think of Marcus and of the things he knew that Edith never understood until it was too late. It was still her greatest regret, that she'd taken the life he would have lived away from him.

The glass cracked and Rbecca brough the knife up to chest height. "Come on, motherfucker," she challenged. One of the Familiars- it was Tituba, Rebecca sensed it in her soul- began to filter through the spidery cracks. She poured through like smoke and convalesced on the other side in a thin column like a snake, the yellow eyes were the first thing to reform. Tituba's hissing intensified. Rebecca heard a shadowy word whispered underneath it.

Mistress.

Mistress mistress mistress.

The others joined in. Sears, Glover, Deliverance, and all the others. Crowding the glass. Others began to seep through. The glass leaked from a dozen different spidery cracks now.

Mistress mistress we've come oh mistress.

Rebecca braced the knife.

"Exinteros!" Edith Penn yelled.

The Familiars shrieked in confusion as a shockwave of rippling lighting hit them. Tituba was forced back through the cracks in the glass.

"Rehat!"

Another burst of sheer power. It wept through Rebecca, making her intestines shudder, and then kept going. The wave hit the window, making the glass rattle, and then struck the shadowy forms on the other side. The Familiar's shadowy forms warbled and then flew apart like a swirl of burnt leaves.

"That won't keep them away long," Edith said. The woman hustled to Rebecca's side. She looked older, more grey creeping into hair that had been brown only a few minutes ago, but Edith didn't move old. She clenched and unclenched her gnarled fingers with assured confidence. Limbering up.

Outside, the shreds of shadow were already pooling back together. Yellow eyes rose up, glinting with new resentment.

"Yes, yes," Edith responded. "I understand you're upset, but life and death are full of disappointments. Walk away while you can, my dears."

Shrieking, the shadows took flight, lunging for the house again. More than that, they flapped forward to exact revenge upon their mistress.

Edith Penn spat on the glass before they could break it and hooked three fingers over her throat. *"Miroy Fey!"*

A wall of translucent gray unfurled out from the saliva. It spread across the glass and solidified. The Familiars hit against it, but couldn't pass through. They scratched and screeched from the other side of the barrier. Rebecca watched them crawl along like the silhouettes of flies trapped in a lamp.

Edith pushed her into action. "Don't just stand there! You have my knowledge. The ingredients will be in the kitchen if you will them. It's an expulsion draught you want. Quickly!"

"But..." Rebecca stammered. She looked around. "None of this is real. The ingredients-"

"The ideas are real, and that's all magic really is. You've got one chance. Now go!

Galvanized, Rebecca ran back. Edith approached the barricade hex.

"Cum Greim Laidir!" she intoned. *"Cum Greim Laidir!"* Edith felt the Familiars bristling on the opposite side of the barrier. Their noxious anger was palpable.

And, beneath it, so was the pain.

Why?

Why, Mistress?

We came back for you.

We didn't leave you.

Edith ached. She loved them all, even now, but there was no other way. She continued to chant, ignoring the way the words were already growing thick in her mouth. They really didn't have long.

Rebecca flung open the cabinets. An expulsion draught. That was what Edith had told her, and the knowledge to make it was already there in her head. Tituba had flooded her with all the knowledge of Edith Penn, and the ingredients she needed had been willed into place. Dried Christ Ladder. Dragonwort. Eye Root. Rebecca grabbed vials and pouches and brought them to the counter.

The magical barrier shuddered with force from the other side. Edith rocked with it, before refocusing her mana and pushing on. *"Cum Theim Laithir!"* Her tongue was swollen, a side effect of trying to hold the spell this long. The woman of forty had shriveled by twenty years. She gritted her teeth, looser in their gums, and held the line.

Rebecca filled a sauce pan with water. *"Beirigh,"* she muttered, bringing it to an instant boil. She threw in the ingredients, boiling water splashing on her arms, and then went to work with the wooden spoon. She stirred clockwise twice. Counter-clockwise three times. The water in the pot took on a murky yellow color. Cloudy vapor rose out from the potion and then sank down to coil around her ankles.

"Amara jibana! Meine zukunft! Amara bhabis yata!"

The Familiars knew what Rebecca was doing. They were attuned to it both by the danger to themselves and to the sheer ecstasy of such a powerful spell. It would almost be a shame to kill her before she could finish it, but they had no choice. They surged together, striking the barrier as one.

Edith had no chance. She had aged another fifteen years. Her back hunched. Her legs cracked. Her mouth had swollen grotesquely as she struggled to maintain the spell. The familiars hit the barrier with all of their combined power and a breach opened in the grey wall of the conjuring. It was not much, little more than a crack the length of an eyebrow, but it was enough. The Familiars flooded through it. Tituba first. Then Danvers, Hobbs, and all the others. They came forward like an oil spill, shrieking their victory.

Ours.

Ours.

She is ours.

They hurtled past Edith. It was Rebecca they hungered for now.

Rebecca sensed the barrier shatter. She felt the dark shades hurtling towards her. *"Kembalikan mereka,"* she muttered. *"Kembalikan mereka ke rumah mereka."* She raised a fistfull of powdered ram's bladder.

"Amara Ekhana!" She threw the last ingredient into the bubbling brew and waited.

Waited.

And then it was too late. The Familiars were in the kitchen. The black flock of them swirled all around her. Yellow eyes found Rebecca and glowed brighter still with ravenous hunger.

Ours.

Our magic.

No more waiting.

"No!" Rebecca screamed. She sought another spell, but there was no time. The thirteen shadows wrapped around Rebecca in a private tornado. She tried to scream, but the creatures poured down her throat before she had the chance.

It was excruciating. The Familiars filled Rebecca's body like gravel down her esophagus. The sensation was heavy and grating... and expanding. The pain pushed from the inside out. She tasted her own blood. The pressure climbed higher, pressing behind Rebecca's eyes.

But even then, even as she felt her brain grinding like peppercorns, it had been worth it to try. Better to-

The potion erupted then. The pot on the stove exploded in a tremendous, sulfuric haze. The smell was revolting, and yet purifying. Rebecca inhaled and, from deep within her body, she heard the agonized wailing. She clutched her chest as the things inside of her shuddered with pain.

Rebecca made herself take another deep breath, sucking down more noxious air and feeling the things crowding her body scream because of it.

Breathe in, Rebecca told herself. *Breathe in...*

Bit by bit, the hideous pressure inside her faded. She felt it moving up through her, heard the screeching rattling in her ear bones, and then Rebecca doubled over, and the Familiars poured out of her like poison leaving her body. The shadows scattered, hiding in cracks behind the refrigerator and underneath the couch.

Meanwhile, the yellow haze kept growing. It filled the kitchen completely. Rebecca had one final glimpse of Edith Penn standing in the doorway. She looked well and truly old now. Perhaps as old as when she'd been discovered on the floor of this same kitchen, devoured by her cats.

But her eyes looked full of life. Edith Penn raised her hand in a final blessing before amarillo smoke consumed them both.

Rebecca coughed. She groped blindly through the all-consuming haze. Searching for something to grab onto.

Her hand closed around wet grass. At the same instant, the fog blew away as quickly as it erupted. Rebecca sat up, breathing raggedly from deep within her chest. She felt completely aware of her body. The grit of mud in her toes. The deep, biting pain of the cold. The crisp night air against her skin. Looking down on the town, she saw no more black glow from the fires. There were no boars rumbling in the distance. The constant screaming of ambulances and gunfire had stopped.

Rebecca stood up, still trying to orient herself. Too much unreality had animated her life. The stillness, the normalcy, was overwhelming.

The sight of the coven anchored her. They were still gathered around the open grave, but the hole in the earth was cold. The thrumming power gathered among them was no longer there.

Neither was the life.

The women, not witches, just women with the bad fortune to be born with just a spark of the extraordinary, were sprawled in the grass. Used up. Cast aside.

They were unmarked, but staring up at the stars with eyes as shallow as puddles of melted snow. Dead. Drained of life so the power of Edith Penn could live.

"I'm sorry," Rebecca mumbled. The eloquence that flowered so easily in her columns would not bloom here. It was the best she could do, and she couldn't dally long.

She needed to see the grave.

There could be no doubt. The open casket revealed the shriveled carcass of Edith Penn, soaking in a shallow pool of brown waste water. Unquestionably dead.

And there, crumpled at the bottom of the casket like a basket of bloody rags, William Hyde moaned piteously up at her. He raised one filthy hand. "Please," he begged. "Help me..."

His other arm hung crooked at his side. Broken in the fall to the bottom of the grave.

Rebecca knelt down. She extended her clean, unmarked hand and clasped his fingers. "Jump," she told him. "Use your legs."

"I can't. Hurts," he moaned.

"Try, damnit!" she yelled.

He did. Hyde dug his bare feet into the dirt wall of the grave. The first try fell short, but Hyde leapt again and this time Rebecca's free hand grabbed the tattered remnants of his sweater. Together, inch by inch, they hauled him out of the ground.

William Hyde sprawled on his back, which Rebecca was grateful for. She'd seen enough of the bloody crop circles the cats had gouged into his back for one lifetime.

If Hyde was in pain, he didn't show it. He simply sucked in air and breathed out gratitudes. "Thank you," he said. "Thank you, thank you."

Rebecca said nothing, but she subtly slid to the left. So there was no chance of him turning and seeing his daughter spread out on the grass like a fallen leaf.

"Hyde, come on." She said.

"One minute," be begged with his eyes closed. "Please, one minute."

But he'd no sooner spoken than he sat up straight on his own accord. He grabbed Rebecca's arm, electric urgency vibrating between them.

"Did you see my daughter?" he asked. "Her name's Alexa." He called it out louder, seeing the dead bodies behind Rebecca, but refusing to make the connection. "Lexie?" he cried. "Where are you, baby!?"

Rebecca forced herself to cup his face. She looked deep into Hyde's eyes and steeled herself. "Hyde," she said. "Senator." He looked into her eyes, and he knew. William Hyde sucked in a deep breath. Agony threatened to rip his features apart, but he took another breath. He braced himself.

And then she stabbed him in the heart, pressing deep with Ginny's paring knife. Rebecca forced the knife all the way in until her thumb pressed against bone, and then she twisted the blade.

Rebecca heard him gasp. Breathy, mumbling words shuffled towards her ear, but she couldn't make out what he was saying. It was better that way, just like it was better not to look at his face. She focused on his chest instead, waiting for the rise and fall of his breath to stop moving.

It didn't take long. Once Hyde's body had stilled, she let it fall limp into the grass. The knife, she left sticking out of his chest. Rebecca would need to retrieve it later but, for now, the hardest part of all awaited her.

Brian.

His body was just a few steps and a thousand miles away. Rebecca made it to his side and touched his hand. The cold ground and night air had already robbed it of its warmth. She decided to drag him by his feet instead.

It wasn't an easy task, and Rebecca made it harder still because she was careful to avoid the rocks and roots in the uneven ground.

She didn't want to hurt him.

By the time she dragged Brian's body alongside Hyde's, it was impossible to tell what was dampness from the river and what was sweat. What wretched, panting noises were exertion and which ones were grief.

Mrow.

Rebecca looked up from her labor and saw the cats waiting for her. The thirteen of them perched on headstones and nestled amongst flowers left for the dead. There was no menace among their members now. No narrowed eyes. Tituba stepped forward hesitantly, her head lowered to be scratched.

"Get out," Rebecca said. "Get the fuck out of here."

Her tone brooked no disagreement. One by one, the felines rose from their perches and fled into the night, as swift and fleeting as the empty promise of false spring.

Tituba was the last to go. And she was the only one to look backwards with baleful recrimination before spinning gracefully into the night.

Rebecca pulled the knife out of Hyde's chest. It came loose with a sound like a boot coming out of the mud.

She recited the ingredients she would need. Wild skunk cabbage, she saw that growing by one of the graves. Sweat from the beloved, it flowed from her brow like melting snowpack.

The heart of a wicked man, killed beneath a full moon on hallowed ground... she would have that soon enough.

In the... Limbo, Bardo, wherever the hell they were, Rebecca had shared in all the knowledge of Edith Penn. The witch had known thousands of spells, but there was only one Rebecca sought. The same one she held onto gamely now, even as all of that knowledge flowed back out of her with every second she spent separate from the Familiars.

"Magic is a cheat."

Edith Penn had said that. The spells were fading, but Rebecca remembered that warning with crystal clarity. *"I believed I could fix things that were never meant to be fixed."* That was what she had said. And if Edith knew that this had been Rebecca's plan from the beginning, maybe the old witch would have never helped her cross back over.

And maybe she would have been right not to.

None of that changed what Rebecca Spencer was prepared to do. She crouched down over the dead body of Senator Hyde and made the first cut.

Chapter 40

2030

SHE WAS AWARE OF him before she opened her eyes. His teeth plucking at her neck. His body taut against hers, holding back just enough of his own weight to keep from crushing her.

"Happy Tuesday," he whispered, shortly before his mouth moved down her chest, lingering only briefly before moving lower still.

She never did get around to opening her eyes. Not until after, when the early light filtered through the window and his sweat-dampened head was nestled against her stomach.

"You're getting grey," she remarked, tracing the well-loved contours of his skull.

"Should I blame you... or the two mini-yous?" He asked.

She smacked his shoulder. "I'm sorry," she crowed. "Something you want to say?!"

"No, no. Not at all." Brian hauled himself out from under the covers and padded off to the bathroom suite.

Rebecca watched him go. He held her with the same strength he always did, but there was no denying the extra freight around his torso and thighs. The pizza and beer didn't burn off as quickly as it used to.

Rebecca smiled and stretched leisurely. A little stomach paunch of her own spreading when she raised her hips. *Count the years and the kids in the stretch marks,* she thought. But he was still hers and she was still his.

Rebecca fished her phone from the nightstand as Brian got the shower going. She skimmed her emails from the night editor. Labor disputes in Japan had delayed the launch of the Playstation X, and the G-9 were celebrating the latest drop in carbon emissions, but there were no major stories that demanded her attention as editor of the Providence Journal. Impulsively, Rebecca fired off an e-mail to her assistant, letting him know that she was going to work from home today, and then slinked off to join Brian in the shower.

Rebecca entered the bathroom. Brian preferred his showers scalding, and the glass was already so fogged as to be impenetrable.

She hadn't bothered with a robe, and now slinked naked across the tile floor. She slid the shower door back with a saucy grin.

"Care to let me get a closer look at those grays?" That was what she wanted to ask, but she saw her husband and all of her carefully laid plans drifted away like so much steam.

Brian lay crumpled in the tub basin, hot water cascading down the broad expanse of his chest. His eyes were closed and his chin was slumped in close against his collar bone.

He wasn't moving.

Rebecca turned off the water. She threw on a robe after all and made her way down to the kitchen. The girls were already making breakfast. "The clones." Not just because they looked exactly like their mother, but because they shared her sharp eyes and absolute refusal to listen to directions. Rebecca went to the special cabinet and immediately felt the keen tension of their eyes pressing into her back. The clatter of spoons and little girl giggling had stopped the moment she opened the cabinet.

"Your father had another fall," Rebecca said calmly. That was it. God willing, that was all it would ever be. It would have been her preference not to tell them anything, but last year it had happened while Rebecca was upstairs reading and Brian was down in the basement with them. How the girls had screamed for her, just four and six then, absolutely unaware of why their daddy had keeled over-

She pushed that memory aside. She gathered up the pouches and vials she needed and turned around. Her daughters wouldn't meet her eyes, and it made her heart twist in her chest. "It's going to be just like last time. You'll see."

Mia just pouted, but her little sister nodded vigorously.

"I know. You're going to wake him up," Sophia recited.

"Exactly. And we're not going to tell daddy, because it makes him feel silly that he falls asleep sometimes."

Jesus that was embarrassing, but it worked for now. She would figure something else out later.

For now, she took the pouches and vials back to the bedroom. Brian was exactly where she'd left him. His chest lay flat as a greeting card, unruffled by the inhale and exhale of breath. As always, her gaze was drawn to the triangle of diamond-shaped divots over his heart. The Druid marks Rebecca had made in the graveyard.

He never seemed to notice them.

Rebecca always did.

She mixed the ingredients in the bathroom sink. Adder's Tongue. Ground Goat's Hoof. Periwinkle Powder. She added just enough water to let her mold the concoction into a small ball of black, clotted sludge.

Brian's lips held the residual warmth from the hot cascade of the shower. They almost felt alive as she smushed the potion ball into his mouth. If Rebecca closed her eyes, she could have pretended she was feeding him a brownie on their anniversary. She slipped two fingers between his teeth, forcing the bundle of dried herbs and animal parts deep into Brian's throat.

Rebecca set a folded towel out for him while she waited. It wouldn't be long. She knew that from experience. In the meantime, she turned away from his crumpled body and leaned against the bathroom counter. Watched pots and all that.

...There was no reason to worry. Absolutely no reason at all.

It was an eternity later when Brian's hands circled her waist from behind. He pressed his lips against her neck, kindled with real warmth this time.

"Busy day today?" he asked. He fished his toothbrush out of the cabinet.

"Actually, I thought I'd work from home today. Since you're off."

Brian's face lit up with genuine, surprised delight. He spat into the sink, seemingly unaware of the rotten shade of froth spattering into the sink.

"That's great!" he exclaimed. "What do you say we let the kids play hooky too? We'll go to the zoo or something."

Rebecca smiled. "I'd say that sounds perfect."

Brian slapped the countertop enthusiastically. "Let me go deliver the good news!" he boomed, already spinning out towards the hallway.

"...Brian?" Rebecca called.

He reappeared in the doorway, practically bouncing on the balls of his feet. "Yeah, babe?"

"You're... you're happy, aren't you?" she asked.

A slow, amused smirk crawled across his face. "Rebecca Davis," he said. "Happy doesn't begin to cover it."

He went to their daughters, leaving Rebecca to clean up the bathroom. They were out of Adder's Tongue. She would need to pick some more at the next solstice.

There were side effects. Edith Penn had known exactly what they were, but the old witch's knowledge had been spilling out of her too quickly, and Rebecca had been too determinedly fixated on holding on to the spell instructions to worry about what came after. Sometimes she wished that she had.

But Brian never needed to be "reset" more than once a year. Sometimes he even made it two years without one of his "falls."

Rebecca sat down on the bed and hugged herself.

It was a small price to pay for the years that they'd had together, to say nothing of the years ahead of them.

And it was him. It was really him.

Rebecca was sure of it.

THE END

About the Author

Sean McDonough lives on Long Island, NY with his wife and daughters. He does not have any pets.
Follow him on Facebook at "Sean McDonough- Horror Author," or on Instagram @houseoftheboogeyman.

Previous Novels by Sean McDonough

Beverly Kills

The Terror at Turtleshell Mountain

Rock and Roll Death Trip

The Class Reunion

CPSIA information can be obtained
at www.ICGtesting.com
Printed in the USA
BVHW040305220423
662811BV00003B/618